Christmas is coming
he who rules over
practice—cannot be
he fails to berate Goc
a water-stained recei ...y aImss,
and the Victorian bc ...uve vows to find out
what.

Join Octavius and his ragtag bunch of friends on their
third adventure as they investigate a shadowy
spiritualist medium recently arrived from
Massachusetts, only to discover that somebody
desperately desires her dead.

The title *Big Bona Ogles, Boy!* roughly translates
from Palari, the nineteenth-century slang, as:
"What great big eyes you've got there!"

BOOKS BY MICHAEL GALLAGHER

Send for Octavius Guy:

Gooseberry:
Octavius Guy & The Case of the Thieving Maharajah (#1)

Octopus:
Octavius Guy & The Case of the Throttled Tragedienne (#2)

Big Bona Ogles, Boy!:
Octavius Guy & The Case of the Mendacious Medium (#3)

Oh, No, Octavius!:
Octavius Guy & The Case of the Quibbling Cleric (#4)

The Involuntary Medium:

The Bridge of Dead Things (#1)

The Scarab Heart (#2)

꙾⸰꙾

Big Bona Ogles, Boy!

OCTAVIUS GUY

&

The Case of the Mendacious Medium

꙾SEND FOR OCTAVIUS GUY #3꙾

MICHAEL GALLAGHER

꙾⸰꙾

BIG BONA OGLES, BOY!
Send for Octavius Guy #3

Published by Seventh Rainbow Publishing, London
First published in paperback 2017
Copyright © 2016 Michael Gallagher.

The moral right of Michael Gallagher to be identified as the author of this novel has been asserted in accordance with the Copyright, Designs and Patents Act, 1988.

Cover design by Negative Negative
Cover photograph *"The Temperance Sweep"*
by John Thomson
Orford Castle by Gernot Keller, www.gernot-keller.com
used under a CC-SA-2.5 Generic License
Monochrome Rainbow by www.rodjonesphotography.co.uk.

ISBN-13: 978-0-9954733-5-5

Printed and bound by Amazon KDP

CONTENTS

ACKNOWLEDGEMENTS

My grateful thanks go first and foremost to Wilkie
Collins, for creating that wonderful chunk of
Victorian fiction, *The Moonstone*, in which Octavius
Guy—AKA Gooseberry—first saw light of day.
Thanks also to my proofreader Lara Thomson and
my website designer Malane Whillock for all your
hard work, support, and encouragement.

The quotations used throughout come from *The Lady
of Shalott* (1833) by Alfred, Lord Tennyson and *She
Moved Through the Fair*, traditional Irish air by Herbert
Hughes and Padraic Colum; alternative lyrics by
Michael Gallagher.

For my friend Malane Whillock.

CHAPTER ONE

London. December, 1852.

IN THE GREAT METROPOLIS of London, nothing heralds the advent of Christmas so much as the shortening of the days, the honking of plump, doomed geese, and the powdery promise of snow on the breeze that's as bracing as a short, sharp slap. Nothing, that is, unless you happen to be accountable to a certain Mr Crabbit, chief clerk to one Mr Mathew Bruff, solicitor of Gray's Inn Square. For us poor souls, nothing heralds the advent of Christmas so much as the shortening of Mr Crabbit's temper, the honking of his voice, and his frequent and oft-fulfilled promises to deliver—well—*a short, sharp slap.*

So, in the lead up to the Yuletide, it was with some trepidation that I presented myself at his office, clutching in my hand something he was bound to find objectionable. In my capacity as Mr Bruff's Investigator-in-Chief, I had just wound up a highly sensitive case involving the theft of some indelicate items—Lady Spenlowe's smalls, to be exact, which had been disappearing with some regularity from her Ladyship's washing line—and, though no one was to be charged with the offence (for it turned out the perpetrator was known to her), I still needed to present my last few receipts to account for the day's expenses. Steeling myself for the onslaught, I cautiously knocked at Mr Crabbit's door.

'Enter!'

I turned the handle and stepped into the tiny office, glancing at the sign that hung behind him on the wall. I didn't need to read it. I could recite the list by heart.

No illegible receipts
No indecipherable receipts
No torn receipts
No crumpled receipts
No defaced receipts
No stained or water-damaged receipts
No receipts with additions or alterations
No receipts requiring further explanation
No duplicate receipts

There was a time when I had coveted this tiny space for myself, in spite of its one small, grubby window and its yellowing walls. I could have turned it into a veritable palace—an office, to wit, with my name on the door—where clients could come and unburden themselves of their woes. I had it all planned out, too. With just a little reshuffling of certain members of staff, I could free him up a room more befitting of a chief clerk's status.

Alas! It was not to be; he refused to take the bait. *The best-laid schemes o' mice an' men gang aft agley*, as I believe some poet once put it (though rather drunkenly, going by how quickly the words descend into intoxicated gargling). For whatever reason, Mr Crabbit seemed content to remain in this squalid little hole I'd set my heart on. If only I could be as content with my own lot…one third of the hard wooden bench in the draughty upstairs corridor, reserved for the use of errand boys (a stinging reminder that, not so very long ago, I was once an errand boy myself). Such are the indignities that an Investigator-in-Chief has to suffer, for all his loyalty, resourcefulness, and diligence!

Sensing my apprehension as a dog might scent fear, Mr Crabbit glanced up from his desk.

'Well, boy? What is it?' he asked.

'I've brought you my receipts, sir.' *And one, God help me, is water-stained.* A tiny speck of sleet had blotted the ink before I'd managed to stash it in my jacket.

'Hand them over, then,' he muttered, 'I haven't got all day.'

There were three all told, and I'd spent quite some few minutes deciding on the best order to present them in. Obviously the water-stained one could not go on top; he would have noticed it immediately. The question was therefore: *should it go in the middle or on the bottom*? In the event I put it on the bottom, in the forlorn hope that the first two might somehow lull him into giving the third no greater scrutiny than a passing glance. It was a receipt for a mere tuppence, but if it failed to meet Mr Crabbit's exacting criteria, that tuppence would be coming out of my own insubstantial pocket.

The chief clerk pulled on his spectacles and studied the topmost receipt. After a few moments, he placed it to his left and began to examine the next. Finding nothing amiss, he placed this to his right, and turned his attention to the last one.

'Well?' he said, removing his glasses and glaring at me as if I were a worm he had just caught crawling out of a freshly-bitten apple. Mr Crabbit may be a man of limited stature, but he can put you in your place with just one look.

'I'm sorry, sir! It was madness, I know! I should have realized I couldn't slip such a thing past you—'

'What are you wittering on about, boy? Where is the threepence you owe me?'

'The threepence I *what*, sir?'

'The threepence you owe me!' Mr Crabbit breathed a sigh of impatience when I failed to respond. 'This receipt is for fourpence-ha'penny,' he was forced to explain, 'and this one, for tuppence-ha'penny. This last one here is for an even tuppence, is it not? Well? Am I right or am I wrong?' He pulled a tight, stern face, challenging me to suggest that he could ever be wrong—and not just in matters of addition.

'Of course you're right, sir.' I'm not sure why, but, as I was saying this, I found myself shaking my head.

'By my reckoning that comes to ninepence, and yet only this morning I handed you a bright silver shilling. So I repeat: *where* is the threepence you owe me?'

I rifled through my pockets and produced the necessary coins.

'They act,' he grumbled to himself as he reached

into his drawer for his cash tin, 'as if money grows on trees. On trees!'

'Sir?' I said, blinking in amazement, and torn between getting out of there while I was tuppence better off and yet wishing to explore the matter further.

Mr Crabbit looked up. 'Are you still here? Well? What is it, boy?'

'Sir, are you feeling…quite yourself?'

'*What*?'

'Are you sure you're not feeling unwell, sir?'

'I'm fine!' he snapped, and, with a wave of his wrist, he banished me from the room.

In the seven years I'd been with Mr Bruff's firm, Mr Crabbit had never been known to overlook a single disallowed receipt. The idea that he might was quite unthinkable. As I mounted the stairs to the first floor corridor, I tried to summon up a one-word description of this unique and perplexing occurrence. By the time I took my seat on the bench next to George, the word "*apocalyptic*" had come to mind.

'Don't tell me,' said George, misreading my expression, 'he gave you a right telling off.'

'Something apocalyptic just happened, George; something I thought I'd never live to see.'

George blinked. 'The end of days has come upon us?'

There was a time not so very long ago when I would have baulked at the notion that the older George—who, together with the younger George, ran errands for our boss, Mr Bruff—might be familiar with the term *apocalypse*, especially when used in its adjectival form. During the four-month period in which I'd been training him up to be my investigative apprentice—unofficially and off the clock, of course—I had learned not to be surprised at anything where George Crump was concerned.

The truth is, he and I were nothing alike. He was a big lad, tall and muscular. I was much shorter, with a small, wiry frame. He had a prominent, square jaw and a broad, fleshy face. I have prominent—some might go so far as to say *bulging*—eyes (hence my nickname Gooseberry, which is what they call me at work). He was dark-haired; I was fair. He was eighteen; I myself had just turned fifteen only the previous week. He lived with his parents; I lived with my younger brother Julius, whom I've taken care of since he was a baby.

'It might as well have,' I said, responding to his query about the end of days. 'Mr Crabbit signally failed to notice the stain.'

'He didn't!'

'I tell you, George, he did! It might have been small, but it wasn't *that* small.'

'What do you reckon's the matter with him?'

'That, my dear George, is the question!' George noticed my playful smile and rapidly read my intentions.

'You mean we're going to find out?'

'It's as good an opportunity as any to flex our mental muscles, don't you think?' It certainly promised to be more intriguing than the sordid matter of Lady Spenlowe's smalls.

'So what's the plan?' he asked, taking out the green leather-bound notebook I'd bought him as an incentive to learn note-taking.

'I think we can rule out any problems here at

work.' Realistically we could. I was able to read our employer, Mr Bruff, like a book, and the man had been in fine spirits of late. Business was clearly on the up, so Mr Crabbit could not be worried about the state of the firm. 'No,' I hazarded, 'I think whatever is bothering him must be happening at home.'

'At home?'

'Trust me, George, if there is something out of kilter, that is where we shall find it.'

This did not sit well with my trainee. The notebook landed with a slap on the bench, where it was likely to remain, given George's propensity for leaving it behind him wherever he went.

'So we're going to spy on him?' he asked in a whine. 'We're going to follow the man to where he lives and then grub about in his private life like pigs in the dirt?'

He did not seem as delighted with this prospect as I might have hoped.

'We're not spying on him, George; we're *helping* him,' I tried to point out.

'Helping?' George's eyes narrowed.

'Mr Crabbit has a problem, and it's our duty to come to his aid. It's what friends do.'

'So we're his "*friends*" now?'

Even I thought I'd overstepped the mark with that one.

'Mr Crabbit has no friends, but we're his colleagues, George. That's almost the same as being friends. And, as detectives, we have a professional obligation to help him.'

'*Hmmm…*'

'What did you just say?' Had my trainee detective just *hmmm*-ed at me?

'Nothing. I didn't say nothing.' George stared at me obstinately.

Hmmm.

I knew Mr Crabbit to be a man of regular habits. He arrived exactly half an hour early for work each morning in order to open up, and was always the last to leave, five minutes to the dot after everyone else had departed. So, as George and I—wrapped up in our scarves—kept vigil outside in the square, I figured we should not have long to wait.

'Pretend to talk to me, George,' I encouraged him. 'It looks more natural if people see us having a casual conversation. Think of us as two friends who've met by chance in the street—'

'I'd happily talk to you if I thought I could ever get a word in edgeways,' grumbled George, just as the chief clerk stepped out on to the pavement. He locked the door with his key, and then, turning up his collar up to the wind, he made his way rapidly out of the square.

'Quickly, now, George. We don't want to lose him.'

Darkness had all but fallen as we set off northwards along the Gray's Inn Road. The air was bracingly cold, and laced with the first tentative snowflakes of the evening. They swirled about us as we walked, so fine, so light, that they never quite touched the ground.

'The important thing when trailing someone,' I whispered, 'is not just to keep them in sight; you have to make sure you keep your distance, too, see? '

George regarded me with disdain, which I probably

deserved. The truth was he was already adept at the art of trailing people. This presented me with a rather sticky problem: what to train him in next? *The art of picking pockets, at which I was once unequalled?* Something told me he would take none too kindly to being offered lessons in that!

At the junction they now call Kings Cross, Mr Crabbit turned left, bearing west this time. He hardly glanced at the glow from the two arched windows in the facade of the brand-new railway station—*the burning eyes of Hell*, as I like to think of them—preferring instead to keep his eyes on the ground, lest he slip and take a tumble on the ice. A boy with a broom tipped his cap to him, then set about sweeping the snow away with a flourish, not that it brought him any recompense. Mr Crabbit forged past him without so much as a nod.

It was somewhere between Church Row and Cook's Row that we lost him, up by the old burial ground.

'Don't worry,' I told my apprentice. 'We can always try again tomorrow night.'

'Why do we need to?' asked George. 'He's probably just gone home.'

'Well, of course he's gone home, George; where else would he go? The trouble is we don't know where that home is, now, do we?'

'Well, you might not, but I do. Mr Crabbit lives round the corner from me…well, from my parents' place, that is.'

'In Camden Town?'

George nodded.

'Why didn't you say so, George?'

'Because you said this was the perfect opportunity

to show me how to trail people.' He scowled and then he pointedly added, 'Again.'

Ho hum.

Twenty minutes later we were standing in the churchyard on Pratt Street, gazing up at a first-storey window in the row of houses opposite, in which we could see—thanks to the light of a strong paraffin lamp—what was undoubtedly the back of the chief clerk's head. I applied my practised eye to each of the trees that the churchyard had to offer. If we were to climb one, we would no doubt get a better view. When I say "*we*", I really mean "*me*", for the topmost branches in every single case were unlikely to support George's weight.

'George, give me a hand up, will you?'

'Don't tell me you're going to climb that tree!'

'That's the general idea, George. How else are we going to find out what's going on?'

'What if he sees you?'

'He won't, George, he won't. A good detective can make himself invisible when he needs to. Besides, it's dark now.'

George frowned, but helped me up into the bottom branches all the same. Swiftly, silently, I climbed the rest of the way, until I could see directly into the room.

'What's happening?' George called to me from the shadows below.

'*Soft voice*, George; *soft voice.*'

'What's happening?' he asked again, this time in a barely-audible whisper.

'I can see Mr Crabbit. He's sitting at a table. I think he's got somebody with him.'

I could see a tantalizing shadow moving back and forth across the wall. Suddenly a pair of hands hove into view, placing a plate of food on the table. *A woman's hands*, I was sure of it!

'George, George! He's got a woman in there with him!'

'What happened to *soft voice, soft voice*?' grumbled George, as the woman in question appeared at the window and promptly tugged the curtains shut. Not before an image of her had burned itself into my memory, I might add. She was tall, rather imperious, in her late forties or early fifties, with long, grey hair that hung down loose, framing a surprisingly narrow, horse-like face.

I scrabbled down from one branch to the next, then dropped to my feet on the ground.

'He had a woman in there, George,' I repeated in a far more tempered voice, albeit with a slightly scandalized tone. 'A woman, I tell you!'

'Tall, big-boned, in her early fifties, with an honest sort of face?'

Of course. When she'd gone to draw the curtains, George had seen her too.

'You saw her,' I said, feeling a wave of disappointment. I'd wanted to be the one to tell him what I'd seen.

'Nah,' said George, to my amazement. 'I wasn't looking.'

'Wasn't looking?'

'Well, I didn't need to, did I?'

'Why not?'

'Well…it stands to reason, don't it?'

'What stands to reason, George?'

'Who she was.'

This required some careful mulling over, not that any solution seemed quick to present itself.

'And just who was she, George?'

'Octavius,' he said, using my real name rather than my nickname—a feat which had taken me no few weeks to achieve, 'it's Mrs Crabbit.'

'*Mrs* Crabbit?'

'It's his wife, Octavius. Mrs Crabbit is his wife.'

Mr Crabbit had a wife? Well, blow me down!

CHAPTER TWO

'I DIDN'T KNOW HE had a wife!'

'You would do, if you showed a bit more interest in your fellow workers,' scolded George.

'We need to get into that building. We need to hear what they are talking about.'

'You expect us to listen at Mr Crabbit's door?' George looked horrified.

'Mr Crabbit is clearly not himself at the moment, and we're only trying to help him.'

'By listening at his keyhole?'

'Sometimes we detectives need to do unpalatable things.'

George glared at me, then turned and stomped out of the churchyard. 'Coming?' he yelled over his shoulder as he crossed the street.

I ran to catch him up. I was about to explain how we should be looking for some form of easy ingress— such as a scullery window round the back of the building that might just lend itself to being forced—when he marched straight up the snow-covered steps and started pounding away on the door. I was so shocked, I froze in mid-stride. The door opened, and there stood a woman in a cloth cap and apron. She took one look at George and burst into a smile.

'George!' she exclaimed. 'Look at you, all wrapped up in your scarf and mittens! What are you doing here, George? Is something the matter?' A look of concern filtered across her face. 'It's not your parents, is it?'

'No, no,' said George hastily, 'everything's fine. I'm sorry to disturb you, Mrs Moody; you were probably at your supper.'

'Well, as it happens, we *were* all just about to sit down.' The woman—whom I took to be the building's landlady—glanced back into the dimly-lit hallway. As I got nearer, the smell of hot, boiled cabbage came wafting out at me from the open door.

'Mr Crabbit dropped this on his way home from work,' said George, producing a white linen handkerchief from his pocket. 'If you're busy, we can return it to him ourselves.'

'Well, isn't that kind of you?' she said, stepping aside to let us in.

I removed my bowler hat and gave her a respectful nod. She smiled and nodded back, and then retired to her quarters, from whence the sounds of everyday domestic life emanated; a squealing girl and the voice of an older, more authoritative sibling, who seemed to be ordering her recalcitrant sister to stay sitting at the dinner table.

'I don't like lying to Mrs Moody,' grumbled George, as we mounted the stairs together. 'She's going to be…' He paused. *Angry? Disappointed with me when she finds out*? Whatever he'd been about to impart, he now decided against it. 'She and I attend the same church together,' he offered instead. 'She's known me since I was a boy.'

'But it got us inside, didn't it?'

George looked unimpressed.

'If it helps, don't think of it as lying,' I suggested. 'Think of it as telling her the truth that she wants to hear.'

'The truth she wants to hear? *Hmmm*.'

For the record, George's finer feelings with regard to listening at keyholes were never put to the test, for when we reached the landing it became abundantly clear we would have no need for such antics. Raised voices were coming from Mr Crabbit's suite of rooms, making it impossible for us not to overhear what was being said.

'Mavis, I utterly forbid this!' came the familiar, crotchety tones of our gruff chief clerk.

'Forbid, Philip?' A deep, determined woman's voice, as icy as the wind that rattled up and down the street outside. 'You think you can *forbid* me? Oh, how I should like to see you try!'

I stared at George. He stared at me. *Who would dare to speak to Mr Crabbit in such a manner?*

'But the cost of it, Mavis! A guinea every time you attend!'

George and I gasped. *What could Mrs Crabbit be attending that would cost a king's ransom?* A guinea! One pound and one shilling! There was only one thing I could think of that might cost that much.

A photograph.

But that made precious little sense, for once you'd had one photograph taken, why would you have need of another? I admit it would be tempting—if financially ruinous—to commission a portrait of yourself at various points throughout your life (say every ten years or so), so you might look back on them all in your dotage and say, "What interesting times I have seen." Of course, such an indulgence is the preserve of monarchs, and not for the likes of Mrs Crabbit— even if she *was* the chief clerk's wife!

'Think of what it will cost us if I don't get this will overturned! Uncle Frederick always led me to believe that his estate would come to me. To *me*, Philip; not to my damnable cousin!'

'But the will clearly states otherwise, Mavis. Thomas is the sole legatee.'

'Thomas is and always was a wastrel! Uncle Frederick disapproved of him in the extreme, so why would he make him his heir? No, there's something rotten here, Philip; I can *smell* it! And I will get to the bottom of it if it's the last thing I do!'

A woman after my own heart, I mused.

'Mavis, please! This madness of yours will see us bankrupted!'

'But think! If it succeeds! We'd have a house of our very own! A house with proper grounds attached …and a most genteel class of neighbour. Why, we could even employ some full-time servants—with Uncle Frederick's money, we could certainly afford to. Surely then it would all be worth it?'

'Worth frittering away our savings? I can't say I think that it would!'

'But we're on the verge of a breakthrough; I can feel it. Just one or two more sittings and we'll have all the proof we need.'

Sittings? You *sat* for a photographer, but how would that get you any sort of proof, other than evidence of what you looked like?

'Is there nothing I can say to change your mind?'

'Nothing. I am going, and there's an end to it. I shall be back some time after ten. Do not wait up for me.'

I'll give George this: he's almost as quick as I am, if a little heavy-footed. We were down those stairs and out that door before the dust could settle, and by the time Mrs Crabbit emerged, we had managed to adopt the slightly breathless appearance of two friends who'd met by chance in the street. She sallied forth, striding southwards through the billowing snowflakes. George glanced at me and raised an eyebrow. I nodded, and the pair of us set off in pursuit.

At the corner of Pratt Street, she turned left, making for the Hampstead Road. The snow was coming down quite heavily now, and it acted like a blanket, muffling the rhythmical swishing of our footsteps. A good thing, too, for visibility was poor, so we were obliged to stay quite close to her, much closer than I would normally have advised.

The route from Camden into Westminster—which is where, it turned out, she was headed—is a fairly long one, but it's relatively straightforward. Hampstead Road becomes Tottenham Court Road, which then becomes Crown Street. Crown Street empties out into St Martin's Lane, just a little north of Long Acre, and it's here that she veered right—down Cranbourn Street, which becomes Coventry Street as it passes by Leicester Square. At Piccadilly Circus, she turned into the southern tip of Regent Street, and from there into Jermyn Street, which is the first street on the right. This seemed to be her ultimate destination, for she pulled up in front of a building approximately halfway along its length.

She spoke briefly to a man in a great coat and hat, who was standing outside in the snow, and then she went in. I tapped George on the arm to signal him to stop, for I recognized not only the kind of establishment she had brought us to, but also the role of the man who was stationed by the door. This was without doubt a private hotel and he was the hotel doorman.

'This is going to require both guile and finesse,' I whispered, as I drew my apprentice aside.

'Where are we going to get those?' he asked, obviously unaware of what they were.

I tried to think of how I could express the subtle nature of these skills in a way that George might understand. 'We need to lie, and we need to do it convincingly,' I replied.

'More lying. I should have guessed.'

'See that man there? He's a hotel doorman, George.'

'I know he is,' he concurred.

'It's his job to keep the likes of us out.'

'But—'

'But nothing, George! We are detectives, and it's our job to gather information in any way we can.'

'By lying?'

'If need be.'

'But—'

'George! You and your "buts"!'

'But—'

'Enough, George, enough! We will approach this problem with logic and inventiveness. That doorman— see?—to him we look like a pair of errand boys.'

'I am an errand boy.'

'Exactly. So that is the role we shall play. A good lie is always founded in truth, George; remember that.'

'I'm surprised you don't want me to write it down.'

I threw him a glance. *Could my trainee detective be capable of sarcasm*, I wondered? Had it been anyone other than the stolid George Crump, I might have said yes.

'All I ask is that you watch and learn, George, for I am a master at this. The first thing you need to do is weigh up your opponent. To which class would you say he belongs? What is this man's station in life?'

'Well, he's working class, ain't he?'

I cocked my head to one side. 'He's not, say, lower middle class, like Mr Crabbit? Or even has pretensions to be?'

George shook his head decisively. 'No, definitely not.'

'Nicely observed, George. You have summed up the gist of this man's mettle in a nutshell.'

'Why's it important?' he asked. I heard a faint budding of interest creep into his voice.

'Well, whichever social group he belongs to, he will have certain expectations of each of the other classes.'

'And that's important how?'

'If he were lower middle class, George, he would look down on us as if we were nothing but a pair of clowns. We, in turn, would need to readjust our demeanour to meet his expectations.'

'What?'

'We'd have to look and act like a pair of clowns, George.'

George frowned. 'Why?'

'Because the greatest threat to any Englishman comes invariably from the class directly beneath his own—or so he fondly imagines. He's only one rung above them on the social ladder, see? And what a tragedy it would be if that rung were to disappear! Why, he would be no better than they were! But once he sees us conforming to his expectations, he'll realize we're no threat to him and he'll swiftly drop his guard. Who—after all—would feel threatened by a pair of worthless clowns?'

'Oh.' George mulled this over. 'And that's what you mean by guile and finesse?'

'It is, George, it is.'

'That's really quite clever, isn't it?'

'Why, thank you.'

'But he's not lower middle class, is he?'

'No, he's not, as you so succinctly observed. Which means we need to adopt a different ploy. We'll approach him as social equals: he has a job to do; we have a job to do. Equals, see? But we defer to him because he's older than us.'

'I think I understand.'

'You'll get the hang of it, George. Just follow my lead…and, whatever happens, make sure you keep your mouth shut. I'm used to these situations, whereas you, my friend, are not.'

We set off along the street again, drawing ever nearer to our mark.

'Equals, remember,' I whispered, but, in spite of the warning, I saw that George was holding himself awkwardly. Head bowed, he stared at the pavement instead of meeting the doorman's eye.

The doorman was quick to notice this and regarded the boy with suspicion. In fact, I felt sure he was about to have words with him, but, before he could, George turned his back and stalked away.

'Sir,' I said, hoping to salvage what I could of the situation, 'we are a pair of errand boys, sent by our good and honest master with an urgent message for his wife.'

Having retreated several yards down the street, George stood squirming with his head in his hands.

'Her name is Mrs Crabbit,' I continued. 'Can you tell me if she's here?'

The doorman glanced at me for barely a second. 'Is this some kind of joke?' he said, addressing himself to my cringing apprentice—or, more accurately, to my cringing apprentice's back.

'Sir,' I said, 'I repeat: we are a pair of trusty errand boys, and we—'

'No, I want to hear it from George.'

'You want...*what?*'

'I want to hear what George has to say. He's got a tongue in his head, hasn't he?'

'I tried to tell you,' muttered George, as he turned around to face me.

'Tried to tell me what?'

'I know him, don't I? He's my brother, William.'

Slowly he came wandering back.

'Your *brother*?'

'Well, one of them.'

Now that it had been pointed out to me, I could see the family resemblance. William was older and taller than George, but both were powerfully built.

'So what's your game, George?' his brother demanded to know. 'What kind of fool's mission are you on now?'

'There's no urgent message. That was a lie.' George threw me a disapproving look. 'We just want to know about Mr Crabbit's wife…that woman who just went in. Is she a guest here?'

Note to self: have a quiet word with George to make sure he's aware that there's more to the delicate art of detection than the straightforward questioning of people he already happens to know.

'And why is that any business of yours?'

'We're trying to help her husband. He's Mr Bruff's chief clerk.'

William let out a low whistle. 'The one who's always giving you grief?'

George nodded.

'And—let me get this straight—you're trying to *help* him?'

'I wouldn't say it if it weren't true.' George fixed his brother with a stare.

'You wouldn't, would you?' William admitted, buckling under the gaze. 'Very well; listen up: Mrs Crabbit's not staying here, if that's what you imagined. She just comes to visit one of the guests.'

'Which guest?'

A decidedly conspiratorial smile appeared on the older brother's lips. 'An American lady who recently arrived here from Boston, Massachusetts…a certain Mrs Maria Harmon.' He emphasized the final three words, as if they should convey some special meaning.

George gasped. 'Not the——?'

William nodded. 'The very same.'

'The very same *what*?' I asked, feeling that I'd been frozen out of the conversation for far too long. Both brothers turned their heads to gape.

'Don't mind him,' said George. 'That's just Octavius. He's my friend. He's all right, even if he does like to lie a lot.'

'The very same *what*?' I asked again.

William looked down his nose at me. 'Are you going to tell him or am I?'

It was George who did the honours. 'Mrs Harmon's a trance medium.'

'A *what*?'

'A trance medium. She holds sittings for people where she contacts the dead.'

CHAPTER THREE

'THE DEAD?' I CONSIDERED the plausibility of this statement, which, I have to say, had been made with every sign of sincerity on George's part. 'You have got to be jesting,' I immediately spat back. 'Surely you cannot be serious!'

Neither brother looked as if he were jesting.

'And people believe in this? Actually *believe* in it?'

'Her sittings are very well attended,' William replied.

And incredibly lucrative, I reflected, *if she's extracting a guinea from each mug that she pulls through the door. I'd seen my fair share of confidence tricks, but this one took the cake!*

'And Mrs Crabbit, she attends these sittings?'

'They only started holding them a few weeks ago, but, yes, since then she's become a bit of a regular.'

Presumably she came hoping for some word from her uncle that would help overturn the will we had heard about. No wonder Mr Crabbit was at his wits' end! I almost felt sorry for the man.

'What's she like, this Mrs Harmon?' In my head I could already see a very straight-backed, elderly widow in a stiffly-starched, lace-trimmed blouse, with a garnet the size of a plover's egg pinned to the throat. There'd be something peculiar about her eyes: they'd be silver or some strange shade of violet, and she'd never look directly at you, or, if she did, it was never quite *at you*, but always over your shoulder.

George's brother scratched his eyebrow. 'She's young, good looking; I'd say about my age. Mr Harmon, he's a bit older, but not by much. They seem a pleasant enough couple—devoted to each other—though I don't get to see a lot of them; they and their entourage generally keep themselves to themselves. They have a suite of rooms on the second floor.'

'Their entourage?'

'There's a young woman who accompanies them; she's Mrs Harmon's secretary. And a lad about your age, who's their general factotum. You should see the colour of his skin!'

'Why?'

'Because it's black…well, not as black as some I've seen…but even so he'd stand out in a crowd. Mr Condon, whose hotel this is, reckons he used to be a slave.'

'And can anyone attend these sittings?' I was already mulling over ways to raise the necessary funds.

'No, you have to be invited.'

Damn! 'So how do you get invited?'

'You need to write the Harmons a request, stating why you want to attend.'

I was about to add, "*And there's no chance you can sneak us in?*" when George gave a loud, disapproving cough. Feeling that it might have been intended for me, I hazarded a glance at his face. His mouth was set, his eyes were stern, and you could almost see the words, "*Don't you dare!*" champing at the bit on his lips. The trouble with providing him with instruction in detection is that he needed to know how my mind works—but the minute he knew how it worked, he could predict what I would probably do. To be charitable, I suppose he was only looking out for his brother's best interests. William's job was to keep the likes of us out, not find ways of smuggling us in.

We bid his brother farewell and began retracing our steps. The snow flurries had finally abated, leaving a cold, frosty night in their wake.

'So what do you think?' I asked, as we passed by the green in Leicester Square.

'If Mrs Crabbit wants to go to these Spiritualist meetings, I don't see how we can stop her.'

'But don't you think they sound fishy?'

'Fishy? How?'

'Well, really, George! The woman claims to talk to the dead…is that not fishy enough for you?'

George gave this his full consideration. 'Actually, we don't know what she does, do we? We know she holds sittings…but who's to say what happens in them?'

As much as it pained me to admit it, I had to agree. 'You're right. We need to see for ourselves.'

'I don't see how we're going to do that,' said George. 'We don't have invitations and we don't have the money.'

'Mere obstacles, George! Mere obstacles! And what, pray tell me, are obstacles?' I cocked my head to one side and patiently awaited his answer.

CHAPTER THREE

'Chances that God sends the jobbing detective to allow him to prove his resourcefulness?'

'Correct. That was almost word perfect.' Actually, it *was* word perfect—he'd quoted *Guy's Taxonomy of Opportunities for the Jobbing Detective* to the letter; I just didn't want it going to his head.

'I still don't see how we're going to do it,' he mumbled.

Neither did I, at least not clearly, though I did have one or two ideas up my sleeve. When we reached St Martin's Lane, we parted company, with George heading back to Camden Town and me crossing the road into Long Acre. My destination was the Lamb and Flag, a public house often referred to as the Bucket of Blood, on account of the bare-knuckle fist fights that used to be held there. My friend Bertha had put a stop to those, much to the landlord's annoyance—not that the landlord had any choice in the matter. You don't say no to the person in charge of London's entire criminal underclass—well, not if you wish to remain upright and breathing, you don't.

Bertha and his underlings, Walter, Alex, and Charley, occupied rooms on the first floor. And, yes, I did say *his* underlings—not that Bertha himself would tolerate such a slip of the tongue—for as gruff and surly as Bertha might be, he thought of himself as a woman.

I first met him some nine years back, when I was but a young lad of six. He had a flower stall in the market, plus a number of less legitimate, oft-times fleeting lines of business on the side. He had always been straight with me (well, except maybe once; but that, as they say, is another story). Apart from my younger brother Julius, he was the closest thing to family that I had. If anyone would stump up two guineas for a good cause, it would be he.

Armed with a paper cone of roasted chestnuts purchased from a vendor in the street, I rounded the corner, and was about to enter the pub, when something up above me caught my eye. The boarded-up window on the first floor, which had stood broken for nearly a year, had finally been repaired. *Well done, Bertha*!

I pulled open the door and went in. Given that this was not a market day, there were a fair few people about. I made my way across the sawdust-strewn floor to the foot of the stairs, where Alex and Charley were on guard duty. In their tailored black frock-coats, and sporting a single white rose each for a buttonhole, they looked like a pair of dapper young bulls.

'I'd be careful, if I was you,' warned Alex, as he stepped aside to let me to pass. ''Er Ladyship ain't too 'appy just now.'

I paused on the stair. 'What do you mean by that?' I asked.

'Ask '*im*,' he said, delivering a swift punch to his sidekick's kidney. Charley turned a bright red; though not from pain, it seemed to me, but rather from an acute sense of embarrassment.

'Charley?' My inquiry only served to make Charley redder. He didn't reply; he just stared at the floor.

I continued on up and found Bertha in his sitting room, reclining on his *chaise longue* with a glass of sherry in his hand. He was dressed in his usual widow's weeds, minus the hat and veil he normally wears in public. His face was the picture of woe, though he brightened considerably when he saw me appear.

'Hello, Bertha.'

'Octopus! Wot brings you 'ere?'

Octopus. Another nickname from my none-too-distant past, and, like Gooseberry, one that will undoubtedly prove hard to shake off.

'I've brought you some roasted chestnuts, Bertha.'

My friend gave a deep, throaty chuckle. 'Always was partial to the odd chestnut,' he declared. 'Come in, come in…'ere, Woll-ah,'—by which he meant Walter, the young lad he'd chosen as his second-in-command—'get Octopus a chair.'

'Please, sir…*take mine*,' said Walter, immediately surrendering his own to me. To all outward appearances, the change in the boy could not have been more dramatic: he wore a nicely-cut suit; he had boots on his feet; and at long last his cold had cleared up. Gone was the snotty nose and the cowering demeanour. But some things aren't so easily fixed—timidity and servility amongst them.

'No, it's fine,' I told him, and hauled myself a chair over from the corner.

'So to wot do I owe the pleasure?' asked Bertha, as he peeled away at the shell of a chestnut with a good deal more dexterity than his fleshy, big fingers looked capable of.

'I was hoping you could help me out with some money,' I replied.

'Money?' The fingers paused abruptly in their task.

'Just a couple of guineas,' I said, uncomfortably aware that what I was asking for was the twice equivalent of what a working man earns in a month.

'Oh, Octopus, it ain't a good time.'

'Is there a problem, Bertha?'

'I went and got the window fixed—see?—'cos it was gettin' bleedin' cold up 'ere. I 'ad a scheme all worked out to pay for it, too. There was this race wot was rigged, right, so I knew from the off 'oo the winner would be.'

'Oh, don't tell me!' I cried, as the pieces of the puzzle began to fall into place. 'You had Charley place the bet for you!'

Bertha grunted and popped the chestnut in his mouth.

'Mr Bertha lost everything,' Walter explained. 'And he still has to pay for the window. Glass don't come cheap, sir…*or so I am led to believe*.'

'Oh, Bertha! I should have warned you about Charley. He's liable to get confused.'

'It's only blinkin' money,' mused Bertha. 'I'll make it back eventually. But wot about you?' he asked. 'Why d'you need the cash?'

I told him about the trance medium in the private hotel on Jermyn Street. It turned out that he'd already heard of her.

'There's this bloke I know, right? 'E's thinkin' of seein' 'er.'

'I don't suppose he needs someone to go with him to hold his hand?' It was a remark said in jest, and yet Bertha looked horrified.

'Oh, Octopus, you oughtn't go joking 'bout something like that!'

'I'm not sure I understand what you mean,' I said.

'This Louis Sligo, he…' Not only had he *not* dropped the "h" from the "he", he also seemed at a loss for words.

'Bertha, are you blushing?'

My friend dithered for another second or two, then looked me straight in the eye.

'Octopus, 'e likes boys like you.'

'Likes?'

Bertha gave a meaningful nod.

Oh. *Likes*.

''E'd take you with him at the drop of an 'at, but you'd always 'ave to be on your bleedin' guard with 'im.'

'How do you know him, Bertha?'

''E sells pictures—don't 'e?—wot they calls "h'oils", out of 'is shop in Great Russell Street. Bleedin' rich as creases, 'e is.'

Rich as Croesus, I conjectured?

'Sometimes 'e'll get a customer wot wants a work by a particular h'artist—a Constable, maybe, or a Frago-nar'.'

A policeman or a what?

''E knows painters wot can knock out a decent forgery, but then 'e's got a problem. 'Ow does the picture come into 'is possession, all legitimate, like? And that's where I come in.'

For the life of me I couldn't see how.

'I goes and sells it to a stall wot does jumble, 'cos jumble can cover a multitude of sins. An 'ouse clearance, 'cos some old codger died…an 'ouse clearance, 'cos the bleeder got burgled; it don't matter none when it comes to jumble! Then Sligo nosies along and buys it for a song—making sure 'e's got witnesses, see? Stall 'older's 'appy; customer's 'appy; and I'm up a shillin' or two. 'Course, these days I don't do the selling meself. I leave that up to Charley.'

'*Charley*? Do you think that's wise?'

Bertha frowned. 'You might 'ave a point.'

'So, can I at least meet this Louis Sligo?'

The frown deepened. 'Oh, I dunno, Octopus. I don't think it's a good idea.'

'Bertha, I can handle myself.'

'Nah, nah, nah! You don't know Sligo.' He wagged his finger at me.

'Please. This may be the only way I'll get to see Mrs Harmon for myself.'

Still frowning and shaking his head, Bertha let out a sigh. 'Woll-ah, go fetch Charley.' A minute or so later, Charley presented himself at the door. 'You know where Louis Sligo lives, Charley?'

'The rooms above 'is shop?'

Bertha nodded. 'You go tell 'im I want to see 'im. Now.'

A subtle change came over the lad's face. He seemed oddly reluctant to leave.

'Wot yeh still doin' 'ere, Charley?'

'Can't you send Alex instead?'

'Why?'

'I don't like the bloke, do I? 'E's always tryin' to paw me.'

'You're big enough and ugly enough to stop 'im, ain't yeh?'

'Well…yeah…'

'Look,' said Bertha, addressing him in a much softer

tone, 'if he tries anythin' on with yeh, you just break 'is arm, right?'

'Right,' repeated Charley, sounding none too convinced.

In due course, when Mr Louis Sligo arrived, he proved to be a clean-shaven fellow in his late forties, with cold, watchful eyes, a sharply receding hairline, and lips resembling those of a fish. He wore a constant smirk on his chubby, pink face, suggestive of how superior he felt himself to other mortals. He was immaculately attired; I'll give him that. There was not a cuff-link, a button, nor a thread out of place. By contrast, Charley was looking decidedly ruffled.

Bertha had decided that the meeting should take place downstairs in the pub. He had also forbidden Walter to attend, which seemed like a sensible precaution, given the man's proclivities. As Mr Sligo approached our table, he rose to make the introductions.

'Louis, this 'ere's me mate, Octo—'

'Octavius,' I said, trying my best to drown him out, and rising to shake the man's hand. The flesh in the glove felt stodgy and lifeless.

'Enchanted,' purred Mr Sligo. 'But where are my manners? Let me introduce myself: I am Louis Bletchford Sligo and, for my sins, I am a dealer in Fine Art.'

We both sat down, facing each other across the table. Bertha went to order us drinks.

'You, young man, must call me Louis. That charming young ruffian over there,'—he made a sweeping gesture to indicate the dishevelled-looking Charley, who had taken up his station by the stairs again—'he leads me to believe that I can be of service to you in some minor fashion. How intriguing!'

I felt the palm of his land on my knee, causing me to sit bolt upright. I'm sure the legendary Sergeant Cuff of Scotland Yard, whom I have had the pleasure of working with twice, never had to suffer such indignities when he was starting out!

'I am your humble servant to do with as you will,' he said, 'so how may I be of help?'

'You are to attend one of Mrs Harmon's sittings at Condon's hotel, sir?' Even as I spoke, I had grabbed him by the wrist and was wrenching his hand off my leg.

'Maria Harmon? The medium? Why, yes; isn't the idea too delicious for words?'

'A friend of mine and I also wish to attend, but—alas!—we find ourselves without the funds to do so, sir.'

'A friend, you say? Ah! Then you shall both be my guests. What an absolute treat it will be!' He abandoned the habitual smirk just long enough to give me a knowing wink. Again I felt his palm land on my knee.

'Take your bleedin' 'and off 'im, Louis.' Bertha was back with the drinks. He placed a ginger beer in front of me and passed the man a sherry. 'You lay another finger on me friend 'ere, and it'll be the last time you lay that finger anywhere.' He set his own glass down on the table. '*Anywhere*. Yeh get me?'

'I do,' said Mr Sligo, this time removing his hand by himself.

CHAPTER FOUR

MR CONDON'S HOTEL ON Jermyn Street was perhaps not the most prestigious hotel I had ever set foot in, but it certainly came close. It was clean and comfortable, and nicely-positioned, being close to The Mall, should one care to take a stroll. As arranged, George and I met Mr Sligo's cab on the corner of Regent Street. George wore his Sunday best; I myself had brushed up my bowler for the occasion. We had agreed in advance on a suitable cover story—a modest little fiction of my own devising, whereby George and I were to be Mr Sligo's young assistants who accompany him everywhere. For those of you reading this who are not in fact detectives, I should perhaps point out that the addition of a simple detail—like how we accompany him everywhere—can lend an air of veracity to the most humble of lies.

George had squared it with his brother that they would not acknowledge each other; I had squared it with Mr Sligo that there would be no funny business where George was concerned. I let it be known that the lad had broken a man's wrist for less, which was true for the most part, though in fairness—at the time—he was saving my life.

We'd barely stepped over the threshold when a woman approached us and asked Mr Sligo if he was here to see Mrs Harmon. She was young, modestly dressed, and spoke with a bit of an accent.

'But what a charming voice you have, my dear,' Mr Sligo purred silkily. 'Boston, if I'm not mistaken.'

'Why, yes! Do you know Boston, sir?'

'Unfortunately, no. But some of my more discerning clients hail from your charming city.'

'May I take your name, sir?' she asked.

'Why, certainly you may. I am Louis Bletchford Sligo, dealer in Fine Art. And these are my assistants, Octavius and Geoffrey.'

George grimaced at being called this, and was about to say something, but in the nick of time he saw me shake my head. *If he thinks of you as Geoffrey, it's probably best to play along with it.*

'Say hello, Geoffrey,' the man urged.

Despite Sligo slipping his arm round his shoulder, George managed a cheery hello.

'And may we have the pleasure of knowing your name, dear lady?' Mr Sligo continued.

The woman blushed. 'I am Miss Sarah Brahms, Mrs Harmon's personal secretary.' She flattened the *"ar"* sounds in both names till they were no more than a sighing *"ah"*. 'There was no mention in your letter about bringing your assistants.'

'Oh? I just assumed you would know…they accompany me *everywhere*. Isn't that so, Octavius?' His other arm snaked its way around my neck. Now he had his paws on the both of us.

'Everywhere, miss,' I affirmed.

'If you wish them to attend the sitting, you realize you will have to pay for the privilege?'

'I *do*,' said Mr Sligo, with a sight more conviction than most bridegrooms can muster. 'But between you and me, Miss Brahms, *it's only money*, is it not?' He gave my shoulder a squeeze. 'How else is one to rid oneself of the Devil's own lucre?' He held out a banker's draft made out to the tune of three guineas.

Miss Brahms beamed at him. 'Then, sir, if you'll be so good as to follow me, I shall take you up and introduce you to Mr Condon.'

She showed us to a room on the second floor, where a party of sorts was in progress. People were gathered in various groups, chatting awkwardly or not chatting at all. A boy whose skin was an extraordinary shade of chocolate moved purposefully between them, carrying a tray of glasses in his hands. He was a year or two younger than me and perhaps a little shorter; his hair was close-cropped and shiny with oil. He wore an expensive-looking suit of red and white livery, with three-quarter length breeches trimmed with buttons up the sides. Noting our arrival, he made his way over and respectfully held out his tray. Mr Sligo eyed every inch of him with obvious approval, from his full, chiselled lips to his sparkling green eyes that glittered not unlike a cat's. He reached out and took the glass nearest him, and then watched as the lad moved away.

'This way, sir,' said Miss Brahms. She led us across to the window, where a tall, self-assured-looking man stood talking to one of the female guests. 'Excuse the intrusion, Mr Condon, but I should like to present Mr Louis Sligo. It's his first time here.'

'Ah, Mr Sligo, welcome! I'm Edward Condon, proprietor of this humble establishment.'

'Oh, you are too modest, Mr Condon! Your hotel is delightful!' He turned to me. 'May I present my two young assistants? They accompany me *everywhere*.'

There's a fine line between adding a hint of compelling detail and flogging your story to death, and Mr Sligo was clearly veering towards the latter. I expect he was exacting his revenge on me for spoiling his fun.

'Well, go on, boy,' he prompted. 'Don't be shy. Introduce yourself.'

'I am Octavius Guy, sir. It's very nice to meet you, Mr Condon.'

'It's nice to meet you, too, Octavius.'

'Come on, Geoffrey.' Sligo nudged George in the ribs. 'Time to earn your keep.'

'Hello,' said George, 'I'm…'

Before he could respond, Mr Sligo swept on. 'And who is this lovely vision with whom you were speaking? Could this delightful lady be our hostess, Mrs Harmon?'

'This is Miss McVeigh, sir, one of the regulars at our sittings. Miss McVeigh, may I present Mr Sligo and his two assistants?'

'Oh, do not concern yourself with my worthless assistants, miss.' He bowed and kissed the woman's hand. 'Trust me, they're no fun at all!'

I didn't catch her reply, just its musical tone, for at that moment my attention was diverted. Miss Brahms was back with a new arrival in tow—and bless me if I didn't know him!

'Excuse me for interrupting, Mr Condon, but may I present Mr Herbert Winter. It's his first time here.'

'Ah, Mr Winter, welcome! I am Edward Condon, proprietor of this humble establishment.'

I watched as the elderly gentleman endured the routine introductions, and chuckled inwardly to myself as his eyes lit on me. *Mr Winter, indeed!*

As soon as he felt able to, he detached himself from the group and went and stood on his own by the fireplace.

'Well, well, well,' I remarked, as I joined him there. 'What brings you here, Mr Death?'

'It's de Ath,' he reminded me gently, 'though tonight I should prefer you address me as Winter.'

'You have need of an alias, sir?'

'An alias can be useful on occasion, as I'm sure you're aware. And in answer to your question, young man, professional interests have drawn me here.'

Ah, I thought, *but which profession?* His clerical post at the Prerogative Will Office, where I'd met him the previous summer? Or something far more mysterious? Call me fanciful, but long had I harboured the suspicion that this mournful-looking character was much more than he seemed. With his deep-set eyes and sunken cheeks, in certain lights his face took on a distinctly cadaverous aspect. Death by name and Death by nature, perchance? *Oh, that was the question indeed!*

'And what, may I ask, brings you?' he said.

'Professional interests as well,' I replied. As I spoke, I spied Mrs Crabbit entering the room.

Eschewing a drink from the lad with the tray, she glanced about at the various groups, then made her way over to join one where all the members were of a similar age to her own. The only exception was an extremely tall young woman, who seemed to welcome her arrival. Mr Death noted my interest in the chief clerk's wife and stood regarding me pensively.

'Sir,' I said, knowing how ridiculous the question would sound, but wanting to hear his opinion, 'let me pick your brain, for you are clearly an expert in such matters: could the testimony of a ghost be used to overturn a will?'

'Overturn a will? *On testimony from beyond the grave?*' He arched a scornful eyebrow.

'But what if that testimony brought to light some new evidence? Actual, tangible evidence?'

Now he stared at me aghast. 'That,' he replied, 'would be an entirely different matter.' Then he added an aside that could hardly have been directed at me, 'So let us all pray it does not!'

'Sir?'

'Oh, nothing, nothing. I was merely reflecting on the fact that we all of us have masters to whom we must answer. Yes, as it happens, even I.'

I found the idea strangely disquietening. 'Sir,' I said, mustering up my courage whilst the opportunity presented itself, 'am I right to imagine you like me?'

'Surprisingly, I do.'

'So you wouldn't wish to see my young life cut short?'

Mr Death blinked, but never quite answered my question, for at that moment Mr Condon made an announcement:

'Ladies and gentlemen, I have just had word that Mrs Harmon is ready to receive you. The sitting is about to commence, so please, make your way through.'

Excusing myself, I went back to my group, who were even now heading into the adjoining room.

Inside, at the head of a large, oval table, sat a young woman in her early twenties. Her fiery red hair was pinned up in a bun, all but a few stray strands that fell in wisps down to her cheeks. In a simple black gown with long, flowing sleeves, she looked pale but oddly beautiful in the light from the tall candelabra. Next to her sat a man a little older than she—her husband, I presumed, for both her hands were clasped in his. Strangely, he did not bother to rise and greet his guests, as one might expect; he seemed content to let his wife to do the greeting.

'Mr Hargreaves!' Mrs Harmon called out, in the same accent as her secretary's. 'How pleasant it is to see you here again.' She extracted one of her hands from her husbands' and patted the chair to her left. 'Will you not come and join me, sir?'

Mr Hargreaves, a man in his thirties with a swarthy complexion, seemed only too happy to comply.

'He always gets to sit at the top of the table,' complained Miss McVeigh in a whisper.

'Tut, tut; there's no mystery there,' Mr Sligo came back in a similar manner. 'Why, the answer's as plain as day, dear lady. Mrs Harmon resents your beauty, and wishes to avoid any comparisons. I mean, just look at the creature she's beckoning to now!'

The tall young woman from Mrs Crabbit's group was being encouraged to sit beside Mr Hargreaves. She seemed rather ungainly and painfully shy, and, even when Mr Hargreaves rose to pull her seat out for her, it still took a great deal of coaxing to persuade her to join him. Mr Sligo indicated that I should sit next to her, and then he took the chair next to me. George ended up in the seat to his left, which put Miss McVeigh in the chair at the bottom of the table, facing Mrs Harmon.

Mr Death made his way round the far side and sat down next to the medium's husband. He was followed by an eminently sensible-looking woman, whom I remembered seeing chatting with Mrs Crabbit. She chose the seat near a small wooden cabinet on which a porcelain bust of Lord Nelson was set. Next came Mrs Crabbit herself, escorted by a middle-aged gentle-man—a doctor or lawyer, by the look of him, for he had a keen, professional eye.

Since all the seats were now taken, it seemed that neither Miss Brahms nor Mr Condon was to join us. The lad who'd been serving the drinks, however, was busy meting out sheets of paper.

'Tonight my good, dear wife will begin the sitting by fielding your written questions,' Mr Harmon explained, with a touch of the brogue in his voice. 'May I remind you all to limit your inquiry to something that can be answered with a simple yes or no.'

Behind me, to my right, there stood a cabinet. I watched as the liveried boy took a dip-pen and some ink from it, and then made his way round to where Mr Death was seated. The mood became serious as, one

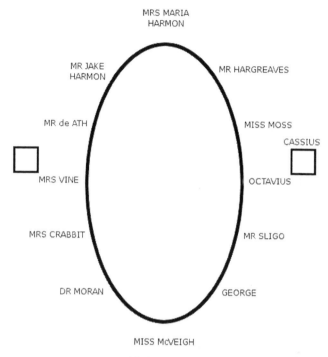

SEATING PLAN
FRIDAY, DECEMBER 10TH, 1852

by one, we each wrote out a question. The resulting sheet was folded once—and then twice—and then placed upon the boy's silver platter.

'Oh, don't bother with him,' sneered Mr Sligo, as the lad offered George the dip-pen.

'No, wait! It's just Mr Sligo's little joke,' I piped up, as the boy began moving away. 'Of course Geoffrey wants to partake in this, don't you, Geoffrey?'

George threw me a look at the use of the name, but applied himself to writing nonetheless.

When the last of the questions had been gathered up, the boy placed the platter in front of Mrs Harmon and then retired to his spot beside the cabinet. Mrs Harmon picked up the first sheet and held it aloft. She glanced round theatrically at everyone present, and suddenly two extremely loud raps were heard.

'The answer is no,' she said, before opening it and reading out what was written there: '*Is my name Mr Winter?*'

Everyone stared at Mr Death.

'You have caught me out,' he said, nodding. He seemed visibly shaken.

'May I ask your true name, sir?' Mrs Harmon inquired.

'Mr Herbert de Ath, Esquire.'

'You are a disbeliever?'

'I am a pragmatist, young lady.'

Mrs Harmon smiled. 'Then there is still a chance we can convert you to the Spiritualist cause.'

'And what does such a cause espouse, may I ask?'

'Why, Equality, sir. There will come a time when brother will take up arms against brother so that *all* men—and women, too—whatever their colour—may be equal on this Earth, just as they are in the sight of God.'

A smattering of dismissive if genteel laughter echoed from the mouths of a few of those present.

Mrs Harmon responded with a tired little smile. 'Go ahead; laugh. Why shouldn't you? Even Cassius doesn't believe me, do you, Cassius?'

I glanced at the grinning lad behind me. 'I'd like to, miss; indeed I would,' he replied.

'But it's true,' she insisted. 'It will come to pass; I have seen it. Slavery will have had its day and all men shall be free.'

She picked up the next sheet of paper. Again she held it aloft and glanced round the table. There was one loud rap this time.

'The answer is yes.' She unfolded it and proceeded to read: '*Does my son miss me?*'

The eminently sensible-looking woman appeared to be on the verge of tears. Mrs Crabbit took her hand and gave it a squeeze.

Mrs Harmon picked up the next sheet. One rap. 'The answer is yes.' She opened it and read out the question: '*Did Cousin Thomas resort to foul play where Uncle Frederick's will is concerned?*'

Again and again she appeared to get the right result as she opened one question after another.

Yes. *Are my wife and baby daughter with each other? Are they happy?*

No. *Will the man I am thinking of make a good, faithful husband?*

And then she came to George. She picked up the question he'd written and held it aloft. Smiling, she glanced around the table. One rap rang out; loud, clear, unambiguous.

'The answer is yes,' she said.

I stole a glance at George. A peculiar light had come into his eyes, and, though he had it under control, I knew him well enough to detect the beginnings of a grin.

'*Is my name Geoffrey?*' she promptly read out.

Hmmm. Nicely played, George! Nicely played!

Mrs Harmon reached for the next sheet of paper, but paused without picking it. The sound of a door being thrust open, followed by an outburst of angry, raised voices, filtered through to us from the adjoining room. She glanced at her husband, who immediately rose and made for the communicating door. Just as he got there, a man barged into the room, followed swiftly by a penitent Miss Brahms.

'I'm so sorry, Mr Harmon,' she bleated. 'I explained the procedure—that he should put his request in writing—but he insisted on attending the meeting regardless. I tried to stop him, but the brute just pushed his way past me.'

'That's all right, Sarah,' Mr Harmon replied. 'I shall deal with this. Sir—?'

The man, who'd been standing and staring at Mrs Crabbit (whose face, I noticed, had drained of all colour), turned towards our host.

For a man in his mid-forties, which he undoubtedly was, he looked remarkably fit and lithe of form. He had short, dark hair, with only the slightest signs of greying, and a neatly trimmed moustache to match. His face was a little gaunt, and the muscles of his jaw were permanently clenched, as if from fighting back some deep-felt emotion. Either that, or he was simply spoiling for a fight.

'What's the matter?' he said, blinking at Mr Harmon. 'Is my money not as good as that woman's?' He pointed across the table at the chief clerk's wife. 'If she can attend your meeting, I demand the right to, too!'

'Sir…'

Taking advantage of the developing quarrel, Miss Brahms skirted round behind me and went and whispered something in the medium's ear. Mrs Harmon looked up with a start and quickly posed a question. My lip-reading skills may be none too good, but I'd have happily wagered it was, "*Are you quite sure?*" Her secretary nodded her head.

'But I will pay double—nay, treble—what she pays,' the intruder was saying, not that Mr Harmon was paying him any heed.

'Sir, I must insist that you—'

'Jake!' Mrs Harmon's voice cut swiftly through her husband's. 'We are Spiritualists, sir,' she said, now addressing the newcomer, 'and, if it is Truth that you seek, then you are welcome here. Jake, while you bring another chair, our guest can introduce himself.'

The trance medium, it seemed, understood the value of money—even if her husband did not!

CHAPTER FIVE

'MY NAME IS THOMAS Patrick Ryman, and I am a man of private means.'

I leaned forward and glanced at George, only to find him already glancing at me. *Mrs Crabbit's Cousin Thomas*, we both thought in unison, and, as one, we turned our gaze on Mrs Crabbit. She still looked exceedingly ill, but two spots of intense colour had appeared in her cheeks. Mr Death, I noticed, had planted his elbow on the table and was shielding his face with his hand. It was as if he were trying to avoid eye contact, but with whom? Mrs Crabbit? Or her cousin? It was hard to tell.

'Welcome, Mr Ryman,' Mrs Harmon said graciously. 'Won't you please sit down?'

Her husband had returned with a chair, which he placed between George and Miss McVeigh. She and the professional gentleman to her left moved around to accommodate him, as did George, Mr Sligo, and myself. Mr Harmon returned to the top of the table and his wife recommenced answering our questions.

I got a resounding "*No!*" to my query, "*Are you a fraudster?*", which everyone seemed to find highly amusing. As the medium worked through her routine, summoning raps out of nowhere, I cast a wary eye over Cousin Thomas. He wasn't fidgeting as such, nor was he sitting perfectly still; his entire body seemed to tremble with a fervour and his eyes kept up an erratic blink. I soon looked away, for it was exhausting to watch.

'We now come to that part of the evening,' I heard Mr Harmon say, 'where—'

'Just a minute,' Mr Ryman interrupted him. 'What about me? Don't I get a turn?'

'Mr Ryman, we—'

'No! I have bought my way to this table, and I should have the same rights as everyone else.'

'Mr Ryman, please—'

Mrs Harmon laid her hand on her husband's arm. 'No, my dearest, Mr Ryman is right. Mr Ryman, please bear in mind that what you ask must be capable of being answered with a simple yes or no. Cassius? Will you please do the honours?'

The boy behind me stirred himself, and promptly produced paper and pen for the newcomer. Mr Ryman took receipt of them, then hunched himself forward in his chair. Palming the sheet close to his chest, he began furtively scratching away on it, penning a question that seemed to go on and on for ever. Every so often he glanced up to see if anyone was watching. Everybody was, though everyone except George put on a good show of pretending that they weren't. Seeing George's obvious interest only spurred him on to greater heights of secrecy. At last he folded his sheet and handed it back, and the boy delivered it to the medium. Some fleeting emotion passed between them as he handed it over.

She held it aloft. Two raps were heard. 'The answer is no,' she said, and then proceeded to open it up.

'*Did I in any way tamper with, forge, or substitute my Uncle Frederick's will, or apply undue influence on him of any sort during his final days on earth?*' She emphasized the words "*in any way*" and "*of any sort*" to indicate the amount of frenzied underlining we had seen him engaging in.

Mr Ryman looked vindicated; Mrs Crabbit looked livid.

'Uncle Frederick would *never* choose you as his heir!' she cried. 'So if you did not tamper, forge, or substitute his will, how is it that *your* name appears as the sole beneficiary?'

'Perhaps he came to forgive me in the end.'

'He'd never forgive you! He would rather have died intestate than leave you a single penny! How old are you now, Thomas?'

'I am forty-five, as you well know, Mavis.'

'Forty-five! And still not married, I take it?' There was venom in her voice, and for some reason it found its target.

'I have yet to find the right woman,' he mumbled, for the first time dropping his gaze.

'One who will put up with your gambling? Who won't blush with shame and humiliation when your creditors come to call? You are nothing but a lowly clerk, Thomas, who frittered his life away at the card tables!'

'You're right. I was. And I regret it absolutely.'

Mrs Crabbit spread her hands out in a gesture of disdain. 'You see my point. Why would Uncle Frederick leave you anything?'

Mr Ryman raised his eyes and stuck out his chin. 'Because as much as he disapproved of me, he detested your mean-spirited ways. You want to know the truth, cousin? You might well have remained his heir, had you not poisoned the very atmosphere of his sick room with your self-righteous pronouncements and your lack of compassion. He altered his will because he saw you for what you really are—an ill-natured, bad-tempered woman. And it was you who caused his change of heart; you yourself peeled the scales from his eyes.'

Mrs Crabbit turned her face away and said nothing. Neither did anyone else, so deeply in shock were we all. Even the unshakable Mr Death seemed at a loss for words. Eventually it fell to Mr Harmon to try to rally us round. He cleared his throat with a self-conscious cough and tentatively began:

'We now come to that part of the evening when my dear wife will attempt to summon one of her many spirit guides.'

He must have been aware of just how anticlimactic this sounded, and yet he went on:

'There is an element of risk attached to this procedure; not to any of you—you may rest assured—but to my dear wife herself. She will put herself into a trance state, so she can be a conduit for whichever spirit it is that chooses to come. The only thing keeping her safe will be you and I, as we form a circle to protect her.

'As my wife prepares herself for this ordeal and Cassius readies the room, I will ask you all to join hands, and I beg you—I *beg* you—whatever comes to pass here tonight, whatever manifests itself in our midst, do not break the circle under any circumstance. My wife's very life depends upon it.'

He glanced solemnly at each of us as we took our neighbours' hands. Mrs Harmon smiled sweetly, then lowered her head, only to raise it again, drawing a lungful of air in through her nostrils. She closed her eyes and opened her mouth, then expelled the breath slowly and rather noisily. Another breath in, another breath out, over and over again, as all the while Cassius went about attending to his duties.

First the lad made sure that the windows were closed and latched. He seemed to have trouble with one of them. I felt the cold outside-air on the back of my neck as he opened and closed it several times until he had managed to fasten it. Next he drew the thick, velvet curtains, blocking out the light from the street. Then he went and locked the door to the adjoining room, and, after pocketing the key, he pulled a curtain across it, concealing it from sight. Lastly he took a candle snuffer from his cabinet and set about extinguishing the candles. As the room grew progressively darker, Mrs Harmon's laboured breathing began to ease. When the last candle flame fizzled and died, pitching us into darkness, her face was relaxed and her eyes were closed, and she looked as if she were asleep.

'Maria, my dear,' came Mr Harmon's voice from the

top of the table, 'are you still with us?'

There was no response.

'Maria? Maria, dearest? Answer me, please.'

Again, no response.

'Maria! Answer me, I beg you!'

And something did answer him—something that was hovering near Miss McVeigh's shoulder, if I was not mistaken; a child's voice—like the hissing of a snake, or the whisperings of a shivering girl gasping for air:

'Maria…is no longer here.'

A jolt went through the group like a physical blow.

'Your hand, Miss McVeigh, your hand.' It was the gentleman with the professional eye who had spoken.

'Sorry; yes, of course. How silly of me! Here.'

'Please!' Mr Harmon cried out. 'Do not break the circle! Whatever you do, do not break the circle!'

A terrified shriek rang out from the woman who was sitting next to Mrs Crabbit:

'*Augh*! It was awful! Awful! I just felt cold, wet fingers on the back of my neck! Mr Harmon, please, can you not do something to prevent it?'

Now others were yelping or crying out as, one by one, we were each subjected to the same ill treatment. I felt Mr Sligo leap out of his seat beside me; an instant later I was jumping too. And yet Mr Harmon was adamant:

'Do not break the circle!'

'Mr Harmon, this is intolerable! I insist that you do something!' It was the professional gentleman again.

'I heartily second that!' came the voice of Miss McVeigh, as a burst of childish giggling was heard high above our heads.

'*Henrietta*?' ventured Mr Harmon, his tone both quizzical and surprised. 'Henrietta, is that you?'

Another burst of giggling, and then, 'It *might* be…'

'Henrietta, if you wish to remain here, you're going to have to behave yourself like a good little girl. I cannot and will not allow you to terrify my guests.'

The voice, which now seemed to be centred on the other side of the table, ignored him entirely. 'I try to get Robert to play with me,' it said, 'but he won't. He says you wouldn't approve.'

'And I don't,' came the stern reply from the woman next to Mrs Crabbit. 'I think you're a very naughty little girl, and I wouldn't want my Robert associating with anyone who behaves as badly as you!'

The crash of shattering pottery rent the air, eliciting shrieks from around the table that seemed to cause Henrietta much mirth. *Farewell the fallen war hero!*

'Do not break the circle!' Mr Harmon implored us.

'Cicely's got a *boy*friend, Cicely's got a *boy*friend!' chanted Henrietta in a whiny, singsong voice, not three feet away from my right shoulder. I felt the arm of the woman next to me flex and stiffen, then, with a gasp, her whole body jolted as Henrietta delivered her cold parting caress.

'Who shall I have fun with next?' asked the girl, mercifully passing me by. 'You? You should be ashamed of yourself, you naughty, naughty man.'

I could feel the tension in Mr Sligo's grip mounting.

'I know what you get up to. I'd never buy pictures from you…Lord only knows who painted them!'

Slowly he began to relax as he sensed her move

away.

'Who's next? You?'

An involuntary shriek erupted from near the bottom of the table; Miss McVeigh, most probably.

'You've got a fair few secrets you keep. Shall I tell people about them? You wouldn't like it if I did.' There was a pause while the girl seemed to consider the matter. 'You're lucky,' she said at last. 'I like knowing secrets. And a secret's not a secret if you tell people.'

'Your hand, Miss McVeigh,' the voice of the professional gentleman prompted.

'Here,' came her flustered-sounding reply.

'I'm not sure I'd give him *my* hand,' drawled Henrietta. 'You would think you could trust a doctor… but trust can be misplaced.'

A brief silence ensued, and then she said, 'How about you?'

I heard Mrs Crabbit gasp.

'I have a message from your uncle.'

'Uncle Frederick?' Her voice sounded eager.

'I don't like your uncle. He smells like death.'

'Please, little girl, I'm begging you. If you have a message from my Uncle Frederick, you need to tell me.'

'I have a name, you know. Why don't you use it?'

'Henrietta? Henrietta, won't you please tell me what my uncle has to say?'

'You said *please*,' observed the girl. 'That means you must want to know really, really badly…just as badly as he longs for *me* to tell you. He's here, you know. Watching me. Watching you. Watching others who are here. He's not very happy. But I think if he's so keen for you to know something, then he should find a way of telling you himself. I don't like him. It's his skin; it stinks.'

'You are a wilful, spiteful little girl!' Mrs Crabbit sounded angry.

Suddenly the voice was no longer high-pitched and breathy; it had become a deep, malevolent bass. 'That's as maybe. Yet I could tell you things and show you things that would make the hairs on you neck stand on end!'

I heard a sharp intake of breath from nearly every single person at the table.

'I'm going to go now,' Henrietta continued, her girlish tones restored. 'You bore me. You're no fun to be with. None of you seem to want to play with me at all. Even so, I'm going to leave you with a present… something to remember me by.'

'Henrietta! Don't!' It was the voice of Mr Harmon.

'Get ready! Here it comes!'

'Hold the circle, people! Whatever is to happen, I beg you, do not break it!'

'Your hand, Miss McVeigh! Give me your hand!'

I could feel the tension mounting in the room, even though I could see nothing in the pitch-black darkness. One second went past. Then another. Then a third. And then—

Crrrrack! With a sharp waft of air and a resounding clatter, something large and extremely heavy hit the top of the table. Even one or two of the gentlemen shrieked.

'Cassius!' Mr Harmon's voice rang out in panic, as a distinctive—though not unpleasant—smell assailed my nostrils…the smell of freshly cooked meat. 'Quickly, Cassius! We need light!'

As Cassius lit a match, the burgeoning flame revealed the most astonishing sight.

Kneeling on the table in his shirtsleeves, knife and fork in hand, was none other than the hotel's proprietor, Mr Condon. It seemed that we had disturbed him at his supper, for there in front of him, swimming in a layer of grease, sat a half-consumed plate of chops and fried potatoes.

CHAPTER SIX

'WHAT JUST HAPPENED?' MR Condon asked sheepishly, as Cassius began to relight the candles. The hotel's proprietor glanced about the room, taking in his surroundings. 'I don't understand it,' he said. 'One minute I was dining in the staff pantry…and now I'm here? Can someone please explain to me what just happened?'

'You're the victim of a practical joke by one of my wife's more troublesome spirit guides,' Mr Harmon replied. 'Sorry about that. Mr Hargreaves, would you be so kind as to help Mr Condon down from there whilst I attempt to revive my wife?'

The medium was slumped across the table, apparently fast asleep. Her flaming red locks were so close to Mr Condon's dinner plate that they'd ended up being splashed by the gravy. Mr Hargreaves rose from his seat, removed the offending plate, and then helped Mr Condon down off the table. Unbidden, Cassius fetched a towel and a basin of water, which he rather conveniently kept in his cabinet. He set them before Mr Harmon, who wetted the towel and applied it to the medium's hair, and then to a spot on her forehead. As he gently proceeded to wash his wife's face, her eyelashes began to flutter. Suddenly she drew a deep breath and sat upright in her chair.

'You're safe. You're here with me,' he murmured, and began tenderly stroking her arm.

'Did I—?'

'Yes.'

'Who was it?'

'Henrietta.'

'Henrietta?'

'That impish little girl.'

'*Her*? *Oh*! What did she do this time?'

'Besides insulting everyone here and causing a major panic?'

'*What*?' Mrs Harmon looked conscience-stricken. She turned and addressed the guests. 'Ladies and gentlemen, I'm so sorry if my spirit guide offended you in any way, but you must understand, I have no control over who I get to channel. They come, and I am just the conduit. Please, please accept my sincerest apologies, won't you?'

'If you care to adjourn to the outer room,' her husband announced, 'Cassius will serve you with refreshments. My wife and I will join you presently, when she is sufficiently recovered from her ordeal.'

One by one we all rose and made our way to the door, which only now was Cassius in the process of unlocking.

'That was quite something,' whispered Mr Sligo in Miss McVeigh's ear. 'Are these sittings always so…'

He flailed his hands in the air as he tried to come up with an appropriate word. '*Fraught*?' he said at last.

Miss McVeigh giggled. 'Hardly. Last time it was an elderly schoolmaster who came through—highly disapproving! Spent most of the evening trying to get us to conjugate Latin verbs. Frankly, I'd take Henrietta over him any day. She was far more diverting.'

She and Sligo passed through the doorway; George and I followed.

'So I take it you're not a true believer, Miss McVeigh?'

'I suppose I'm what that old man called himself.' She indicated Mr Death with a slant of her eyes. 'A pragmatist. One can meet such interesting people at these gatherings, I find. That man over there, for instance'—she nodded briefly at the professional-looking gentleman who'd been seated to her left, who was now standing talking to Mrs Crabbit—'he's a doctor. Lost his wife and baby daughter in childbirth. He's not too old to remarry. And that man over there—'

'Mr Hargreaves, is it not? Mrs Harmon's favourite?'

'Quite the eligible young bachelor! Though what he sees in that bungling, oversized dormouse, Cicely Moss, I cannot begin to imagine.' She eyed the awkward young woman standing next to Mr Hargreaves with disapproval. 'I mean, really! Those hands belong on a giant, and that dress might have been designed for a doll! Do you think perhaps she made it herself? As for her comportment, why, just look at the way she holds that towering body of hers! It's as if she's willing the floorboards to swallow her up!' An idea seemed to come to her and she frowned. 'Do you think Henrietta was right?' she asked.

'About what, dear lady?'

'About Cicely having a boyfriend.'

Mr Sligo regarded the couple thoughtfully. 'No,' he said, after a moment's reflection. 'See the way they avoid each other's eyes? He's merely being chivalrous.'

Miss McVeigh's face brightened as she saw Mrs Crabbit's cousin enter the room.

'Now, that Mr Ryman is definitely interesting,' she observed. 'Forty-five isn't old, it's merely distinguished; I believe he merits my further attention. Shall we go and make his acquaintance, Mr Sligo? It would be a shame if no one spoke to him, and I've a feeling no one will.'

Mr Sligo smiled mischievously and linked his arm through hers. 'At your service, my dear,' he said, and the pair of them set off, leaving George and me on our own.

'So, what do you think, George?'

'I felt sorry for her.'

'For that woman over there? Cicely Moss? They were rather cutting, weren't they?'

'No, I meant Henrietta.'

'*Henrietta*? Why?'

'Well, she didn't have any brothers or sisters, did she? Or if she did, they weren't proper brothers and sisters; they would have come from an earlier marriage. Their mother died and their father remarried, and his new wife gave birth to Henrietta.'

I stared at George, astounded. Was it possible that he and I had attended entirely different events?

'Why do you say that, George?' I hazarded to ask.

'Well, she was spoilt. Spoilt rotten, in fact. Proper brothers and sisters see to it that you don't get spoilt. That's what family is all about, isn't it?'

I gave this some thought. *Yes, most assuredly different events.* 'You may be right,' I said, 'but do bear in mind why we are here, George.'

'We're here to help Mr Crabbit. But I don't see how us being here helps him much. I reckon after what happened tonight Mrs Crabbit will only want more.'

We stole a glance in Mrs Crabbit's direction. She was deep in conversation with the doctor, her eyes glittering feverishly every time that she spoke. Most of her sentences were punctuated with furious glowers at her cousin.

George was right about one thing. The events of the evening had only served to whet her appetite.

'What we need to do, George, is prove that Mrs Harmon is a fraud. That would put paid to Mrs Crabbit's costly visits, at least.'

'But is she a fraud?' he asked. 'That girl, Henrietta, seemed very real to me.'

'Of course she's a fraud. You yourself went quite some way to proving it.'

'How?'

I narrowed my eyes and urged him to think.

'Oh,' he said at last. 'She called me Geoffrey.'

'Exactly! She got it wrong because she *thought* your name was Geoffrey.'

George frowned. 'Even so, how did she know what question I wrote?'

'That, my friend George, is what we in the profession call a "*stumbling block*". And what, pay tell, is a stumbling block?'

'A chance that God sends the jobbing detective to allow him to show just how clever he is?' George recited faithfully, if a little stiltedly for my liking.

'Correct.'

'Go on, then,' he challenged me, in not exactly the friendliest of tones, 'show me just how clever you are.'

'Very well,' I replied, and duly set about considering the matter with logic and precision. Putting aside the issue of how she went about making the rapping sounds, it seemed to me that all the questions asked fell into either one of two categories: those from the non-believers present—typified by mundane inquiries, such as *Is snow cold?* or *Is my name such-and-such?*—and those from the people who did believe—typified by questions demanding reassurance, such as *Are faithful pets allowed into Heaven?* or *Does my daughter remember me fondly?* Answers to the former would require a certain amount of foreknowledge. Answers to the latter would depend on what the petitioner wished to hear. Answers to both categories, I soon came to realize, still relied on her knowing what was written on those blasted sheets of paper.

Oh! And this was actually the simplest part of the sitting, I reflected. I had yet to deal with the problem of Henrietta's freezing cold fingers, how she managed to soar not only around the table but high above it, and lastly—and hardly least—how she contrived to conjure Mr Condon out of thin air.

'I'm going to need some time to think about it,' I

announced.

'What? Five minutes isn't long enough for the great jobbing detective?' he replied.

Hmmm. 'Look, tomorrow's Saturday. We could meet up in the afternoon, put our heads together, and see if we can't come up with a possible explanation of how she does it.'

'I can't,' said George. 'I have plans.'

'Plans?'

'Just something I have to do,' he said evasively.

'What? Again?' He had had something he had to do two Saturdays ago as well. 'Would you care to tell me what it is?'

'No. And don't go trying to worm it out of me, 'cause I'm not going to say.'

Fair enough. My worming skills as a detective left much to be desired.

Suddenly an idea took root that once having sprouted refused to be weeded out. 'George, you wouldn't happen to be taking on private cases on your own, would you?'

''Course not!' said George, looking highly offended.

Hmmm. Then just what could he be doing that was so much more important than attending to his training?

At that moment Cassius passed by with his tray and, without thinking, I reached out and picked up a glass. I regretted the instant it was in my hand, for George harbours suspicions that I might be a bit of a drinker. To my surprise, instead of the anticipated lecture, I saw his hand reach out, too. He raised the glass to his lips and took the smallest of sips.

'*Ughh*, it's so sweet,' he complained. 'What is it?'

I raised my own glass to my lips and applied a little of the rich, brown liquid to my tongue.

'Sherry wine,' I replied.

'And you *drink* this muck?'

'I have been known to on occasion.'

'Try it again, young man,' came a deep, melancholic voice from behind George's shoulder. 'It's an acquired taste, I'll admit, but who knows? You may grow to like it. This particular sherry is really quite good.'

'George, I'd like you to meet an acquaintance of mine. This is is Mr de Ath.' Though I pronounced the name the way that he himself pronounces it, in my mind the jury was still out as to whether I'd pronounced it correctly. 'Mr de Ath works at the Prerogative Will Office. Mr de Ath, this is my friend and associate, George Crump.'

Mr Death slyly arched an eyebrow. 'So your name isn't Geoffrey?'

'No, sir. It's George.'

'Fascinating! You'll forgive me, I hope, but I couldn't help overhearing portions of your earlier conversation.'

Note to self: when discussing cases with an apprentice, always bear in mind that walls have ears.

'It seems that our professional concerns align,' he continued. 'You suspect Mrs Harmon of perpetrating a hoax, and you fervently wish to debunk her; my employer, for reasons of his own, wishes to do the same.'

'Your employer, sir?' I queried.

'Why, yes; he has quite a vested interest in the matter. His good reputation is at risk of being impugned.'

'Ah.' *Exactly who…or even* what…*was this mysterious employer?*

'Since I represent him *in absentia*—in his absence, that's to say—I feel certain he would wish me to offer you any and every assistance that I can.'

'Sir, can you shed any light on what we just witnessed here?'

Mr Death shook his head sadly. 'I must confess that what we experienced tonight stumps me whole-heartedly, and I do not much care to be stumped. On the face of it, it all seems impossible. And yet reason demands that it *must* be possible, though I'm blessed if I can see how. There is but one small point that suggests itself—'

'Sir?'

'Before I say more I should first like to ask you a question. Was Mrs Harmon expecting your presence at this sitting?'

'No. We managed to—' I was about to say *weasel our way in*, when I realized how unprofessional it might sound. 'To accompany a guest who had already been invited.'

'Well, it occurs to me,' he said, 'that, thanks to this young man here, we now have a significant lead to explore.'

'A lead? And what would that be, sir?'

Even as I asked this, my eyes were drawn to the door connecting the two rooms. Having abandoned serving the drinks, Cassius emerged from it, carrying what I took to be Mr Condon's plate. I say *took to be*, because all I could see was its rim; the rest was hidden beneath a fair-sized saucepan lid.

'George and I both asked much the same question,' Mr Death explained. 'Is my name such-and-such? I asked if my name was Winter, and she said it was not—and in a most decisive manner, you will recall. George asked if his name was Geoffrey, and she said that it was—and again she seemed perfectly sure of herself. You see the significance in that, given that I myself had followed the required procedure?'

I didn't at first, but then I slowly began to.

'She'd had you investigated. When you wrote her the letter asking to attend, she sent someone out to investigate you. But we arrived unannounced; she didn't have a chance to investigate us.'

Mr Death smiled. 'Which rather raises the question: why would she need to investigate anyone, if her powers are indeed as genuine as she claims?'

Why, indeed?

The hour was getting late and people were beginning to depart. For appearances' sake, George and I took our leave with Mr Sligo, who professed loudly and volubly all the way down Jermyn Street just how much he'd enjoyed the evening.

'I've already pledged to attend their sitting on Tuesday,' he admitted, as I tried to hail him a cab—a thankless task, for it was snowing again, and all the passing cabs were taken.

I glanced at George. He returned my glance with a nod.

'Sir, if you please…may we be allowed to accompany you?'

Sligo pursed his lips to form an unattractive smirk. 'And what would I get out of such an arrangement?'

I had to think quickly. *The satisfaction of aiding a fellow human being* seemed unlikely to cut it. 'You'd get to sustain the little fiction you made use of this evening. We are your two assistants. We accompany you everywhere.'

'*Your* little fiction, not mine!' he snapped. 'I shall just say I became bored with you both and dismissed you from my employ. It is, after all, the truth. And just where do you think you're going?' he added, when he saw George and me walking away.

'Home,' I called back over my shoulder. 'Good luck hailing yourself a cab at this time of night and in this appalling weather, *Misss*-ter *Sss*-ligo!'

CHAPTER SEVEN

ONE OF THE DRAWBACKS of being a Chief Investigator (or Chief-and-Sole Investigator, since George was still an errand boy and I had no official staff) is that my weekends are no longer routinely my own. I'm often obliged to work through them, even on the Lord's day, as if the Sabbath were no different from any other day of the week. There's a saying amongst us chief investigators: "*An errant cat waits for no man*". Well, no, you're right, there isn't; but there should be—along with: "*The maid who filches food doesn't cease because it's Sunday*", "*Bad butlers pay no holiday heed*", and "*A dog in season cares naught for time*".

From this list of sayings alone, you may well be able to deduce the range and breadth of my more recent cases, all of which have eaten into my weekends with precious little regard for my own personal wants and needs. Consequently this Saturday was something of a landmark, being the second in three weeks that I'd had to myself.

After my brother Julius left for work—taking his

dog with him—I rose and tended to the stove, then set about tidying the room. Twenty minutes later, the fire was burning brightly, the bed-rolls were furled up and stacked in the corner, and the floor was swept and spotless. I put on my bowler hat and went and sat at the table, where I picked at the remains of the kippered herrings from the night before.

As I ate, I applied my mind to the problem of Mrs Harmon's written questions. If Mr Death was right— and I felt certain he was—the so-called medium must have had him investigated. It would be a simple enough thing to do—after all, any newcomer wishing to attend was first obliged to submit a request in writing…a request that would of necessity include a residential or business address. How easy it would be to visit their neighbours or co-workers and make a few general inquiries.

George and I, however, had turned up unexpect-edly…as had Mrs Crabbit's cousin, I suddenly realized. She could therefore know nothing of our backgrounds. She'd answered George's question incorrectly because she *believed* his name was Geoffrey. It was what she'd heard me call him when Sligo stopped him joining in. Which brought me back full circle: Maria Harmon knew what was written on those accursed sheets of paper!

I sighed, then went and retrieved my notebook and pencil. On the first blank page that I came to I wrote following the heading:

The Case of the Mendacious Medium

Mendacious, for those of you who do not know, has nothing to do with darning and repairs. It is more to do with lying or being routinely dishonest, despite the way it sounds. I studied the title for some minutes, then considered what I should write next.

Nothing came to mind.

I glanced at the dog's water bowl. It was practically full; but then, Julius would hardly forget to fill it. I got up and inspected our own reserves. They were fine; they would last us through the day, and then into the next, at which point one of us would need to make a trip to the pump. I paced the room and then went and sat down again, and tried once more to apply my brain.

Mrs Harmon had held each question up in the air before making her pronouncements. Could she have read what was written—or even seen the odd keyword—*through* the paper, aided by the light of the candles? No. It was impossible. The paper was thick and expensive. And it was folded twice-over.

I stared out the window. The sky was clear and bright. There'd been some flurries of snow during the night, and the light glared sharply on the fall that had settled. I opened the window and leaned out. *Anything to avoid thinking about how she'd known what our questions had been!* In the distance I could see a steam trail billowing from an unseen train, the clatter of its wheels squealing plaintively as it snaked its way out of the railway-yards. From closer to, there came the occasional bellow from the cattle being driven to market, their peculiar earthy smell wafting up to me on the breeze. I closed the window and went and sat down again.

One of the drawbacks of having time on your hands, I mused, is that you are invariably required to fill it—in this instance with profitless speculation about a seemingly impossible conundrum. I took up my pencil and wrote:

Fact : Mrs Harmon did not leave her seat while we were writing our questions.

Conclusion : Mrs Harmon could not have seen what we had written.

Fact : The paper we wrote on was thick and was folded not once but twice.

Conclusion : No matter how many candles there were,
no words would have shown through.

It wasn't as if it was rice paper, I reflected.

And yet she knew.

How though? The only person who could have told her was Cassius, the lad with the mischievous eyes. He'd had every opportunity to read them. But he hadn't said a word to her—not a single word. He'd set the tray before her and then retired to his place by the cabinet.

I got up and stoked the fire in the stove. I sat

down and picked at the kippers again. I opened the window; I closed the window. I paced restlessly about the room. Even if I were to have some massive revelation—to solve this insoluble puzzle—my apprentice was not here to bear witness. What could he be doing that was so much more important than watching me solve the case?

Once again I applied my mind to the problem in hand; once again I was ignobly defeated. I considered putting another log on the fire; instead I rose and donned my jacket and tucked my notebook in my pocket. Then I wrapped a good many scarves around my neck and, locking the door behind me, I set out for Camden Town.

George and his family lived in the house on the corner of Albert Terrace and—I kid you not—George Street. *Could his parents not think of a suitable name and had christened their son after a road?* I knew where he lived because I had accompanied him home once or twice. Though he'd never invited me in, I did not take this as a slight. I myself had been debating for several months the wisdom of introducing George to my own circle of friends. He'd met my brother Julius, of course, but how would he react to Bertha? The hat and veil that Bertha now wore might well hide his big, manly face, but nothing could disguise that voice of his, nor conceal his fondness for habitual swearing. And even if George *was* to be accepting of Bertha, there was a chance—nay, a veritable *likelihood*—of Bertha bringing up my criminal past. And what would George think of *that*?

George's house is not far from the canal, which, in

summer at least, provides a pleasant, straightforward route between my lodgings and his. The trouble with keeping it under any kind of surveillance is that there is precious little cover to be had, this being an area where buildings, trees, and fences come in short supply. In the event, I had to make do with a low stone wall on the corner diagonally opposite, which belonged to one of the outlying annexes of the local veterinary school.

When I say "*low*", I mean I was obliged to crouch behind it if I was to stay hidden. After half an hour of that, I gave in and simply sat on it, reasoning that, if I saw the front door opening, I could easily dive behind the wall.

I sat there till my bottom threatened to go numb—*such is the life of the truly dedicated detective*—then I went and stood behind it, reasoning that I could always bob down. George's door remained stubbornly closed.

Judging by the position of the sun, it was now roughly eleven in the morning. Had I arrived too late? Had George already left to fulfil his important and secretive mission? I didn't think so. From the little he'd said, I had the impression that this was an afternoon affair.

Suddenly I saw the front door open and I dropped to my knees.

A young girl stepped out. She was maybe fifteen or sixteen years of age, with dark blonde locks and an untroubled face stamped with a faintly mocking air. She wore a grey woollen cape over a plain charcoal dress, with a muffler to protect her ears. On her arm she carried a basket.

Not only did George have an older brother, he also had a younger sister! George, I decided, was quite the dark horse!

She carefully descended the steps—which, though cleared of snow, were probably quite icy—then disappeared up Albert Terrace. Some ten minutes later she was back, her basket now bulging with provisions.

More time elapsed. It went by so inordinately slowly that, in order to fill it, I found myself dwelling on Mrs Harmon again. *How could she have known? How? How?* HOW? When my mind was at last as numb as my bottom had been, the front door opened, and out stepped George.

He was dressed as he had been the previous evening—in his Sunday best—and was accompanied by a woman, who, going by her age and her facial resemblance, I took to be his mother. Looking slightly abashed, he helped her down the steps, and then linked his arm through hers. She turned and whispered something in his ear—which only served to make him look more embarrassed—and the pair set off down George Street, walking at a leisurely pace. Naturally I followed, keeping my distance.

They turned first into Camden Street and then into Pratt Street, by the corner of the churchyard where I'd climbed the tree. Then they did something that nearly made my heart seize up in my chest. They crossed the road and knocked at the door where the Crabbits lived.

Oh, what was my trainee detective up to?

As much as I've grown to like him, I have to be honest and say that George can be a tad too

honourable. He will get an idea into his head and—
once it's lodged there—you are stuck with it until the
next one comes along to unseat it. The trouble is that
they are all such *worthy* ideas. George, bless him, suffers
from that terrible thing called "a conscience". Was he,
at this very minute, explaining his actions to Mr and
Mrs Crabbit under the watchful eye of his mother?
Worse, was he *apologizing* for them? Had I instilled in
him nothing of the detective's code in his five long
months of training?

I had little choice; at the risk of being seen in full
daylight, I needed to climb that tree again. I went and
grabbed hold of the lowest branch and then hauled
myself up. Higher and higher I clambered, till I had a
view directly in through their window.

Mr Crabbit was seated at the table. He appeared to
be reading a magazine. Mrs Crabbit was pottering
about the room. She seemed to be tidying up. There
was no sign of George or his mother. I waited a
further ten minutes, and still they did not appear.

Where were they?

Defeated, I made my way down again and took up
position behind one of the gravestones. Watched by a
succession of small birds and animals, an hour passed
by while my feet turned to ice. Women arrived bearing
flowers for the church. The vicar stuck his nose out,
but only to check on the sky. At long last the front
door opened and George and his mother emerged.

Mrs Crump shared a word or two with the
landlady—a Mrs Moody, if my memory served me
correctly—and then set off, presumably for home. As
I adjusted my bowler whilst preparing to follow, I was

suddenly confronted by a very red, very irate George.

'Are you trailing me?' he demanded to know in the most pointed of tones.

'Of course I'm not,' I said brightly. I don't think he believed me because I saw him rolling his eyes.

'Really? Then why are you here?'

It was a perfectly reasonable question that required a perfectly reasonable answer.

'I'm keeping a watch on the Crabbits,' I said.

'Why?'

'Because I've made an important breakthrough in the case, and, having time to spare, I thought I might use it productively.'

'What breakthrough?'

'I worked out how Mrs Harmon knew what the questions were,' I announced, a little too grandly.

Again George rolled his eyes, and—would you believe it?—suddenly I *did* know! And the solution was so simple, so ridiculously simple! We'd been looking at everything the wrong way around.

'How?'

'She didn't know them, George.'

'I don't understand.'

'We just *thought* she did, see? She didn't need to know the questions; she only needed to know the answers.'

'I still don't understand.'

Distractedly I shook my head. 'Listen, we need to find a way to attend the next sitting. I have a theory— a *very* good theory—but I need to make sure that I'm right.' I was already beginning to walk away from him, for not only was my story about the Crabbits unlikely to stand any scrutiny, it was essential I had some time on my own in which to think matters through. 'Keep Tuesday night free,' I called back to him, turning my head just enough to see the puzzled expression on his face.

I sought out the nearest bridge and made my way down to the canal tow-path below. What was it that Mr Death had said? *On the face of it, it all seems impossible. And yet reason demands that it* must *be possible.* It seemed impossible for Mrs Harmon to know what our questions were, but, if I was right, she'd had no need to; like everyone else, I'd simply believed that she did. What more might I have been fooled into believing, I wondered?

I had reached one of the lock keepers' cottages, and, as nobody seemed to be about, I availed myself of an outdoor stool and whipped out my notebook and pencil. I decided to tackle the most astonishing event of the evening first: the sudden appearance of Mr Condon on the tabletop. I licked the tip of my pencil and wrote:

Question : If Condon didn't materialize out of thin air, how then did he get there?
Answer : Under his own steam.

If that were indeed the case, how had he gained entry to the room? The lad, Cassius, had locked the door and removed the key. We'd *seen* him do it. Simplicity itself. *Mr Condon had a duplicate key.*

Again I licked the pencil.

Question : How did he enter without us hearing him?

Answer : The curtain would have helped mask the sound of a key being turned, especially if our attention was diverted, say, by somebody shrieking.

Question : Why did we not immediately smell the chops?

Answer : The plate was covered with a saucepan lid. I'd even seen Cassius carrying it out when he was clearing the room.

Question : How had Condon managed to get up on the table through the circle of linked hands?

Answer : Someone had let him up.

Who? Mrs Harmon herself, most probably. She and her husband could have easily parted hands. There was, however, an even more ingenious explanation: Mrs Harmon was not even in her seat. She'd been roving round the room in the dark, playing the horrid Henrietta. *If that were the case, Mr Hargreaves must be in league with them too.* They needed him to sit where he sat so he could pretend to be holding her hand. Once more I took up my pencil.

Question : If Mrs Harmon was Henrietta, why did Henrietta sound English?
Answer : Maria Harmon was an actress with a natural ear for accents.

Question : We'd heard Henrietta soaring high in the air above our heads. How was that possible?
Answer : Easy. Mrs Harmon had been standing on the table.

Not that I could prove any of this, of course, and there were a few things it didn't explain. Henrietta's frozen fingers, for instance, and how the loud rapping sounds were produced. But if my theory about Mrs Harmon *not* knowing the questions was correct, then that was something I *could* prove, at least to my own satisfaction. All I had to do was figure out a way for George and I to attend.

CHAPTER EIGHT

FOR THE SECOND TIME in less than a week, my apprentice and I found ourselves waiting in the bitter cold on the corner of Jermyn Street and Regent Street. Although we were awaiting the arrival of a cab, it was not in fact a cab that pulled up.

It was a hearse.

Drawn by four plumed black horses, a carriage with a long, glass compartment at its rear—mercifully empty, I was most relieved to note—creaked to a halt in front of us. Mr Death lowered himself on to the pavement, muttered a few words of thanks to the driver, then sent the man and his singular vehicle on their way.

'Ah,' he said, turning to address us at last, 'my two young assistants who accompany me everywhere!'

'You came in a hearse?' I felt unable to let such behaviour pass without mention.

'I have just come from attending a funeral—a sad but regrettably frequent duty for someone in my profession. The funeral director was kind enough to offer to drive me here.'

'A funeral? At this time of the evening?'

Mr Death chose not to answer this. He merely grinned at me unreassuringly. 'So,' he said, his eyes still sparkling, 'what is our plan of action to be?'

'Once we're upstairs, I want you to stand near the communicating door, so that—as soon as it opens— we'll be the first ones into the room. I need you to sit where you were sitting last Friday, next to Mr Harmon. I will take the seat next to you, and, George, you can sit next to me. When it comes time to write out your questions, ask something simple, and, whatever you do, make sure that the answer is yes. I myself will ask one where the answer is no.'

'And this will prove Mrs Harmon a fraud?' Mr Death gazed at me somewhat incredulously.

'It will, sir…if I see what I expect to see.'

'What do you expect to see?' queried George.

'I expect to see Cassius,' I told him truthfully. I could see he was dying to ask more, but it was time for us to be going.

Once again his brother William was stationed at the entrance; once again he ignored us as we made our way in.

'Do I have to be Geoffrey again?' whispered George, as Miss Brahms scurried forward to greet us.

'You do, George, you do,' I whispered back. 'That's how everyone thinks of you.'

'I wish that they thought of me as George,' he replied.

'Mr de Ath! So very nice to see you again,' chirruped Miss Brahms. 'And with Mr Sligo's two young assistants in tow! Goodness gracious, isn't that... a little *unusual?*' Despite her best welcoming manner, the greeting was unmistakably a challenge.

'*My* two young assistants now, Miss Brahms. Happily they have quit Mr Sligo's employ.'

'Of course, of course,' she concurred, though she still seemed perturbed by the arrangement. 'You do realize you will have to pay for them to attend?'

'At a guinea per head; yes, I am fully cognizant of the fact. Here,' he said, handing over a not inconsiderable fortune. 'They do, after all, accompany me everywhere.'

Don't overdo it, Mr Death. A gentle touch is all that's required.

'Let me take you up,' she said, and ushered us towards the staircase.

'I am sure we can find our own way,' Mr Death assured her, and, waving her away, ascended the stairs with George and me bringing up the rear.

The room, when we arrived, was hardly what you might call animated. People were standing about in pairs: the horrid Mr Sligo with the hypercritical Miss McVeigh; Mrs Crabbit with the bereaved doctor (there was no sign yet of her other friend, the woman who'd been so vocal in her disapproval of Henrietta). The painfully-shy, rather tall young woman—Cicely something-or-other, Miss McVeigh had called her—was again to be found in the company of Mr Hargreaves, who, if I was right, worked hand in glove with Mrs Harmon and her husband. Mr Condon, the hotel's proprietor—who was also in league with them—moved from group to group doing his best to inspire conversation, but he was fighting an uphill battle all the way. Cassius, resplendent in his red and white livery, circled the room with his tray of drinks.

As per my instructions, Mr Death strode casually across the floor and took up his position by the door to the adjoining room. Mr Sligo's jaw dropped open when he saw George and me following. Mr Death raised his hand in salute to him and, with a wry sense of humour I had not quite anticipated, mouthed the words, *"They accompany me everywhere"*. Mr Sligo seemed to catch his meaning, for his face succumbed to a scowl.

Before long, Mr Condon approached us with some cheery words of welcome and summoned Cassius over to offer us drinks.

'Do try some, Geoffrey,' urged Mr Death, as both he and I reached for a sherry. 'At your time of life, you should be actively seeking out new experiences. How else, as a man, are you to know what your tastes might be?'

George turned bright red, but took a glass anyway. He thanked Cassius and raised it to his lips.

I expected him to pull another face as he took a sip. He didn't. He held the liquid in his mouth for a few moments before swallowing it down, then, with his Adam's apple still bobbing, he stole a glance at Mr Death, who was watching to see what his reaction would be.

'It's all right,' said George. 'It's not as bad as I thought.'

'Did you manage to discern the subtle taste of almonds on your palate?'

George's eyes widened. 'I did! I tasted almonds! And something else besides. Was it cherries?'

Mr Death smiled at him. 'Quite a complex little wine, is it not?'

I took a sip from my own glass. Almonds and cherries, my foot! It just tasted sweet and a little bit sickly.

'Ladies and gentlemen,' Mr Condon announced, 'I've had word that Mrs Harmon is ready to receive you, so please, do make your way through.' Cassius, who by this point was standing by the doorway, relieved us of our glasses as we all filed inside.

Once again Mrs Harmon was seated at the top of the table. Tonight she wore a dress of serpent-green brocade, a much more flamboyant kind of gown than we had last seen her in. The colour flattered her red hair, which in the candlelight looked especially radiant. She seemed vaguely surprised to see me and George there with Mr Death, but she smiled very graciously, and indicated that he should come and take the seat beside her husband. It will come as no surprise to anyone that Mr Hargreaves was invited to join her in his usual spot. The doctor entered next and sat down by Mr Hargreaves. Then came Mr Sligo and Miss McVeigh, with Mr Sligo taking the chair opposite me, and Miss McVeigh, the one opposite George. They were followed by the gawky Miss Cicely, who took the seat next to Miss McVeigh's. Mrs Crabbit was the last to enter. She glanced briefly at George, and promptly assumed the place at the foot of the table, leaving the chair next to George unoccupied. Other than the seating arrangements, the only practical difference as far as the room was concerned involved the cabinet on which the porcelain bust of Nelson had stood; seemingly in excess to requirements, it had since been removed, leaving the space behind me entirely free of clutter.

The medium's husband was in the process of suggesting that we all shift round a little in order to facilitate the holding of hands that was due to come later, when the door was rudely pushed open—quite violently, in fact—sending Cassius, who was attempting to close it, into the back of Mrs Crabbit's chair.

In marched Mr Ryman.

'Am I late?' he asked, evidently oblivious to the distress he'd just caused. With a great deal of dignity, Cassius extricated the braiding on his sleeve from Mrs Crabbit's necklace, then went and stood in the corner, awaiting his opportunity to shut the door.

'Mr Ryman, is it not?' It was the medium who spoke. 'You're not late at all, sir. Please, do sit down. You are most welcome at our table.'

'Not beside me, he's not!' Mrs Crabbit exclaimed, as her cousin made for the one remaining seat. 'This is intolerable! I must protest! Why should I be made to sit next to *him*?'

Mr Harmon did his best to placate her. 'My dear Mrs Crabbit, we are all Spiritualists here, and, as such, we must strive to see beyond this earthly plane. We are but brothers and sisters to each other, are we not…all equal in the eyes of God?'

'There are things that God will never forgive,' she responded darkly, 'and things that I shan't forgive either! I refuse to sit anywhere near this man!'

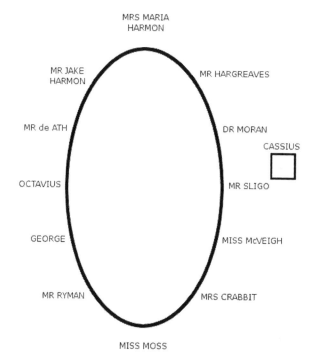

SEATING PLAN
TUESDAY, DECEMBER 14TH, 1852

'Excuse me,' Miss Moss piped up. 'Perhaps you would care to change places with me?'

A murmur of approval swept around the table, which made the poor thing blush. To prevent anyone seeing it, she swiftly lowered her head.

Mrs Crabbit seemed taken aback. 'You'd do that for me?' she asked.

'Really, I'm only too happy to oblige.' Keeping her head bowed, she rose and vacated her chair.

'So very kind of you,' Mrs Crabbit remarked, as the

two of them exchanged seats. Miss Moss acknowledged her with a bird-like twitch of her head and a smile so fleeting, it was gone before anyone noticed it.

'As usual, my dear wife will begin the sitting by fielding your written questions,' Mr Harmon announced. 'May I remind you all to limit your inquiries to something that can be answered with a simple yes or no. Cassius, will you please do the honours?'

Having at last managed to close the door, the young man began distributing sheets of paper. Once everybody had a sheet, he fetched his silver platter and his dip-pen and ink, and presented it with great ceremony to Mr Death. One by one, we each wrote out our questions; one by one, Cassius collected them and arranged them on his tray. As soon as Mr Hargreaves had finished writing his, the lad set them in front of the medium, and retired to his spot by the cabinet. I had an ideal view of him from where I was sitting. He was positioned a little to the right of the doctor, his face as impassive as ever.

Mrs Harmon picked up the first question and held it aloft. I kept my eyes on Cassius, who was gazing in an abstract fashion in the general direction of Mr Hargreaves.

Mrs Harmon glanced slowly around at everyone present, and then one loud rap rang out.

'The answer is yes,' she said. She opened it and read out Mr Death's question: '*Is Christmas eleven days away?*'

Delighted sighs and some quiet applause issued from those present.

Smiling, she picked up the next question, which,

you can probably guess, was mine. Cassius, I noticed, had shifted his attention to the doorway. He was also scratching his ear.

Mrs Harmon glanced slowly around at everyone present, and then two loud raps rang out.

'The answer is most definitely no,' she proclaimed. She opened it and read out my question: '*Is it hot outside?*'

People laughed politely.

Next Mrs Harmon picked up George's question. Cassius, at this point, was staring at the ceiling.

Damn it! Could I have possibly been wrong?

Two half-hearted raps were heard.

'The answer is no,' she said, before opening it and reading it out: '*Did I taste cherries in my sherry wine?*'

Grrr! Simple questions, George, simple questions!

Now it was Mr Ryman's turn. Cassius was still staring at the ceiling.

Mr Ryman, as was his wont, had been secretive in its writing. As at the previous sitting, he'd shielded his paper throughout. *Could staring at the ceiling be a sign that Cassius did not know the answer, forcing Mrs Harmon to simply guess?*

One knock. 'The answer is yes.' Slowly, almost reluctantly, she unfolded the sheet in her hands. '*At the very end, did Uncle Frederick forgive me for the wrongs I'd done him?*'

The relief on Mrs Harmon's face was palpable. She reached for Miss Moss's question. Cassius had transferred his gaze to the doorway again.

Two raps, loud and unambiguous. 'The answer is no. *Do people feel pain in their final moments if their deaths are agonized and brutal?* No, my dear, they do not. They see the Gates of Heaven opening before them and their hearts rejoice; their loved ones are there to welcome them into their arms and they suffer not. Do not imagine for an instant that your parents suffered when they died.'

The sound of muffled sniffling was coming from the bottom of the table. Like everyone else, I turned to look, and saw tears streaming down Miss Moss's cheeks. In the embarrassed silence that followed, Mrs Crabbit placed her hand on the young woman's shoulder and murmured:

'There, there, child. You have suffered a terrible loss and you have shouldered it bravely. I'm sure your mother and father are very proud of you. Take comfort in that. I know they would want you to.'

The words may have been designed to soothe, but disastrously they had quite the opposite effect. The woman's face twisted into an ugly, red mask as she began to sob hysterically. Mr Ryman, who looked visibly shaken, reached into his pocket and pulled out a handkerchief. She snatched it from him with her big, clumsy hand and used it to mop her eyes. Thank God it was a gentleman's handkerchief; had it been a lady's, it would have been sodden by the time she gave it back.

'Thank you,' she said, as she handed it to him. He smiled and asked if she was feeling better now. 'I'm fine…it's all fine,' she replied. 'Can we not just get on with it, please?'

'You're sure?' Mrs Harmon asked gently.

'I'm sure. I'd rather not have any fuss.'

I glanced at Cassius. He was looking in Mr Hargreaves's direction and tugging on his earlobe.

There came one explosive rap as Mrs Harmon picked up the next question.

'The answer is most definitely yes. *Will Uncle Frederick ever appear to us, and settle this dispute for once and for all?* I should tell you, Mrs Crabbit, that I have been praying on the matter all day, and this evening I have every hope of making contact with your uncle.'

A look of triumph flashed across Mrs Crabbit's face. I'm not sure Mr Ryman even heard the medium, for he was still being solicitous to the teary Miss Cicely. Cassius, meanwhile, had turned his attention to the door.

Two raps. 'The answer is no.'

I was right about the code. Whenever Cassius looked at Mr Hargreaves, the answer was yes; when he looked at the door, it was no. My theory was confirmed as Mrs Harmon worked her way round the remaining participants. Since this was clearly a trick, then it followed that everything else was too.

'We now come to that part of the evening,' Mr Harmon was saying, 'when my dear wife attempts to summon one of her many spirit guides. But tonight she will try something new.'

Cassius had drawn the curtains, locked the door and screened it off, and was now going around extinguishing candles. Mrs Harmon had begun taking deep breaths.

'Tonight my wife will attempt to extricate her spirit—her very life force—from her body, so that she may cross from this existence to the next and guide Mrs

Crabbit's uncle back here from the spirit plane. She will need your protection more than ever this night, if she is to survive such a journey. Please, will you all join hands?'

Two candles—one candle—a brief fizzing sound followed by a lingering afterglow, then utter, utter darkness all around.

'Maria, my dear, are you still with us?'

There was no response. I fancied that I heard the faintest noise—the swish of a velvet curtain, perhaps—from somewhere by the door.

'Maria? Maria, dearest? Answer me if you can hear me.'

Suddenly a shriek erupted from the foot of the table, followed by another: 'OW! *OW!* ' I felt a jolt eddy out around the circle, passing from one hand to the next.

'Hold the circle!'

'But something just stung me on my temple, Mr Harmon, and then it went and stung me on my wrist!'

'Mrs Crabbit? Is that you? Are you quite all right, dear lady?'

'No, I am not all right,' she replied tartly. 'Something just stung me, I tell you! Surely it can't have been a wasp? It's far too late for wasps! I do hope it's not that dreadful Henrietta again!' I could hear her briskly rubbing the skin on her hand. 'May I not have some light so I might at least examine the damage?'

As if in response, there came a kind of a cough and a gurgling from where the medium was sitting.

'It's just not possible, don't you see? Even now my wife is departing her earthly body…her destiny is sealed. For her sake, complete the circle, I beg of you.'

I heard a muffled *humph*! and felt a little jostling as Mrs Crabbit complied. A bare instant of silence ensued, and then:

HONK, HONK! HONK, HONK!

'What on earth was that?' shrieked Mr Ryman, as I felt another jolt go through the circle. 'The damnable thing was right in my ear!' I got the distinct impression that he'd sprung to his feet.

'Why, I do believe it was a trumpet,' Mr Harmon informed him, his voice brimming over with awe. 'The spirits are inordinately fond of music!'

'If they're so fond of music,' Mr Sligo sniggered, 'you'd think they might at least learn how to play!'

All at once there came a gasp…and then another, and another.

'Look!'

Floating high in the air by the doorway was the disembodied head of Mrs Harmon—and, believe it or not, it was *glowing*! Only faintly, I'll admit, but certainly enough for us to see it. Slowly the eyes began to open and the lips began to part, and from the mouth there issued what appeared to be a kind of vapour.

'Ectoplasm,' declared Mr Harmon, and, when I instinctively turned to look at him, I nearly leapt out of my seat, for there, face-down on the table—barely visible in the light from the spirit-face, but visible nevertheless—was the medium herself, her distinctive red tresses splayed out across the table's surface. I could see an object—and at that moment I could only speculate as to what—sticking out from between her shoulder-blades.

The disembodied head had seen it too, for it let out a piercing shriek and promptly disappeared from sight. Sensing that something was terribly wrong, Mr Harmon called for Cassius to light the candles. As soon as the first one was lit, the truth became all too apparent.

Mrs Harmon had been stabbed to death—for the thing that was protruding from her back was nothing less than the hilt of a dagger!

CHAPTER NINE

THE CIRCLE OF SHOCKED, disbelieving faces might have been carved from stone. For a good few seconds nobody moved a muscle.

Then, eyes bulging, Mr Harmon let go of his wife's hand, but rather than trying to comfort her— undoubtedly a rather pointless exercise, though certainly a human one—he sat blinking at Mr Hargreaves, who for some odd reason seemed to be the more upset of the two.

Finally Mr Harmon spoke, but his words sounded contrived and wooden. 'My dearest, darling Maria,' he said, 'what terrible evil has befallen you?'

At this, Mr Hargreaves's head shot up. He had not yet let go of the woman's hand; indeed, he'd reclaimed his other hand from the doctor and was using it to stroke her palm. 'It's Sarah, God damn you!' he cried. 'Have the decency to call her by her proper name!'

'James—'

'She's dead, Jake, she's dead! And it's one of these people who murdered her! Stabbed her in the back in cold blood!' His eyes snaked around the table. 'Which of you was it? Who was it, I say! Own up, you blasted coward, or I'll have your lights out!'

Miss McVeigh rose to her feet and pointed a tremulous finger at Mrs Crabbit. 'It was her!' she exclaimed. 'It had to be! She was the only one to break the circle; the only one who had the opportunity!'

'Don't be ridiculous!' Mrs Crabbit protested. 'I never left my seat! Besides, why should I wish to hurt Mrs Harmon?'

'Let's say she did manage to produce your uncle; you were terrified of what he might say.'

'But Uncle Frederick would tell the truth!'

'Whose truth, Mrs Crabbit? Yours or Mr Ryman's?'

While everybody glanced at Mr Ryman, who was looking slightly green about the gills, the doctor rose and made his way around the table to the body. Mr Harmon tried to stop him, but found himself being thrust back against the wall by the furious Mr Hargreaves. As the pair of them tussled in the corner, the doctor drew back the woman's hair and placed two practised fingers on the vein in her neck. After a respectful amount of time had elapsed, he removed them and shook his head. Suddenly he frowned. He bent forward to inspect the woman's hairline.

'Oh, my!' came the gasp from everyone's lips, as he took hold of her locks and yanked them clean away.

'It's a wig!' shrieked Mr Sligo.

'And that isn't Mrs Harmon!' cried Miss McVeigh.

It wasn't. Supporting the woman's forehead with the palm of his hand, the doctor lifted her head from the table, revealing the face of the medium's secretary,

Miss Sarah Brahms.

I glanced to my left. All the fight seemed to have gone out of Mr Harmon. With a final effort he pushed Mr Hargreaves away and staggered back to his seat.

It's at this point the hotel's proprietor arrived, summoned, I assumed, by Cassius, who had slipped quietly from the room a short while before. Despite being the one in authority, Mr Condon seemed to have no idea what to do, and it fell to Mr Death to take charge, as the eldest, most experienced man present.

'As regrettable for you as it may be, sir,' he said, 'you will need to send for the constables.'

Since constables are little more than peace-keepers, and often poor at doing even that, the two who responded merely took a note of our names and occupations, then kept us waiting there in silence for their superior to arrive.

Sergeant Snipe of the Metropolitan Police's Detective Division was a man so charmless and yet snappily-dressed, you might have mistaken him for a fairground tout. Though hardly any taller than me, he gave the impression of height by rising up on the balls of his feet and staring down at those seated before him with wide, mistrustful eyes. For one so scrawny, he had a bull-like neck; but with cheeks like overwintered apples and barely any chin, he looked less like bull and more like a stoat on the prowl.

He introduced himself in the most perfunctory manner, then consulted the list that his underlings had drawn up. One by one he read out our names and had us raise our hands to identify ourselves. Once he'd familiarized himself with every aspect of the respondent's appearance, he would ask him or her to state why they were there and give a brief account of what had occurred that evening. Having gained some idea of the order of events, he then set his constables to work taking our formal statements while he himself made an examination of the body.

From the inside of his jacket he withdrew a magnifying glass, a sturdy model approximately five inches in diameter, and applied his eye to the lens. After much poking and prodding of her shoulder region, he eventually withdrew the dagger. First he scrutinized the handle, which was made of ivory inlaid with a crescent-moon design in mother-of-pearl. Then he focused on the blade, a thing of steel approximately six inches long. Suddenly he leaned in closer. He let out a grunt. Pulling the candelabra towards him, he produced a pair of tweezers and used them to tease away a few strands of hair that appeared to be caught on the hilt. He held them up to the light. Satisfied, he compared them to Miss Brahms's own hair, and, finally, to those of the wig.

Despite my misgivings about the man, I have to say I was fascinated. Although I had worked with the police before (indeed, with the great Sergeant Cuff himself), it was seldom I got the chance to observe detective work up close—and frankly I could not have been much closer. I smuggled my notebook out of my pocket to record my observations.

Make your introduction short and sharp.

Expect people to have heard of you, even if you know they won't have.

Don't bother with the niceties of calling people "sir" or "miss". You are the most important person in the room, and everyone must respect this!

I glanced up to make sure that I wasn't being watched, and then licked the tip of my pencil.

Assign the donkey-work to those under your command.

I took a sneak look at George, and then added:

If they make a mess of things, as they probably will, you can always reprimand them later.

Treat everyone as if they were the murderer, then suggest none too subtly that you have their measure and it's only a matter of time before you come to arrest them.

'You, boy! What do you think you're doing?' It was Sergeant Snipe.

'Me, sir? Why, nothing.'

'You were writing something in that book of yours.'

'No, sir. You are mistaken.'

'You have a pencil in your hand and I saw it moving. That means you were taking notes.'

'I was simply making a likeness of you, sir…for posterity, see?' *Not for "prosperity", which is something quite different.*

'Fancy yourself as an artist, do you?'

'You flatter me, sir.'

Our few seconds of banter had given me just enough time to thumb back through the notebook to the page where my brother Julius had drawn a portrait of me. I humbly held it aloft.

'Why, it's just a great big circle!'

'That's your face, sir. See? These two circles are your eyes…and that line there is your nose…and this one here is your mouth.'

'Call yourself an artist? My five-year-old could do better than that!'

'Sir, I never claimed to be especially good at it!'

At long last the room was locked up to preserve the corpse *in situ* (for the jurors at the forthcoming inquest to examine) and we were permitted to leave. Having bid Mr Death a goodnight, George and I plodded the empty streets towards our respective homes.

'We can rule out Dr Moran,' I observed.

'Why?'

'Because he was holding hands with Mr Hargreaves.'

'So?'

'Did you not see how distraught Mr Hargreaves was? If the doctor had let go of his hand for even a second, he would have been the first to accuse him.'

'Oh…'

'We can also rule out Mr Death.'

'I thought his name was de Ath.'

'It is…though that's only when we're addressing him in person.'

'Really?' A moment later George was scowling. 'No, that's rot! You're pulling my leg!'

'Of course I'm not, George; I'd never do that. But, tell me, why can we rule him out?'

'Because he was holding Mr Harmon's hand?'

'And mine, George; don't forget that. Likewise we can rule out Mr Ryman.'

'Because he was holding my hand?'

'Exactly.'

George frowned. 'Is there anyone else we can rule out?'

We were heading up the short stretch of Regent Street towards Piccadilly, and George had just posed this question, when a movement in the shadows caught my eye. Persuading him to go on without me, I crept back along the shop fronts till I came to the entrance of a narrow alley. Cautiously I poked my head around the corner.

Although the light from the gas lamps barely penetrated a foot or two into the filthy, cluttered walkway, there was still a faint gleam to the snow's powdery surface, enough for me to distinguish the crouching figure in red behind the assortment of overflowing bins.

'You can come out now, Cassius,' I murmured gently. 'You've nothing to fear. There's nobody here but me.'

Slowly the boy rose. He was holding his hands in the air in a gesture of surrender, as if I'd had a pistol trained at his heart.

'There's no need to do that,' I told him. 'See? I'm not armed.' I held my own arms aloft to prove it.

'What do you want?' he asked.

'Tell me why Miss Brahms changed places with Mrs Harmon.'

He didn't reply, but the reason was easy enough to guess. Whatever preparation the medium had applied to her skin, the glow it gave off provided sufficient illumination for a stand-in to be required.

'No? Then perhaps you can tell me *when* they changed places? At what point exactly?'

Still no response.

'I know how you work the trick with the questions,' I informed him. 'You look to your right if the answer is yes and to the left if the answer is no.'

The lad stared at the ground. 'Is Sarah really dead?' he asked in a tired, tiny voice.

'Miss Brahms? Yes, Cassius, she is.'

'Who killed her?'

'I was rather hoping you might be able to shed some light on that.'

'It wasn't one of us. We all loved her.'

'But, of all of you, Mr Hargreaves loved her the most?' It was as much a stab in the dark as the murderer had been obliged to make, and yet it found its mark, for Cassius nodded.

'He and Sarah were engaged to be married.'

Just as I thought.

'Did the police come?' he asked, sounding more than a little worried.

'They did.'

'Have they arrested anyone?'

'For the murder...or for the fraud?' It was the wrong thing to say, for once again the boy shut his trap like a rudely-prodded oyster. 'Mr Harmon and Mr Condon claim they had no knowledge of Mrs Harmon's more dubious activities. I'm not sure the police believe them.'

As unwilling as he may have been to discuss the sittings, it seemed he still had questions. 'What will happen next?' he asked.

'Tomorrow there'll be an inquest to determine the cause of death, but there's no doubt what the verdict will be. It's clear Miss Brahms was murdered. The police will be charged with finding the culprit, but I don't hold out much hope of that. The sergeant assigned to the case seems wholly inadequate to the task.' I gave the lad a second or two to digest this before continuing. 'I imagine there'll be a separate investigation into the goings-on at Condon's Hotel. The police will be hunting you down—you and Mrs Harmon both. And it's not just the police who'll be looking for you.'

'What do you mean?' he gasped.

'Whoever stabbed Miss Brahms, she was not his intended target.'

A challenging voice promptly rang out: 'Stop it! Stop it at once! Can't you see you're scaring the lad? Shame on you!'

I heard the swish of heavy material and the thud of suddenly-displaced snow. With her hair all but hidden under the hood of a thick woollen cape, Mrs Harmon stepped forward to join Cassius. The skin of her face looked raw from scrubbing. Whatever ointment or preparation she'd used to cause it to glow, it seemed she'd had trouble getting it off.

'What does he mean?' the boy asked her.

'He means that somebody was trying to kill me, Cassius. No one outside our circle knew that Sarah and I were planning to trade places, so that dagger was really meant for me.'

It occurred to me that, despite her youth, the woman had a very good brain in her head. 'Do you know of any reason why somebody would wish to kill you, miss?'

'No, but whoever it was, they must have got quite a shock when they saw it wasn't me.'

A very good brain, indeed! I tried to think back to the moment when the doctor pulled off Miss Brahms's wig. Had anyone's face shown a look of great consternation? *Hmmm.* It begged the question: does consternation look any different from surprise?

'So,' said Mrs Harmon, 'what do you plan to do with us? Shout…and betray us to the constables?'

As an Investigator-in-Chief, my duty was clear.

'You will remain silent and you will follow me,' I instructed them. 'And keep your heads down, both of you!'

Proceeding by a circuitous route along the unlit, lesser-trodden back streets, I led them to the Bucket of Blood and the kind of sanctuary that only Bertha alone could provide.

The next day started off as one of those days that are generally best avoided. I like to think of myself as bright and quick-witted, but how was I to explain to my employer our involvement in a murder, and moreover our need to take time off to attend the resulting inquest?

As it turned out, George and I were not the only ones beset by this particular problem, and by half past eight we were ensconced in Mr Bruff's office, together with Mr and Mrs Crabbit, confessing all.

Well, not *all*. I certainly didn't admit to what had drawn us to the hotel in the first place. Even the good, honest George seemed to shy away from mentioning *that*. I thought we were doing rather well for ourselves—too well, as it happens—for just as I was explaining how we'd paid for our admission out of a legacy left to me by my late, lamented uncle, who should knock on the office door but Mr Death!

He was accompanied by a gentleman in his very early forties, whom he introduced to us as Mr Smalley, of the firm Skipp and Smalley, Solicitors at Law. It was a name I had come across before, though in a different context. Mr Death began by acknowledging Mrs Crabbit (as did Mr Smalley) and then he went on to explain that, at the behest of Skipp and Smalley, as well as that of his own employer, he too had been present at Condon's Hotel.

'These boys,' he said, gesturing to George and me, 'had agreed to furnish me with proof that Mrs Harmon was a fraud in return for my paying for them to attend.'

Mr Bruff regarded me coolly, and addressed me with a quizzical, 'Gooseberry?'

'Sir?'

'One day you must tell me all about this dear, departed uncle of yours.' He gave me a grim little smile.

Somewhat puzzled by this remark, but sensing that my employer was done with his reprimanding for the time being, Mr Death carried on. 'As it transpires, the woman herself provided the proof by absconding. As a consequence of their involvement, however, my colleague here has a proposition he wishes to put to you.'

Mr Smalley brushed some imaginary lint from the sleeve of his coat, and then turned and addressed me directly. 'There is a small matter we would like you to investigate,' he explained. 'Well, not exactly a *small* matter,' he added, as he caught Mrs Crabbit's eye. 'Mr Bruff, you will be paid handsomely—*handsomely*—for your trouble, and we will advance the boy a generous sum for any expenses that might be incurred—'

This was clearly too much for Mr Crabbit. 'Any *reasonable* expenses,' he interjected, 'and be aware that you will still submit your receipts to me, and I shall be scrutinizing them thoroughly.'

'Hold on! Hold on!' It was Mr Bruff. 'Sir, you speak as if this were a done deal. Believe me, it is far from being that.'

Mr Smalley approached my employer's desk, took up his dip-pen, and scrawled a figure on a sheet of paper.

Mr Bruff's eyes widened. 'The weekly rate, I take

it?'

'The *daily* rate, sir. So if both the lads will be so good as to present themselves at my offices the first thing tomorrow, my colleagues and I will endeavour to take them through it.'

George blinked. 'What? You mean me too? You want me to be a detective?'

'An *investigator*. And, yes, we expect you as well.'

George glanced at Mr Bruff. 'And I won't have to run no errands?' he asked.

Now it was Mr Bruff's turn to blink. 'I suppose you won't,' he replied.

Whereas George looked elated, Mr Bruff's expression was decidedly gloomy. With George off, the younger George would be his one and only errand boy, and, Lord, I pitied him for that.

When the meeting eventually broke up, my employer called me back into the room.

'Gooseberry, a word.'

Ho hum; I should have expected it. 'About my late uncle, sir?'

Mr Bruff shook his head. 'No, not that. You know what that man Smalley is, don't you?'

'He's a solicitor like you, sir, is he not?'

My employer's face hardened. 'He may be a solicitor, but he is not like me. He is but a cheap imitation. He believes money can buy him anything he wants, and woe unto him who should fail to come when he's beckoned. Be careful, won't you? I shouldn't care to see you or George getting hurt.'

'Hurt, sir?'

'There are more ways of hurting you than giving

you a punch or a kick. You have been warned.'

I should point out that Mr Bruff has seldom had the need to resort to punching and kicking. That said—cheap imitation or not—Mr Smalley was prepared to hire George and me both, and to furnish us with a generous allowance. *Generous allowance*. Two of my favourite words!

CHAPTER TEN

AS YOU MAY HAVE expected, the inquest into Miss Brahms's death was held at Condon's Hotel, though not upstairs in the Harmons' suite, but in the ground-floor dining room. Though really quite spacious, it was only just large enough to accommodate everyone who was obliged to attend. Due to the sensational nature of the case, the police had no trouble empanelling the full twenty-four jurors; they sat two rows deep with their backs to the windows down the right-hand side of the room. Facing them on the opposite wall—where the coroner's clerk had set up his table—sat Sergeant Snipe and his two constables, looking rather rough from lack of sleep. The rest of us, huddling in our respective groups, found chairs where we could. George and I sat with the Crabbits and Mr Bruff, who now seemed tight-lipped but resolute. Mr Death and Mr Smalley were joined by two other gentlemen, whose easy manner marked them out as their colleagues. Mr Harmon, Mr Condon, and Mr Hargreaves were accompanied by a cocksure young man, who was, I was later to learn, their lawyer. Mr Ryman, Miss McVeigh, Mr Sligo, and Miss Moss found themselves clinging together for support, having brought no separate counsel of their own.

The coroner, a man with a grizzled face and a shock of white hair, surveyed the room with an acerbic eye.

'We seem to have a surfeit of lawyers with us today,' he observed, nodding to Mr Bruff, Mr Smalley, and the man in Mr Harmon's party in turn. 'Can the Inns of Court survive such an exodus, I ask myself? I suppose they will jolly well have to! Very good, let us begin.'

I happen to be quite the old hand at inquests, whereas for George it was an entirely new experience, so I felt it only fitting that I should give my apprentice some advice.

'See that chap over there, George...the one with the quill?' I whispered.

George grunted in response as he glanced in the man's direction.

'He's going to take down your statement—see?—so you need to talk slowly.'

'What?'

'He's going to take down your statement—see?—so you need to talk...oh, never mind.' It hardly mattered, since George talked slowly as a matter of course.

'He said you have to talk slowly,' observed the coroner, fixing me with a look that would have turned the sweetest butter rancid. 'And the boy is right. When each of you is called upon to give your evidence, you will enunciate slowly and clearly so my clerk here can take down a faithful account of your statements. As these will become your sworn depositions, do I need to remind you to speak truthfully? I trust I do not, for the outcome of any other course would be perjury. I frown on perjury and will not abide it in any form. Now, lad, unless you have any further advice to mete out to this inquiry, may we be allowed to begin?'

The constables were the first to be called. They told of how they'd been approached by one of the hotel's employees whilst making their rounds and summoned to an upper-storey room. They described— with, to my mind, quite lacklustre detail—what they found there and how they then sent to the station house for Sergeant Snipe.

Next Mr Harmon, Mr Hargreaves, and Mr Condon were called upon to explain the nature of Mrs Harmon's sittings. I could see that the coroner was none too happy with their testimony. When he asked how Miss Brahms came to be sitting in Mrs Harmon's seat, none of them could offer a satisfactory explanation.

'Sir,' said the young man who'd been sitting with them, 'may I please address the court?'

The coroner treated him to one of his looks, and said, 'Young Mr Cox, is it not?'

The fellow rose. 'Edward William Cox at your service. If it please the court, I have been retained to represent the interests of these three gentlemen. They know nothing of how the substitution was effected, or of Mrs Harmon's current whereabouts.'

'Really?'

'Truly, my Lord. They are as mystified as everybody

else.'

My employer, Mr Bruff, stroked his eyelid with his finger; Mr Death and his associates were doing likewise, whilst trembling with laughter, it seemed to me.

The coroner smiled. 'Young man, while I may be Her Majesty's Coroner for Westminster, I have yet to be made a Lord Justice. As a mere Sergeant, you may address me as "Sir"…or even "Your Honour", should you feel so inclined.'

'Yes, your Honour,' Mr Cox replied, and meekly reclaimed his seat.

One by one the rest of us were called upon to testify. With remarkably few variations, this was the story that emerged.

How did you know the deceased?

Only in her capacity as Mrs Harmon's personal secretary. Miss Brahms would greet me at the hotel's entrance, take my money, and show me up to the suite.

When was the last time you can positively say you saw Mrs Harmon?

Just before the candles were extinguished. She was seated at the top of the table. She was going into a trance.

And you are sure it was she?

Perfectly.

Then presumably Mrs Harmon was the intended victim?

That would certainly seem to follow.

Do you know of any reason why someone would wish to murder Mrs Harmon?

Most people answered that they did not, with only one exception worthy of note: Miss McVeigh.

She remained adamant that Mrs Crabbit was fearful

of what her uncle might say, were Mrs Harmon to manifest his spirit. Luckily for Mrs Crabbit, the coroner seemed to take a dim view of the medium's powers, and was inclined to think of Miss McVeigh as being hysterical. I say "*luckily*", because, of course, *if* Miss McVeigh was right—*and if* Mrs Crabbit were a true believer (which she certainly appeared to be)—then that would still constitute what we detectives refer to as *a motive*.

It was only when the doctor was called to give evidence that a new fact came to light. Like everyone else who testified, he was seated in a chair beside the coroner's desk, for there was no official witness box as such.

'Will you take us through the events that led up to the discovery of the body?'

'As was usually the case, Mrs Harmon began by fielding our written questions, then she put herself into a trance, the door was locked, and the candles were extinguished.'

'The door was locked, you say?'

'Yes, by the boy.'

'What boy?' the coroner demanded to know, for it was the first time there'd been any mention of Cassius.

'The one who serves the drinks. I think they call him Cassius.'

'And where is this boy now? Why isn't he here?'

'Sir,' said Mr Cox, rising from his seat, 'after informing Mr Condon of what had come to pass, it seems the lad slipped out of the building. We don't know where he is.'

'How irritating,' the coroner remarked. 'Doctor,

pray continue.'

'Soon after the candles were extinguished, Mrs Crabbit cried out that she'd been stung. She made quite a fuss about it, but Mr Harmon refused to take the matter seriously. Presently three—no, four—loud blasts were heard, sounded on a trumpet from somewhere near the bottom of the table. Then Mrs Harmon's glowing head appeared, floating high up near the ceiling.'

'Just her head?'

'Just her head. Suddenly the ghostly apparition let out a blood-curdling scream and disappeared from sight. When the candles were relit, we saw the dagger, sticking out of the young lady's back. At first we thought it was Mrs Harmon, on account of the wig she was wearing. It was only when I got up to ascertain whether the poor woman was truly dead did I see through the deception.'

'The dagger—had you ever seen it before?'

'No.'

In fact everyone's response to this question was a resounding no. When asked whether anyone had broken the circle, however, both Miss McVeigh and Miss Moss swore that Mrs Crabbit had, and for a good two or three minutes, to boot. Furthermore, she was apparently the only person to do so, for everyone else claimed that their neighbours had never once relinquished their grasp.

Mrs Crabbit gave a fairly creditable performance when she was eventually called, but then Mr Bruff had spent over an hour that morning preparing her for the ordeal.

'Keep your answers short and to the point,' he'd

advised her, 'and do not be tempted to turn the inquest into a platform for besmirching your cousin.'

'But—' she'd replied, or tried to reply, for my employer cut her short.

'Mrs Crabbit, a young woman has been murdered. This inquest is the start of a legal process to bring her killer to justice. You understand that, don't you?'

'Yes, but—'

'You want justice for her, do you not?'

'I do—'

'So how will you answer the coroner's questions?'

Mrs Crabbit sighed. 'I'll keep my answers short and to the point, and I shan't refer to my cousin.'

'Unless—?'

'I'm sorry?'

'You shan't refer to your cousin, unless—?'

'Oh. Unless I'm specifically asked to do so.'

'Good. I'm so glad we understand each other, dear lady.'

And she kept to her word, for the most part. She made no direct mention of Mr Ryman, and only once did she speak without prompting. It was on the subject of stings.

'I'm not stupid,' she said. 'I know what you're all thinking.'

Mr Crabbit turned ashen; Mr Bruff lowered his head and massaged his eyes.

'You think because I let go of your hands that I was the one who stabbed her! I was *stung*, I tell you! Look, I can show you the bruise!'

She held up her hand. On the fleshy part, where the thumb adjoined the forefinger, there was undoubtedly a big, nasty bruise.

'But it can't have been me,' she went on. 'It can't have, for I never once budged from my seat! You all heard me talking, the lot of you! You know I never moved. If you're so keen to find a killer, then I suggest you need look no further than—'

'Mrs Crabbit, enough!' It was the coroner.

It did the trick; it brought her to her senses. She gazed about the room, blinking, as if surprised to find herself in such surroundings. She stared at one jury member after another. Horrified by her outburst, they each of them refused to meet her eye.

'Thank you for your testimony,' said the coroner. 'I think we've heard all we need to hear from you for the present. Madam, will you please take your seat?'

Mrs Crabbit staggered back to her chair. When at last she was sitting, Mr Crabbit took hold of her hand and gave it a squeeze; Mr Bruff patted her gently on the shoulder.

George and I were presently called upon to give our accounts. He had little to add to what had already been said. I might have talked about how Mrs Harmon achieved her myriad tricks, but instead I followed Mr Bruff's advice and kept my answers brief and to the point. The last person to be called was the weaselly sergeant. He described how he'd examined the dagger and found three strands of human hair attached to the hilt.

'Long, grey hair,' he added meaningfully, staring directly at Mrs Crabbit.

All this weighed badly with the panel of jurors. When they returned from their deliberations, you could see the way the wind was blowing.

Mr Bruff rose to intervene, but with an, 'I know, I know, I know,' the coroner waved him down. 'Before you utter a single word,' he said, addressing the jury's foreman, 'you may not—nor *will* not—attribute this crime to a particular individual. Since I have heard no evidence given that would warrant such an action, *you cannot have, either.* Do you understand me? Nod if you do.'

It was a highly disappointed jury that brought in a verdict of murder by person or persons unknown. The coroner directed Sergeant Snipe to investigate, not just the murder, but the disappearance of Mrs Harmon and Cassius, too. *Ha! Good luck with that, Sergeant Snipe!* He was also instructed to look into the sittings with a view to deciding what charges might be brought. The coroner then thanked the jurors for their service and called the inquest to a close. As the room began to empty, the sergeant made his way over.

'I imagine you'll be seeing a lot of me, Mrs Crabbit,' he smirked, before turning and scuttling away.

'Why does he think that I murdered her, Philip?' Mrs Crabbit asked tearfully.

'I don't know, my dear. I honestly do not know.'

For a long time George had been remarkably quiet— even for George, who can spend his whole day saying nothing. It was only when we got out on to the street that I finally learned why.

'I think I might have done a terrible thing,' he whispered to me, as we trailed behind Mr Bruff and the Crabbits.

'What terrible thing, George?'

'I think I might have lied.'

'Either you lied or you didn't—so which is it to be?'

'I don't know,' said George, looking torn.

I decided to try a different tack. 'What *might* you have lied about, George?'

'About Mr Ryman not letting go of my hand.'

'*Did* he let go of your hand?'

'That's the thing. He might have. I can't remember. But if he did, it was only for a second.'

'A short second...or a long second?'

'Just a second. And that's only if he *did*.' We trudged silently through the snow for a while. 'What if I done what the judge said?' he asked. 'What if I've...'—he wrinkled his nose and thought for a bit— 'what if I've done some perjury?'

'What if I've *perjured myself*?' I corrected him. 'And he's a coroner, George, not a judge.'

'What do you think they'll do to me? Do you think they'll put me in prison? Oh, what will my mum say? What will—?'

'I shouldn't worry about it, George,' I broke in. 'As detectives, we have a duty to perjure ourselves.'

Was it too late to include it in *Guy's Taxonomy of Opportunities for the Jobbing Detective*, I wondered? It would make a rather neat inclusion. *And what, pray tell, is perjury? A chance that God sends the jobbing detective to present a superior version of the truth*! What a ring to it that had!

'Who do you think I should tell?' asked George.

'You've told me, haven't you? I don't see why you need to go telling anyone else. Besides, what if you're just imagining it, and he didn't let go of your hand?'

'Oh…'

'Exactly! And here's another besides for you: I am quite sure in my own mind that another person perjured themselves…actually, no, two people, if I'm right.'

'Two people? And one of them's the murderer?'

'I wouldn't go so far as to say that, but it certainly means they had the opportunity.'

'Who?'

'If I told you, it would prevent you from working it out for yourself, so it would be most unfair of me to say.'

'Oh, go on; tell me.'

I confess I gave in all too readily. 'Miss McVeigh, George! Miss McVeigh! And, as a consequence of that, Mr Sligo too!'

'How do you know?'

'I don't know for certain, but I can deduce it.'

'Deduce it? How?'

'Because, in my experience, people's behaviour seldom changes.' I tapped the side of my nose and left him to figure it out. He didn't—not at first, and even then, not for several days to come.

CHAPTER ELEVEN

THE OFFICES OF SKIPP and Smalley, which can be found just off Temple Lane—that gently sloping thoroughfare that runs from Fleet Street to the river— were neither as large nor as prestigiously-placed as those of Mr Bruff's. In their defence, however, I am bound to say I noticed a spirit of kinship amongst the staff that is entirely lacking from Gray's Inn Square. George and I were met by their chief clerk, an amiable, young man (yes, *amiable* and *young!*) who introduced himself to us as Mr Candy. He accompanied us up to Mr Smalley's room, where, despite the earliness of the hour, Mr Smalley and Mr Death were already assembled with the two colleagues who had been with them at the inquest. The lamps had been lit, for it was not yet fully light outside, and a new fire burned sluggishly in the grate. Once the three of us were seated, Mr Smalley began the introductions.

'This is my partner, Mr Skipp,' he said, gesturing to the man sitting beside him, who was roughly the same age as himself. 'And this is my proctor, Mr Devlin, who handles my civil cases.'

Mr Devlin was considerably older than either of the partners and was dressed in robes of black with ermine trim. I spied George looking rather perplexed. *Note to self: Explain to him later how a proctor is the only kind of lawyer qualified to prove people's wills.*

'Mr de Ath—Mr Devlin's man at the Prerogative Will Office—you already know,' Mr Smalley continued, 'and I imagine my chief clerk will have introduced himself—'

'On the way up,' affirmed Mr Candy.

Having dealt with his colleagues, he now tried to introduce me. 'This young fellow here goes by the name of Gooseberry,' he explained, with an overly-bright and somewhat annoying chuckle.

I adopted my most professional face and countered, 'Not true, sir. Although I'm often *called* Gooseberry by others, my name is in fact Octavius. I am Octavius Guy, and I am at your service.'

'Ah!' said Mr Smalley. 'My mistake. And this young man is George.'

'George Crump, sir,' said George.

'Gentlemen, these two lads have kindly agreed to help us with our Eldritch problem.'

Mr Skipp's eyes widened. He turned to his partner and said, 'Richard, you cannot be serious. They're so…'

Young? Uncultured? Working class? Rough? I wondered which description he was about to apply.

Mr Smalley held up his hand. 'I know. And yet they seem to have stumbled into the case all on their own. Mr de Ath here tells me that, when he came upon the pair, they'd already taken it upon themselves to investigate the Harmon woman.'

'And how did that go for them?' The question was delivered with a great deal of sarcasm.

'Why don't you ask them yourself?' suggested Mr Death.

Mr Skipp seemed unconvinced. 'What say you, Devlin?'

'Oh, I trust my clerk's judgement implicitly,' the black-robed proctor replied. 'He has an instinct for this sort of thing.' Mr Death acknowledged the compliment with a bow of his head.

'All right,' said Mr Skipp, addressing himself to me. 'You investigated the medium. Tell me, what did you find?'

'You heard at the inquest how she would answer written questions without knowing their content, sir?'

'I did.'

'The truth is she didn't need to know their content, for her accomplice, Cassius—the lad who absconded with her—knew what the questions were, and knew how to answer them.'

'But the boy barely said a word,' Mr Death pointed out.

'He didn't have to. He just had to stand there. If the answer was yes, he'd look to his right; if no, he would look to his left.'

Mr Death blinked. 'But that's…*ingenious*! Ingenious! How on earth did you figure it out?'

'With a little help from my colleague here.'

George stared at me and gaped. I could sense his lips about to move, to form the incredulous, baffled words, "*What help?*" I raised my hand just in time to prevent him.

Note to self: Teach George the useful art of accepting compliments, deserved or undeserved.

Mr Skipp was less enthused; in fact he was downright dismissive. 'That just sounds so simple.'

'It is simple, sir, when you know how it's done. But if you don't know, it seems wholly impossible.'

'He's got you there, Skipp,' Mr Devlin observed.

'So, Arthur, do we take them on?' Mr Smalley gazed quizzically at his partner.

'Oh, very well,' Mr Skipp replied, though I can't say he looked very happy.

'Good, then let me give these lads the facts. Our late client, Mr Frederick Eldritch of Hampstead, died of natural causes on the twelfth of November last.'

'Natural causes, sir?' I queried.

'What the doctors refer to as organ failure. There's no question of foul play; the man was old, and had been warned that his death was imminent. When he knew the end was near, he sent for his niece, Mavis Crabbit.'

'She was his closest relation?'

'Yes. His wife, Estelle, passed away some years ago, as did his younger brother and sister. He and Estelle had had a child together, but the boy died in childbirth. He and his sister's son, Mr Ryman, had once been close, but there'd been a falling out. Gambling debts, I believe. Which just left—'

'Mrs Crabbit.'

'Exactly. His brother's only child. For the past twenty years or so, she's been his sole heir.'

I scratched my head. 'Yet, if I understand the

situation correctly, it's Mr Ryman who has inherited his fortune.'

'On the day before he died, Frederick Eldritch tried to summon me. Unfortunately I wasn't here; I was engaged on some lengthy business down in Devon.'

'Do you know why he summoned you, sir?'

'I can only assume he wished to alter the terms of his will, for, when I failed to make an appearance, he seems to have taken matters into his own hands and composed a new one himself.'

'Holographic wills!' groaned Mr Devlin and Mr Death in unison.

'He *seems*?' I queried. Mr Smalley's choice of words was certainly interesting.

'There's been some suggestion that this will might have been forged.'

'Mrs Crabbit's suggestion, I presume.'

Mr Smalley nodded.

'Sir, *is* the will forged?'

'We don't think so.'

'May we see it for ourselves, please?'

Mr Candy rose and left the room, and presently returned with a folder. He opened it up and pulled out two sheets of paper, which he handed to me. I edged my chair a little closer to George's so that he and I could read them together.

I was glad to see that George had taken out his notebook, and was preparing to make a copy of the text.

The Last Will and Testament of
Mr Frederick Leonard Eldritch, Esquire,
of Blackthorn House, Hampstead

I, Frederick Leo Eldritch, being of sound
mind and body, revoke all former Wills and
Codicils made in my name and affirm this
Will to be my Last Will and Testament.

I appoint as my executor
Mr Richard Smalley, my lawyer,
trusting that he will carry out my wishes to
the letter without question or dispute.

In light of recent experiences, I bequeath the
entirety of my Estate to my nephew,
Thomas Patrick Ryman, son of my late,
beloved sister Patience, to do with as he sees
fit.

Though it pains me to adopt this
extraordinary course of action, I find myself
driven to it by the spiteful, petty
nature of the woman I am forced to call my
niece.
May she reflect at length on my decision,
in the hope that it might cure her of her
mean, uncharitable ways.

Signed by me, this day,
Thursday November 11th, 1852:

Frederick Eldritch, Esq.

and witnessed by my two faithful servants:

Agnes Butterworth (Cook)

Gladys Bland (Housemaid)

The body of the will was penned in a scratchy, decrepit hand that even the most novice forger might replicate with comparative ease. The style was hardly distinctive; any number of literate people might write this way. There were no extravagant flourishes, no curlicues to underscore particular passages; the letters were neither especially cramped nor excessively spaced apart, and even the inkblots seemed innocuous—and unlikely to be covering up some word that might change the document's essential meaning. In short, it appeared to be exactly what it purported to be: the testament of a dying man who was suffering from pain.

I studied the second sheet at length, paying meticulous attention to the signatures. Whereas Mr Eldritch's matched the ragged nature of the rest of the writing, the cook's and the housemaid's were both spotlessly rendered. Did either show signs of hesitation, as one might expect to see if this were a forgery? Certainly not in the cook's case. She'd signed the will with a practised hand. The housemaid, however, had signed her name slowly, and each stroke of the pen was considered. This *might* be an indication of forgery; then again, it might simply signify that the girl was unused to signing her name. My verdict? As an adept at the beguiling art of forgery—not that I could admit to such an accomplishment in the company I presently found myself in—I would bet my boots that the signatures were genuine.

And yet, as a whole, I felt there was something slightly off about it—something that was staring me in the face and crowing at my supreme lack of insight.

Hmmm.

'I've known Mr Eldritch since I was quite a young man,' Mr Smalley confided, when I was done reading it. 'I've transacted much of his business for him over that time. I am prepared to swear that *that* is his signature.'

'What about the witnesses—the cook, Agnes Butterworth, and the housemaid, Gladys Bland? Did you think to interview them?'

'It was the first thing we did.'

'And?'

'They examined their signatures most carefully, and duly confirmed they were theirs. We have their sworn statements to that effect.'

'What made Mr Eldritch change his mind?' asked George. 'I mean, there had to be a reason. Something must have happened for him to want to leave his money to someone else.'

It was a perfectly good question, and one that I myself would have asked, had I been given half the chance.

Mr Smalley wriggled in his chair. 'I really couldn't say.'

'Richard,' his partner urged him, 'you've told the boys this much…you might as well tell them everything.'

Mr Smalley studied the lengthening flames as the fire kindled itself into life. He seemed to come to a decision, and rather annoyingly addressed himself to George.

'The minute Mrs Crabbit set foot in the house, she rubbed everyone up the wrong way—the cook, the housemaid, the nurse…even the attending physician.

She behaved abominably towards Mr Ryman. The only person she showed the slightest deference to was Miss Moss, Mr Eldritch's neighbour.'

'Miss Moss? Miss Cicely Moss?' George looked puzzled. 'Miss Moss was Mr Eldritch's neighbour?'

'Indeed. She owns the Limes, the property next to Blackthorn House.'

'And you think Mrs Crabbit's behaviour was the reason Mr Eldritch changed his will?'

'The wording Mr Eldritch used paints a rather sorry picture, wouldn't you say?'

George nodded sagely. 'And he wrote this will the day before he died?'

'Yes. He passed away the next night, alas, on the eve of my return to London. By the time I finally answered his summons, his body was already cold. The first thing I did after paying my respects was to go through the bureau in the drawing room where I knew he kept his will. When I found the envelope bearing his handwriting, I was dismayed but not surprised.'

I saw a chance to pose a question—albeit a weak one—and, with it, to reassert my authority. 'You opened it and read it, sir, there and then?'

'Not then, no. I waited till the family had gathered for the formal reading—'

'Family? Mrs Crabbit and Mr Ryman, you mean?'

'Yes. I asked them both to come into the drawing room. It was only mid-afternoon, but the sky was already dark, and the rain kept battering the terrace outside the window. It's then that I opened the envelope in front of them and learned of its extraordinary terms. I found myself blushing with embarrassment, for I was obliged, you see, to read it out in front of Mrs Crabbit, word after hurtful word.'

'How did they react, the pair of them?'

Mr Smalley frowned. 'Neither of them spoke. They simply sat there in a kind of stupor. Eventually Mrs Crabbit turned to her cousin and said, "You did this, Thomas; I know you did. This will is *your* doing." It seemed a reasonable enough comment, given what she had just had to sit through, but then she went on, "And, by that, I don't mean that you put our uncle up to it; I mean that you wrote the entire thing yourself! Mr Smalley, I appeal to you! It's absurd! Uncle Frederick would not have left Thomas a penny...under any conceivable circumstance! He knew what he was like!"'

'Mr Ryman rose and gave her a piteous look, then left the room without saying a thing.' Mr Smalley sighed and adjusted the cuffs of his shirtsleeves. 'Obviously we cannot be seen to ignore her complaint,' he continued. 'We still have a duty of care to our client.'

'Your client?'

'The late Frederick Eldritch.'

'Here's the difficulty,' his partner chipped in. 'There may not be a shred of evidence to back up her story, *but that's not to say she's not right.*'

'Which brings us to my own particular problem,' Mr Devlin explained. 'If he did what she claims he did, then I need to know. I cannot risk moving forward with probate until I am certain of the will's authenticity.'

'So where do you want us to start?' asked George. *That was my line, George, I'll have you know!*

'By interviewing everyone who was there when Mr Eldritch made his new will. I've taken the liberty of writing to them and warning them to expect you. My chief clerk has drawn up a schedule with their names and their various addresses.'

Mr Candy delved into his folder again and pulled out a neatly-written list. I snatched it from him as he tried to hand it to my apprentice, and George was forced to content himself with peering over my shoulder as I casually perused its contents. This afternoon we were to meet with Mrs Crabbit. Tomorrow it was the turn of the doctor, the nurse, Mr Ryman, and Miss Moss.

'What about the cook and the housemaid?' I asked, having noticed their surprising omission.

'Sadly, Mr Ryman let them go. But we have their sworn statements, if you care to read them.'

This time Mr Candy handed them directly to me. I read them through, though they held no real surprises. Both women had been called on to witness the will, and both were positive that the signatures were theirs.

'So,' said Mr Smalley, 'have you any further questions?'

'You haven't told us yet how Mrs Harmon comes into this.' I'd hardly got the words out before the chief clerk was flushing crimson.

'That would be my fault,' he admitted sheepishly. 'In the days following Mr Eldritch's death, Mrs Crabbit became a regular visitor here.' I could tell from the expression on his face that what he really meant was *a pest.* 'I grew so tired of her constant petitioning, I advised her that her only chance of overturning the will was to have her uncle testify from the grave. I never expected her to take me seriously.'

'When we learned what she was doing,' Mr Smalley took over, 'we thought it only prudent to send a man along…just to observe, you understand. Mr Candy couldn't go because she knew him by sight. It was, of course, out of the question that Mr Skipp or myself— or our colleague Mr Devlin—might attend—'

'Which rather left me,' Mr Death observed, shrugging his shoulders sadly.

'Do you think your Eldritch problem, as you put it, has anything to do with Miss Brahms's murder?' The hasty denials all round told me they feared that it might.

'I would stress that we are hiring you to investigate the will's authenticity,' Mr Smalley emphasized, '*not* the murder of that unfortunate young woman.'

'But if we were to uncover her murderer in the process?'

'Let us cross that bridge when we come to it.'

'Be assured that we shall do our level best,' I promised, and rose to leave. George took his cue from me and rose too.

'Don't forget your notebook, George,' I warned him, for he was about to leave it sitting on the arm of his chair.

After much handshaking and not a few votes of appreciation, Mr Candy showed us to the door.

'It doesn't seem right,' said George, as we trudged up the snow-covered lane back to Fleet Street. 'They should have hired us to find out who killed Miss Brahms.'

'Of course they're hiring us to find her killer,' I replied. 'They just don't know it yet. Why, they've even arranged for us to interview half of the suspects.'

George blinked. 'Oh. I never thought of it like that. So what now?'

'We have an hour or two in hand before we are due at Mrs Crabbit's. I think we should find ourselves a good chophouse and treat ourselves to a spot of dinner.'

'But it takes at least an hour to trek to Camden when the roads are like this!'

'Not if we take a cab, George.'

George nearly slipped on a patch of ice as he turned to stare. 'We're going to take a cab?'

'Of course we are. We owe it to Mr Smalley to take cabs *everywhere*.'

George gasped. 'How do you figure that?'

'He's paying our expenses, George. When he scrutinizes the receipts that Mr Crabbit sends him, he'll be relieved to see that we do things professionally.'

George's eyes turned to saucers as he began to follow my reasoning. 'Oh,' he said, '*professionally*...'

CHAPTER TWELVE

'HELLO, MRS MOODY. WE'VE—' is as far as George got before a great wave of water tossed from a pail hit us both squarely in our faces.

'Oh, my gawd, oh, my gawd! I'm so sorry George! I thought you was that blasted policeman again, didn't I?' Mrs Moody appeared to be on the verge of tears. 'He's been hounding me ragged, that horrible man, with all his questions and his prying! Is Mrs Crabbit *this*? Is Mrs Crabbit *that*? Is Mrs Crabbit *three bags full, sir*!'

'Sergeant Snipe?' guessed George, water dripping from the tip of his nose.

'Sergeant Snipe!' she replied. 'He's been haunting my doorstep all morning—peeking through my windows and going through my bins—why, at one point he even climbed a tree in the churchyard! How can a man like that live with himself? Tell me that!'

Rather than telling her—and despite being soaked—George ran his censorious eye over me.

'But you're here to see Mrs Crabbit, aren't you

dear? She mentioned somebody from her husband's work might be dropping by; I never thought it would be you, though. Oh, but you're drenched to the skin! The pair of you will catch your deaths if you stay in those wet clothes! There's nothing for it; you'll have to dry off. I've got some old towels you can use. Go on through, go on through.'

To George's consternation, she put down her pail and bustled us into her own suite of rooms.

'Don't worry,' she said, as she closed the door, 'there's nobody home but me. Take off those jackets and shirts, and I'll dry them by the fire.'

While she went to fetch the towels she'd promised, I slipped off my mittens and started unfastening my buttons. George, I noticed, seemed reluctant to join me. When Mrs Moody returned and saw that he was still fully dressed, she began to tear a strip off him.

'Now, don't you go getting coy with me, George Crump! Just you think of me as your mother...now, out of those things this instant!'

Unwillingly, he peeled off his jacket and pulled his shirt over his head.

'Singlet too!'

She handed us towels, picked up our garments, then draped them over the clothes-horse. Judging the distance with an expert eye, she installed them in front of the fire.

'I think she's sweet on you, George,' I whispered, when she went to the kitchen to make tea. George looked none too pleased at the prospect, and sat glowering at the room.

Tea, when it came, was a strained affair. Mrs Moody

passed the sugar bowl; I took two lumps, George took six.

'Mr Moody, when I married him, he had a sweet tooth like yours,' she observed. 'It took me a year, but I managed to whittle him down to three in the end. I expect when you—'

We never got to learn what it was she expected, for George burst abruptly into speech. 'Mrs Moody, are our clothes dry yet?'

The woman peered at the steam coming off the clothes-horse and said, 'Not yet, dear; no.' Again she tried to strike up a conversation; again George made a point of interrupting her. After twenty minutes of this constant battling back and forth, I too couldn't wait for the clothes to be dry. It was a relief when at last she pronounced them fit to wear and handed them back to us so we could get dressed again.

With a face on him as dark as a storm cloud, George finished buttoning his jacket, muttered a few words of thanks, then lumbered out into the hallway and disappeared up the stairs. I gave a commiserative shrug and followed in pursuit.

'Who's going to knock?' growled George, as we eyed the Crabbits' door together.

Despite the surliness of the delivery, it was not an unreasonable question. Which of us was brave enough to rouse the chief clerk's wife?

'You do it,' I whispered.

'You're the chief investigator,' he snapped back. 'You should be the one to knock.'

'You're the one who's always going on about wanting more responsibility. Well, here's your chance,

George. Take it! Grasp the nettle firmly while you may!' *Touché, my touchy friend, touché!*

'You think you're so clever, always twisting the truth with your words! If I didn't know better, I'd say you were scared!'

I was left with one last trump card in my hand, and decided the time had come to play it.

'I'm just trying to give you an opportunity, George...and *what*, pray tell, are opportunities?'

George's face darkened by several degrees. If we were still talking of storm clouds, then a deluge was imminent.

'Chances that God sends the jobbing detective of battering his teacher into the ground?'

'What's the matter with you, George? Why are you acting so—?'

Suddenly the door flew open, revealing a furious-looking Mrs Crabbit.

'What's all this shouting?' she cried, and then she saw it was us. 'Well?' she said, 'What are you waiting for? Come in, come in.'

I cannot begin to convey how extremely odd it felt stepping into the chief clerk's rooms—his *personal* residence...the place where he lived and slept and ate. I truly believe there are some things that should never be seen...the insides of your own body, for instance. I count the chief clerk's home as being amongst these. Entering this private space felt like I was intruding in the man's own head.

George, now that his temper had been deflated, appeared to feel much the same as I did. When told to sit, we both found ourselves seeking out the least offensive spot on which to perch our worthless behinds. We strenuously averted our eyes from the faded velvet curtains, the small but well-stocked bookshelf, the three or four hunting scenes that hung on the walls. I suddenly remembered I was wearing my bowler, and furtively removed it. George watched in silence as I balanced it on my knee. I tried to think of what words to use to start off the interview, but nothing came to mind. Luckily for us, Mrs Crabbit needed no such prompting. She installed herself on one of the straight-backed chairs and came straight to the point— albeit *her* point.

'Before we talk about my cousin, Thomas Ryman,' she said, 'you need to know a little about my family's history. Mr Frederick Leonard Eldritch was my father Robert's elder brother. Patience Eldritch was their younger sister. Much younger, in fact, for when their parents died, she was still in her adolescence. As the head of the family, it now fell to Frederick to find Patience a suitable husband. He introduced her to any number of his eligible friends, but she found fault with them all. They were, she claimed, too old. My father was then availed upon to find her a suitable match. Patience, however, was a wilful girl and none of his acquaintances were deemed good enough. Then, quite out of the blue, she announced that she'd become engaged to a man named Cyril Ryman.

'"But who *is* he?" both Frederick and my father demanded to know.

'"He is the man I am going to marry," she replied, and very soon she had—and only just in time, if you grasp my meaning. Cousin Thomas entered this world in an inglorious birth a paltry seven months later.'

George shot a nervous glance in my direction. I returned it with a knowing nod.

'I was thirteen at the time; quite old enough to count the months and calculate their meaning. Father was naturally scandalized, and began to distance himself from his sister. The same cannot be said of Uncle Frederick, more's the pity. His own baby son had died in childbirth some years before, and he and his wife Estelle welcomed—*welcomed*—the Rymans into their home. They doted on the baby, and came to love the child he grew to be.

'I imagine you'll be too young to remember the first outbreak of cholera. February 1832, it was. They called it "blue cholera" back then. It didn't do as much damage as the outbreak four years ago, and yet, at the time, it felt like family after family was being snuffed out in its wake. Ours certainly was. Uncle Frederick's wife, my own father, and both of Thomas's parents fell victim to the disease.

'Uncle Frederick saw to it that my mother and I were provided for—though hardly in the manner to which we were accustomed; Cousin Thomas, however, he embraced as a son. Nothing was too good for Cousin Thomas. Little did he know, when he installed him in Blackthorn, that his cherished nephew had already fallen into dissolute ways!

'He found out soon enough, though, when the young man's creditors came knocking, and not just from the gaming tables and taverns, but from bordellos and houses of ill repute! Oh, how Cousin Thomas begged and howled! How he wailed and pleaded and beguiled! He could change, he *would* change, he'd become a new man, if only his uncle would pay off his debts. The funny thing is, those debts never stopped coming. Fresh creditors arrived at the close of each month, as did Thomas's tears. Eventually, Uncle Frederick could see only one way past it. Thomas would be married off post-haste. If marriage couldn't cure his nephew of his profligacy, then nothing ever would. And so he arranged for him to wed the daughter of his late wife's cousin. I imagine you can guess how that turned out?'

This time I glanced at George and he glanced back, giving the slightest shrug of his shoulders.

'How, miss?' I asked. My mouth was so dry, I fairly croaked the words out.

'Why, he jilted the poor girl at the altar!'

George shifted uneasily in his chair. For a moment I could have sworn he was blushing.

'Uncle Frederick never forgave him,' she continued. 'He banished him from the house. He published notices in every journal in London saying how he'd no longer be held accountable for what his nephew owed. As for me, well…he named me as his heir.'

If I'd understood Mrs Crabbit's story correctly, he had no other choice. All the others were dead. At a pinch, he *might* have picked Mrs Crabbit's mother, who was his brother's widow, or his wife's cousin's daughter, whom Thomas had jilted, but, as neither of them were tied to him by blood, it seemed a little unlikely.

'Now you can see it, can't you?' she asked.

Again I felt stumped. 'See what, miss?'

'Why this will can be nothing but a forgery. My uncle would never leave a penny to a man who'd betrayed him so.'

I had to admit she had a point.

'Mrs Crabbit,' I said, 'would you be so good as to take us through what happened at your uncle's house? From the time you first arrived, please?'

Mrs Crabbit sniffed loudly and straightened her shoulders. 'When I received word of Uncle Frederick's condition, I naturally set off right away. I should like to be able to report that I found him in the best of care, but it would be a lie. I dare say the nurse was doing her best, but really! With only Miss Moss from the neighbouring house to give her any respite, the woman was clearly run off her feet. Well, I soon put that right; I started organizing. And by the very next day I had the servants pitching in and things began running like clockwork.'

'Was Mr Ryman there at that point?'

'No. He turned up three days later.'

'Was he not sent for at the same time as you?'

Mrs Crabbit let out a bitter laugh. 'Haven't you been listening to me? My uncle had banished him from Blackthorn! He wasn't sent for at all!'

I frowned. 'Then why did he come?'

'Isn't it obvious?' she exclaimed. 'To worm his way back into Uncle Frederick's good graces before the poor man could draw his last breath!'

'Was your uncle disposed to receiving him?'

'Not at first. But Thomas can be persistent. He refused point-blank to leave the house until he'd seen his uncle. And eventually Uncle Frederick gave in.'

'Were you present at this interview, miss?'

Mrs Crabbit's face hardened. 'No,' she replied, 'but as a result of it, Thomas was permitted to stay.'

'Do you think they made it up, miss? Did your uncle choose to forgive him?'

'Hardly! The interview, as you call it, lasted all of five minutes. Even Thomas would have difficulty working his wily charms in such a short space of time.'

'And yet the fact remains, miss, your uncle made a new will.'

Mrs Crabbit stared at me. '*Somebody* made a new will, but I'm telling you it wasn't my uncle. Don't you think he would have informed me if that's what he was planning to do?'

'If I may point out, your uncle's solicitors have examined the document thoroughly, and they don't consider it to be a forgery. They interviewed the two witnesses and obtained their sworn statements: the signatures are undeniably theirs.'

'The doddering old cook and the halfwitted housemaid? The cook's such a goose, if you told her the world was flat, I swear she'd ask you, "*Where there be dragons?*" And as for that slovenly housemaid, I dare say her honour could be bought for a wink and nod. Don't you see?' she cried. 'They were in on it, the pair of them! They had to have been! If the will was truly genuine, why would my cousin need to be rifling through the bureau in the drawing room?'

'The bureau, miss?' I glanced at George. He too was sitting on the edge of his seat.

'On the very day my uncle died, I saw Thomas going through the bureau. It's where the will was kept…the real will, that is,' she added.

'And when was this?' I asked.

'A little after four in the afternoon. I came downstairs to ask when tea would be served, but I couldn't find Cook anywhere, nor was there any sign of a teapot, or sandwiches, or a cake. That alone should tell you just how slipshod she was! Anyway, I was about to head back upstairs when I heard sounds coming from the drawing room. The door was slightly ajar, so I peered in. And what do you think I should spy? Why, Thomas, searching through the bureau, in what can only be described as a highly suspicious manner.'

'Did you challenge him over it, miss?'

Mrs Crabbit's head shot up. 'I…' The word trailed away tellingly.

'You didn't challenge him, miss?'

'No. No, I did not.' She flushed with embarrassment.

Why not? From the little I knew of this woman, this was extremely out of character. However, given the look on her face, I let the matter lie. A good detective knows when and when not to press his advantage.

'Why not?' asked George, shrugging at me when I shot him a well-deserved scowl.

'I didn't think anything of it at the time,' she replied, in a most unconvincing manner. 'It was only later when this so-called new will emerged, it got me thinking.'

'Thank you for being so candid with us, miss. I realize it can't have been easy. I only have one more question for you. When you first approached Mrs Harmon, how did you expect her to help you?'

Mrs Crabbit's eyes narrowed. 'I am by no means a

fanciful woman,' she replied, 'so don't go getting it into your head that I am. I am, however, a Good Christian. I believe in the Life Hereafter. And you saw for yourself what Mrs Harmon can do.'

I had indeed…and—to some extent—I'd also seen *how* she had done it.

With the interview concluded, George and I took our leave.

CHAPTER THIRTEEN

FRIDAY MORNING DAWNED BRIGHT and cold, if not especially early, with the sun pushing its head above the eastern horizon a goodly time after us working mortals had risen, washed, dressed, and breakfasted. I had no problem hailing a cab, and by the time half past eight had rolled around, I was on my way to Camden Town to pick up George. I found him waiting for me on his front steps. He waved at the three faces watching from the window, then ran down and hauled himself up in beside me.

'They didn't believe me when I told them I was getting a cab to work,' he explained, his breath forming frosty white vapour clouds within the confines of the carriage. 'So who are we seeing today?'

'The doctor, the nurse, then Mr Ryman and Miss Moss. All the Hampstead lot.'

The going was slow and treacherous on the climb up Haverstock Hill, with the wheels getting caught in the deep icy ruts that were now a feature of every major road in the land. Passing the parade of shops on the high street, we turned left into a narrow lane, which brought us to our first destination, named for its row of picturesque houses leading down to a splendid parish church.

'Take a deep sniff, George. What do you smell?'

'Clean air?'

'Clean air?'

'Well, it don't smell as bad as what it does in London.'

I shook my head. 'No. That, George, is the smell of the hunt; today we shall track ourselves down a criminal!'

I paid the driver out of the funds Mr Candy had furnished us with and obtained a receipt; George, meanwhile, scouted up and down the street in search of the doctor's residence.

'Found it,' he cried.

I went to join him, and together we perused the brass plaque on the door.

Dr Felix Kauffmann
Doctor of Medicine, Emeritus Professor of the College of
Physicians (Frankfurt), and Member of the Institute of
Frankfurt (in Perpetuum)

'Where's Perpetuum?' asked George.

'You should really be asking where Frankfurt is,' I replied, for I wasn't entirely sure about Perpetuum.

'All right, then. Where's Frankfurt?'

'It's a town just outside Paris,' I informed him sagely, 'not far from Florence and Vienna.' *Perhaps Perpetuum was the name of the district they were in.*

While he seemed impressed by my superior geographical knowledge, he still sounded a little doubtful. 'Do you think Dr Kauffmann speaks English?' he asked.

'Of course he does. Everyone from France speaks English, George. They have to. How else would they make themselves understood when they come over here?'

'Tell me again why we're seeing the doctor?'

'We need to ascertain that there was no funny business with regards to Mr Eldritch's death.'

'Is that all?'

'It's a small question, George, but a vital one.'

'Who's going to knock? You or me?'

'Stand back, my friend. I shall do the honours this time.'

My curt little rap with the knocker brought a swift response, though not from the doctor himself, but rather his housekeeper. She showed us into the waiting room—which was in reality nothing more than a parlour—and instructed us to wait. After a short space of time, the doctor appeared: a corpulent man with a luxuriant beard and a pair of wire-rimmed spectacles. He asked us through to his surgery—which to my mind was naught but a study.

'So,' he said, in an accent so harsh that it might well be considered guttural (making me think that Frankfurt might lie a little to the north of Paris), 'you come to make the inquiries about my former patient, Mr Frederick Eldritch?'

'Sir, we were told by his lawyers that Mr Eldritch died of natural causes. Can you confirm that this is indeed the case?'

He looked me up and down before replying. If he found my youth surprising, he was kind enough not to remark upon it.

'That is perfectly correct, young man. Mr Eldritch's kidneys were failing him, his heart was failing him, and it was only a matter of time before his liver failed him too.'

'And there's no chance that someone might have hurried his demise along?'

Dr Kauffmann frowned deeply, to the point where his straggly, grey eyebrows knitted together.

'Someone is suggesting foul play was involved?'

He extracted a cigarette from a box on his desk, struck a match, and lit it.

'But that is an idea most ridiculous,' he went on. 'It is idiotic, imbecilic, indefensible! *Nein, nein! Es ist unsinnig!*'

Nine, nine, what did he say about sinning?

'Why,' asked the doctor, in a more reasonable tone of voice, as a thin stream of smoke issued from his lips, 'why would anyone wish to kill a man who is destined to die at any minute?'

They might, if they had an inkling he was about to change his will and they wished to forestall him, I reflected.

Dr Kauffmann rose and flicked the spent match into the fireplace. 'Young man,' he said, 'who is it that has put these ideas into your head? Eldritch's niece?'

Quite the contrary, since I was considering the possibility that Mrs Crabbit had learned that the lawyer had been summoned, guessed what was in the wind, and had taken steps to prevent it. Again, it's what we detectives think of as "*motive*".

'No, sir,' I replied.

'That woman is quite unhinged,' he informed me. 'If anyone helped the poor man to his death, it was she! Ach, a thousand pities she will not face such a charge, for I repeat: Frederick Eldritch died of natural causes. You have my word on that!'

Since the doctor seemed disinclined to be swayed from this view, we respectfully asked for directions to the nurse's house and made our exit.

'Do you really think somebody murdered Mrs Crabbit's uncle?' asked George, as we trudged our way back to the high street.

'No; it was just a possibility that I wished to rule out.'

'And have you?'

I stopped to consider the question. 'I *think* so,' I said at last.

'You don't sound very certain.'

'It's too early to be certain of anything, George. We're still collecting the facts, remember.'

We crossed the high street and, after a brief search of the snow-covered thoroughfares, we presently found Flask Walk and the little lane leading off it. Nurse Tully's cottage was the fifth on the right, a squat brick edifice with a garden the size of a proverbial matchbox.

'They don't look much like cottages to me,' mumbled George, as he eyed the row of tightly-packed buildings. 'You'd think out here in the countryside they'd know how to build themselves a proper cottage!'

I was inclined to agree. Still, it was a step up from my own humble lodgings. Feeling in a magnanimous mood, I suggested that George might do the knocking this time. It was a mistake I shall not repeat, for he took it as a sign that he might also do the questioning.

'Hello,' he said, when the door was opened by a pleasantly rotund woman in a clean, white apron and a matching cap. 'Are you Nurse Tully?'

'I am,' she replied, with a touch of caution in her voice. 'And just who might you be, may I ask?'

'My name's George Crump, miss. This here's my colleague, Octavius Guy. Mr Smalley sent us to interview you.'

She regarded us with suspicion for quite some few moments before eventually inviting us in.

'I was expecting someone older,' she said, as she showed us through to her kitchen. A pot of soup was bubbling away on the black coal range, watched—it seemed—by a man in a chair, though he never once rose to attend to it. The little room was as cosy as cosy could be, and yet the man's lower limbs were tucked up in a blanket.

'My husband,' Nurse Tully said simply. 'He used to be a stonemason until the accident. Now, sit yourselves down and tell me how I can be of help.'

'We've come to ask about Mr Frederick Eldritch,' George replied, before I could get a word in. 'About the new will he made, miss.'

In response, Nurse Tully moved to the dresser and drew down a cloth-bound folio from the highest shelf.

'What's this?' he asked, as she returned to the table and laid it before him.

'My scrapbook,' she said, flipping it open to a point near the middle.

I leaned closer to take a look. On the left was the beginnings of a sampler, with the letter "A" stitched in a peacock-blue silk; on the right, a half-finished bookmark, bearing the words, "*THE LORD IS MY SAV*". Nurse Tully flipped over the page.

I stared; George stared. What we saw was a fragment of blotting paper.

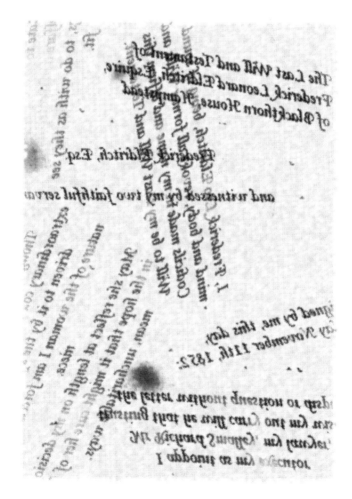

'I retrieved it from the bin in Mr Eldritch's room as a memento. I take a keepsake to remind me of all the patients I nurse in their final days.' While George took out his notebook and pursued a frankly pointless line of questioning, I slid the folio across to me and, trying my best to ignore the child's drawing that sat next to it, I made a study of the blotter. It was extremely hard to read, and I found myself wishing I had a mirror.

'Your friend doesn't have much to say for himself, does he?' Nurse Tully observed, as George brought his interrogation to a close.

'I do have a few questions for you, miss,' I replied.

'Yes?' She looked at me expectantly.

'You say you retrieved this from Mr Eldritch's room—do you mean his bedroom?'

'Yes. It was in the bin beside his bed.'

Ah! *So it was reasonable to assume that he'd put it there himself.* I moved on to a different line of inquiry.

'May I ask what you thought of Mrs Crabbit, miss?'

Nurse Tully's lips set into a tight, grim line. 'I shouldn't care to say.'

'What about Mr Ryman?'

'Our paths seldom crossed, though he always seemed personable enough. Knows how to stay out of the way.'

'Thank you, Nurse Tully, for sparing us your time. A word of warning, and then we'll let you be about your business. Guard your scrapbook with your life, miss; I fear it may turn out to be of the greatest importance.'

Nurse Tully stared.

'I mean it, miss. Come, George; we should go.'

We rose and she showed us to the door. George suddenly realized he'd left his notebook behind and ran back to the kitchen to get it.

'What was that about?' I asked, as we returned to Flask Walk, and thence to the shops on the high street in search of a quick bite to eat.

'What was what about?'

'Thinking you can ask all the questions! Please bear in mind that you are my apprentice, George; it is I who will take the lead.'

'So I don't get to ask any questions?'

'Of course you do, George; but if you wish to become a proper detective, you need to know the right ones to ask. So, for the remaining interviews, I will allow you to pose one question at each. When I have finished my inquiries, you can say: "What led you to consult Mrs Harmon?"'

'*What led you to consult Mrs Harmon*?' George looked disgruntled in the extreme. 'Why do I have to ask that?'

'You don't *have* to ask it, George. I'm quite happy to ask it myself.'

'Why's it even important?' he demanded to know.

'Since somebody tried to kill Mrs Harmon, I should very much like to know what drew these people to her sittings in the first place. It's a question they won't be expecting. Coming out of the blue, it might throw them off their guard.'

'*Hmmm*.'

'Did you say something, George?'

'No, I was just muttering.'

'Well, find yourself a different way to mutter!'

After a scratch meal of bread and cheese—which barely satisfied my own appetite, let alone George's—we set out for Mr Ryman's place. Blackthorn House on the East Heath Road proved to be a rambling two-and occasionally three-storey mansion that backed on to the heath itself. It had barely gone noon as we made our way through the gates and up the icy path to the house.

'Oh,' said Mr Ryman, as he opened the door to us. He was kitted out with scarves and a coat, and appeared to have just arrived home, for his boots were making puddles on the floor.

'*Oh*,' he said again, when he realized who we were. 'It's you two. Mr Smalley said he was sending his investigators round to see me, but I never imagined it would be you.' The muscles of his jaw tensed. 'Aren't you a bit *young* for the job?'

My heart fell. Not only did he think us too young, he'd addressed his comment to George.

'Don't ask me,' came George's grumbled reply. 'Apparently I'm just the apprentice.'

'We may be young, sir,' I quickly took over, 'but we have solved many a puzzling case together.'

'Really?'

'Oh, yes, sir. Most assuredly.'

'Then you must tell me about them.' The smile and the general cheeriness did not match the coolness in his eyes. 'Come in, why don't you? Go on through into the drawing room; it's just through there.' "*Step into my parlour,*" *said the spider to the fly*!

The entrance hall was spacious and airy, and may

have once been jolly and welcoming, but not any more. The pictures and mirrors that had adorned the walls had been taken down, and now sat waiting to be boxed up in crates. The oval drawing room, with its large, round bay window that looked out on to a snow-covered terrace, had already been stripped of its furnishings. The only thing that remained was an old-fashioned writing bureau that stood all alone in the corner. If I were of a suspicious nature, I might suggest that Mr Ryman had been selling off the family chattels—even before he'd been granted probate, the naughty man!

Realizing there were no available chairs, he pulled three of the packing cases in from the hall and placed them close to the fire. I briefly considered removing my hat when he bade us to sit down, but decided against it, for the fire was low, there was a draught from the window, and the room was rather chilly.

'So,' he said, as he lowered himself on to his allotted crate, 'tell me why Mr Smalley puts his faith in you.'

Somehow I didn't think tales of tippling butlers, pilfering maids, or even the disappearance of Lady Spenlowe's smalls would cut it. I needed to make an impression.

'Sir, my colleague and I have twice been of service to Mr Franklin Blake, the Member of Parliament.' George stared at me, his eyes narrowing further by the second. 'Prince Albert himself has been a client of ours.' Now his jaw dropped as they sprang wide open. 'More recently we were engaged to investigate the death of the celebrated actress, Miss Isabella Prynn.

You see, Mr Ryman? I assure you our credentials are quite impeccable.' *George for the most part had not been involved in these cases, so it was only a tiny white lie.*

Mr Ryman still looked sceptical—as did George, I'm sorry to say. Even so, the man agreed to take our questions.

'You heard your uncle was dying and you came back to Blackthorn House in order to be reconciled with him. Is that correct?'

'Who told you that?' he asked. His eyes blinked erratically. 'No, when I came back here, I had no idea the old chap was so close to death.'

'Then why did you come? It is my understanding that the two of you were estranged.'

'We were,' he answered candidly. 'And yet he was the only person I could think of to turn to. I was in a dreadful bind. I'd borrowed a vast sum of money; the repayment was due, so I came to beg him for help.'

'At first he refused to see you, I believe.'

'That's right.'

'But then he relented?'

'He did.'

'And how did that meeting go?'

Mr Ryman treated me to a mocking smile. 'How do you think? The atmosphere was a little strained, though secretly I think he was rather pleased to see me. We were very close once.'

'Did he accede to your request for money, sir?'

'I didn't broach the subject. It's not the sort of thing you ask a dying man.'

'Did you know that your uncle was planning to alter his will in your favour?'

'Not exactly. But I had hopes. The day before he passed, he was hell-bent on seeing his lawyer. I myself went up to town to fetch him. As you probably know, he was away on business.'

'Which forced Mr Eldritch to pen the will himself?'

'So it would appear.'

'You weren't privy to his intentions, then?'

'No.'

'What made him change his mind, do you think?'

'Not me, if that's what you were thinking. If I had to guess, I'd say it was my cousin herself. In the will he called her petty and spiteful, and that's exactly what she was. It was quite insupportable, the way that she treated the servants—bossing them hither and thither, and finding fault with all that they did. I imagine it came as quite a shock to the old boy, seeing her show her true colours. Ah, well. I can't say I'm especially sorry.'

'Sir, on the day of your uncle's death, you were observed going through that bureau.' I pointed to the huge, old-fashioned writing desk in the corner.

Mr Ryman's body went rigid. 'By whom?' he asked.

'By your cousin.'

Mr Ryman sniffed, then began to laugh. 'Oh, trust Mavis to go snooping!' He grimaced distastefully and turned his head away.

'You don't deny it, then?'

'What point would there be in denying it?'

'So it's true?'

Mr Ryman gave a terse nod.

'What, may I ask, were you looking for?'

'I was looking for money, God damn it!'

BIG BONA OGLES, BOY!

'You weren't looking for the will?'

'*No*! I had a loan to repay, remember! I thought if I could offer my creditors something—anything, even a paltry amount—it might just stave them off for a week or two, until—'

'Until your uncle was dead and you came into your inheritance,' I interjected in a suitably reproachful tone, 'an inheritance that would have gone to your cousin.'

'Listen, I may be a terrible specimen of a human being, I may have done things of which I am truly ashamed, but I swear to you by all things holy that I did nothing whatsoever to try to sway my uncle's hand.'

I rose and began moving randomly about the room, touching a patch of faded wallpaper, studying the brass handles on the bureau. Mr Ryman's eyes followed me wherever I went.

'Are you planning to relocate, sir?' I asked. 'You seem to have boxed up all the furniture.'

'It's going to the auction houses, if you must know; I still owe a substantial amount. If I can raise enough capital, I may yet hold on to the house.'

I ran my finger along the wall's dado rail and examined it for dust. 'I hear tell you've let the servants go.'

'Before he died, Uncle Frederick made provisions for his cook and his housemaid. They left of their own accord. I haven't sought to replace them; I'm quite happy doing for myself.'

I watched a robin on the terrace foraging in the snow, then crossed to where George was sitting and patted him on the shoulder.

'Sir, my assistant has something he'd like to ask

you…don't you, George?'

Thomas Ryman looked the lad in the eye. George peered up at me with a resentful expression, then sullenly returned the man's gaze.

'Why did you go to see Mrs Harmon?' It wasn't the *exact* wording we'd agreed on, but it would do.

'I got wind of what Cousin Mavis was up to, and I wanted to set the record straight.'

'You got wind? *How?*' asked George, and I mentally gritted my teeth. *One* question, George, *one* question; that's what we decided!

Mr Ryman blinked. 'Mr Smalley's clerk alerted me to what she was doing,' he replied. 'Helpful chap. I believe his name is Candy.'

CHAPTER FOURTEEN

'ONE QUESTION, GEORGE, AND one question only! "*What led you to consult Mrs Harmon?*"'

'What led you to consult Mrs Harmon,' he repeated back to me, so lifelessly it had ceased to contain a query.

'Try to put a bit more feeling into it, George. People notice if your heart's not in it.'

'But my heart's not in it, is it? It's not my question, see?'

We tramped along the winding lane, keeping to the middle of the road, for the snow was banked up in drifts on either side. I estimated the hour to be no later than two. The day was still clear and bright, heralding a cold night to come.

'Would you prefer that I ask it, George?'

'Would I get to ask something else?'

I shook my head.

'Then no.'

The Limes, where Miss Moss resided, was a boxy, white three-storey mansion, so much more regular in its features than its next-door neighbour. Whereas Blackthorn sprawled with curving rooms and hidden spaces, the Limes was uncompromisingly steadfast and upright; indeed, it would have been as symmetrical as a doll's house, had it not been for a later extension to its eastern side. Moreover, unlike Blackthorn, the Limes was fully staffed. A footman opened the door to us and took our hats and coats, and informed us that Miss Moss was expecting us. He led us through to what he called "her studio at the rear", where she was biding her time until we arrived by working on her latest tapestry.

The room was generously proportioned and brightly lit, for there were two large picture windows that looked out on to the heath, and a mirror on the opposing wall, so large that it reflected the light back and effectively doubled it. Facing the mirror, with her back to the windows, Cicely Moss sat at her loom, passing bobbin after bobbin through the vertically-strung warp threads and then carding the new strands into place. At first she appeared to be staring into the distance, but then I perceived that she was actually looking in the mirror at the view outside. This was the source of the design she was weaving, a stylized pattern of what she could see, a landscape of fields and trees and snow.

'You must excuse me,' she said, annunciating her words with a great deal of care—not that it made her lisp any less noticeable. 'I must tie off each bobbin with a half-hitch or they will probably come unravelled on me.'

Her large hands worked quickly and with an

assurance that I wouldn't have expected. Today she was dressed all in white and wore a circlet of pearls around her head. She seemed more confident than I had ever seen her before, though, in truth, she could hardly seem less. Perhaps it was because she was in her own home, the mistress of all she surveyed. Or perhaps she didn't consider us threatening; who can say?

A maid entered the room, bearing a tray of tea things. She set it down with a brittle clatter on the table by the fire.

'Please, won't you pull up a chair?' said Miss Moss, as she herself took a seat on the settee. 'I believe you have some questions for me about my late neighbour.'

George glanced round the room, looking for a chair that would support his weight. He quickly saw that there wasn't one, and had to settle for a spindly, bow-legged thing that looked as if it had been squashed by some former incumbent.

'Thank you for seeing us, Miss Moss,' I began, as I perched myself on one of its equally unfortunate cousins. 'Perhaps you could start by telling us how well you knew Mr Eldritch.'

'I've known Mr Eldritch all my life. This was my parents house; I grew up here next door to him. He was very kind to me when Mama and Papa passed away.'

'Your parents are dead, miss?' Even though I could recall some mention of this, it still surprised me; she seemed extremely young to have lost them both.

'Two years ago last August. In a freakish accident. They were on their way to the opera when their carriage overturned.'

From these few words alone, I realized I knew of the crash that had taken them. It had been the talk of the town at the time; everyone who'd witnessed it could speak of little else. Whilst stuck in a line of banked-up traffic, the horse had been attacked by a rabid dog and, with nowhere else to go, it had taken to the pavement to make its escape. In the ensuing flight, the carriage had been dashed against the railings of Bow Street Magistrates' Court, and had then over-turned when one of its wheels mounted a flight of steps, splintering like matchwood under its own weight. The driver had survived the ordeal only because he'd been thrown clear of the vehicle when the horse first bolted.

'Tea?' It was the maid who spoke, a girl a little younger than Miss Moss. She handed me my cup and then went to serve her mistress. George, I noted, already had his; he sat rather awkwardly, trying to balance his cup and saucer on his knee.

I posed another question to the lady of the house. 'Are you acquainted with Mr Ryman, miss?'

'Oh, yes,' she replied with the tiniest nod, a kind of nervous, bird-like, pecking motion. 'He was a regular visitor to Blackthorn when I was a child.'

She took a sip of tea, then quite unexpectedly burst into a snort of the most unladylike laughter. Even George couldn't help but stare.

'You know, many is the time his head would appear above the boundary wall,' she giggled, 'whilst I was hosting a tea party for my dolls.

'"Spare a cup for me?" he'd say, and Cynthia, Dorothy,

Clarissa, and Anne would fix me with their glassy eyes.

"'The pot is nearly empty," I'd reply, earning their deepest disapproval for acknowledging him. "I shall have to send the maid to fetch more water."

"'Oh, please don't put the girl to any trouble on my account," he'd always come back. "I shall make do with taking tea with my uncle…though I dare say I shan't find the company half as convivial.'"

'Sandwich?' came a jarring voice that dragged us all back into the present. Miss Moss's short splash of exuberance vanished like the receding tide, leaving her to shrivel like seaweed washed up on the shore. She blinked woodenly at the maid, who was standing over George, offering him a sandwich from her plate.

'What are they?' he asked, eyeing the daintily-cut fingers.

'Egg and cress,' the girl replied. 'They're very good.'

George took two and placed them on his saucer.

'Go on,' she urged him. 'A big lad like yourself should be able to manage three!'

George blushed, but took another one nevertheless. I was given no such encouragement when it was my turn. The plate was whisked away before I could even nab a second. There are limits to what a reformed pickpocket can do, no matter how skilled and accomplished he may once have been!

'Miss Moss,' I said, 'I am led to believe that Mr Ryman and his uncle had a falling out.' I took a bite of my sandwich.

'That is so.'

'Over what, may I ask?' I spoke with my mouth full—not that I cared. The maid was right; the sandwiches were delicious.

'I was never privy to what occurred between them.'

'But you can guess?'

Again that bird-like movement of her head. 'Oh, no…I shouldn't care to speculate.'

'Will that be all, miss?' Having performed her duties—and rather less than fulsomely than she might have done, for there were still sandwiches she could have offered around—the maid was preparing to leave us. *At least with her gone*, I reflected, *there'd be a damned sight fewer interruptions*.

'It will, Gladys. I will ring if I need you again.'

'Very good, miss.' She pulled the door closed behind her.

'Miss Moss, how well do you know Mrs Crabbit?'

Our hostess pondered the question for a moment. 'Not especially well,' she said at last. 'I knew who she was, of course. When I was growing up, I'd see her from time to time when she came to visit her uncle— always at a distance, though; from the windows of the nursery, or through the front gates. I don't recall ever speaking to her directly.'

'And yet you seem to know her now, miss…'

'When Mr Eldritch fell ill, naturally he sent for his niece. I was in the habit of visiting him regularly to read to him for an hour or two, and I just happened to be there when she arrived. She seemed…' Her eyes strayed to her tapestry as she struggled to find the right phrase.

'Less than happy with the arrangements?' I prompted.

Miss Moss nodded. 'That's it exactly. But I'm sure it was only out of concern for her uncle. It must have been an extremely worrying time for her, and worry does take its toll, don't you think?'

'In what way, miss?'

'Mrs Crabbit was…' Again she became hopelessly tongue-tied.

'A little over-zealous in her ministrations?'

A shy smile crept across her lips. 'To say the least. The night before Mr Eldritch died,' she confided, 'she worked herself up into such a state that I thought she might have a seizure. I did what I could to settle her, but the poor thing was overwrought.'

'Did you know that Mr Eldritch had changed his will in favour of Mr Ryman?'

'Not then. I only found out later.'

'What about Mrs Crabbit? Did she know?'

'She may have had an inkling. I do not know for certain.'

'And Mr Ryman?'

Miss Moss shook her head. 'You'd have to ask him that yourself.'

I already had. He'd claimed he'd had "*hopes*".

'Miss Moss, let us move on to the day of Mr Eldritch's death. I hear tell you were called upon to help out?'

'Poor Mr Eldritch had come down with a fever, and there was some silly nonsense about Mrs Crabbit not being allowed in his rooms.'

'She wasn't allowed in his rooms?'

'No.'

Mrs Crabbit had failed to mention that in her

interview!

'I believe there may have been some unpleasantness,' she went on, 'so I refrained from asking. Whatever the case, the nurse had been up with him all night applying cold compresses. Cook and I took over from her so she might get a few hours' sleep. That was shortly before noon.'

'Was Mr Eldritch lucid, miss? Did he manage to say anything?'

'I wouldn't say so, no. He would mumble the odd word, of course, but nothing of any significance. He was delirious, you see.'

'And were you there when he passed away?'

'Oh, no. Mr Eldritch died later on in the evening. The nurse relieved me around half past four, and, as it was nearly dark, Mr Ryman was kind enough to escort me home.'

'I see. Well, I think that about covers everything. My assistant has one last question for you, if you will be so kind as to answer it.' I looked expectantly at George. The line, when it came, was delivered in a resentful monotone.

'Can you tell me how it is you came to attend Mrs Harmon's sittings, miss?'

Miss Moss blinked. Whatever she'd been expecting, it wasn't this.

'Why, I attended them on Mrs Crabbit's recommendation. She thought they might help draw me out of my shell.'

I quickly took over the questioning. 'Mrs Crabbit introduced you to them? So you and she keep in touch?'

The young woman frowned and shrugged. 'I've

never really thought of it that way. I suppose we do.'

'She must have told you about the sittings quite recently, miss. They only started a few weeks ago.'

'It was the day she came to interview Gladys.'

'Gladys?'

'My maid.'

'Your *maid*? The one who served us tea?'

Miss Moss nodded.

'But what would Mrs Crabbit want with your maid, miss?'

'I suppose she wanted to know if Gladys had seen anything untoward…you know…where Mr Ryman was concerned.' Noticing our blank looks, she added, 'Gladys is new to my employ. She was in Mr Eldritch's service…until he passed away.'

'So you took over his staff?'

Miss Moss blushed. 'Nothing like that, no. Towards the end, Mr Eldritch kept only two servants, his cook and his housemaid. The cook had been with him nearly all of her life, so he gave her an…' And here she began to flounder, trying to form a word that was apparently unfamiliar to her. 'En…end…endow… endow-*net*? Endown-*met*?'

'An endowment, miss?'

'Yes, that's right; a lump sum so she could live her life in comfort, wherever she might choose. But Gladys is young; she'd not been with him long. Still, he wanted to make sure she went to a kind and decent household, so he made me promise to take her in.'

'That was very thoughtful of him, miss.'

'Mr Eldritch was a good and thoughtful man.'

'Miss Moss, I believe Gladys was one of the

witnesses to Mr Eldritch's will. Might we be allowed to interview her?'

'I have no objection,' she said, 'so long as I am there to oversee it.'

She rose and moved to the corner, and gave the bell-pull a tug. As she returned to her seat, her eyes fell on the mirror. I followed their direction, and saw what it was that had caught her interest. Through one of the reflected windows, a boy and girl were throwing snowballs at each other on the heath. The boy had accidentally strayed on to Miss Moss's back lawn.

While we waited, I pondered Mr Smalley's attitude towards Mr Eldritch's two servants. While he recognized their importance as witnesses to the will, he failed to see their true value. No one could speak with greater authority as to what had gone on in the house. It was Providence that led me to Gladys Bland, of that I had no doubt.

'You rang, miss?' It was the maid, looking expectant as she appeared in the doorway.

'Come in, Gladys. These two young men have some questions they wish to put to you.'

'To me, miss?' The girl sounded pleased at the prospect.

'We do,' I said, forcing her to abandon her cow-eyed glances at George and face me instead. 'Tell me, what did Mrs Crabbit want with you when she came to see you?'

'She wanted me to tell her about the will the master made. She thought Mr Thomas might have forced him into writing it.'

'And did he?'

'Of course he didn't! But would that vinegary old so-and-so believe me?'

'Gladys…' Miss Moss's tone was gentle, yet it held a warning.

'Sorry, miss, but I must speak as I find…and, from what I saw, Mr Thomas was always the perfect gentleman. If anyone moved the master to change his will, it was that horrid woman herself!'

'Be that as it may, Gladys, she is Mr Eldritch's niece, and as such she deserves your full respect.'

That stopped the fiery Gladys in her tracks.

'Yes, miss. Sorry, miss.' She glanced at George and gave a little shrug.

'Tell me,' I said, 'you seem very certain that Mr Thomas did not exert undue influence on your late master—'

'Undue what?'

'He didn't force him to change his will.'

'I already told you he didn't.'

'Yes, but what makes you so sure?'

'Well, he can't have done, can he? The whole time he was in the house, he and the master barely spoke to each other. And when they did—well!—there were servants present, weren't there?' She glanced at her current employer. 'Begging your pardon, miss, but we *do* have eyes and ears, not to mention a tongue in our heads, and it's only to be expected that we'll talk amongst ourselves. We're only human, after all.'

'So you discussed these meetings amongst yourselves?' I asked.

'Well, someone had to look out for the master's interests, didn't they? He was in no state to look out for himself, poor man, so it was only right and proper!'

Miss Moss smiled and twisted her head away with another of those bird-like jerks.

'Gladys,' I said, 'you witnessed the will—'

'*Me and Cook* witnessed the will,' she corrected me. 'Yes, we did, and we were happy to do it!'

'Were you aware that it favoured Mr Thomas?'

Gladys smirked. 'We had an idea.'

'But you didn't know for certain?'

'Well, not until that lawyer fellow read it out, no.'

'So you were there at the reading of the will?'

The question put her on the defensive. 'Don't you go thinking I was snooping!' she cried. 'Someone had to serve the tea, didn't they? And you can say what you like, I'm glad it went to him! So was Cook. "Oh, I *am* relieved," she told me, when I broke the news to her. "I was scared he might go and leave it all to some Home for blinkin' wayward cats and dogs! Money should stay in the family, that's what I say. It oughtn't never go to no strangers!"'

'Gladys, can you tell me what became of Miss Butterworth?'

'Cook? Oh, she retired to the seaside. Her brother was a fisherman. When he died, he left her his cottage…if it's any business of yours.'

'*Gladys…*' came another gentle reprimand from Miss Moss.

Gladys sniffed. 'Sorry, miss.'

'Do you know where she retired to?' I asked.

The girl pursed her lips at me and answered, 'Somewhere on the coast.'

There must be thousands of miles of coastline round Britain, I thought. 'Where on the coast, Gladys?'

She grinned a wicked grin and said, 'I couldn't say, I'm sure.'

CHAPTER FIFTEEN

'SO, WHAT DID WE learn from that?' I asked George, as he pulled the gates shut behind us. The sky was already starting to get dark and the air bore the promise of snow.

'Other than the fact that Thomas Ryman is a gentleman and Mrs Crabbit isn't well liked? Not a lot.'

'That,' came a familiar voice, 'is because your funny little friend there asked me all the wrong questions. Let me guess…he told you not to speak, and you chose to obey him. You should be ashamed of yourself, a big lad like you!'

Both our heads turned in unison. A figure standing in the shadow of the wall stepped forward. It was Gladys, swathed in a thick woollen cloak, holding out a neatly-wrapped brown-paper package.

'What is it?' asked George, taking it from her.

'Open it and see.'

He peeled back the layer of paper to reveal the bevy of sandwiches bundled within.

'I could see how much you were enjoying them,'

she remarked, before turning to me. 'Don't worry, there's some for you, too.'

'Thank you, miss,' I mumbled, as I tore into the packet she handed me. 'Most thoughtful of you. So, if I asked the wrong questions, what are the right ones, pray tell?'

'The ones that he asks,' she replied, staring directly— and most provocatively—at George.

George blushed and mumbled, 'I don't know what kinds of questions to ask.'

'Well, you could ask me what I'd like to do on my afternoon off…I take it from your silence that that's a no? Then I have a question for *you*. What do you think of big families?'

'I come from a big family myself,' muttered George.

'I'd like to have a big family,' she said, and, ignoring the cold, threw open her cloak to display her ample skirts. Her hips were swaying rhythmically and suggestively, not that George appeared to appreciate it.

'Now don't take on so,' she begged, as he clapped his hands over his eyes. 'I was only kidding with you.' When that didn't work, she tried a different tack. 'Surely a big lad like you must have *some* questions for me? Ask away, and I'll tell you no lie.'

George raised one hand and took a cautious peek. Seeing that she was behaving modestly again, he deigned to remove them both.

'Why did Mr Eldritch change his will?' he asked, his voice sounding vaguely mistrustful.

Gladys smiled. 'Now, there,' she replied, 'is a *very good* question.' She cast me a look of triumph and wrapped her cloak about herself once more. 'It was on account of the fight they had over the curtains, the day before the master died.'

'A fight?'

'One of many such squabbles since old Vinegar Lips moved in. But this one was the straw that broke the camel's back.'

'Tell me about it,' he said.

Gladys pulled her cloak tightly about her and began. 'Well, it wasn't long after breakfast, see? The master had taken a bit of his oatmeal—though, to be honest, it was only because the old crow insisted on spooning it into his mouth. I returned his tray to the kitchen, then I came back to tend to the fire. Since Nurse and Mother Crabbit were busy folding the bed-sheets, the master called me over, saying, "Gladys, be a good girl and pull the curtains back for me?"

'I went to do as he'd asked, when suddenly Mrs Crabbit flew into a rage. "What do you think you are doing?" she cried. "This is a sickroom, girl! Those curtains are to remain closed at all times!"

'At first I thought she hadn't heard the master, so I started to explain what he'd said. The next thing I knew, she was at me again: "If I say the curtains are to remain drawn, then they remain drawn. I know what my uncle's needs are, girl, and don't go suggesting I don't."

'"I wouldn't suggest anything of the sort, miss," I replied, as coolly as I dared, and then she really started to jump down my throat. It's then that the master spoke up.

'"Mavis," he said, and it would have broken your heart to hear how much it pained him to speak, "if I am to die, I should like to feel the sun on my face one more time. Is that too much to ask?"

'Then Nurse put in her tuppence-worth: "There is no reason—no *medical* reason—why Mr Eldritch should not have sunlight," she said.

'"The doctor made himself perfectly clear on the subject," she came straight back. "Uncle Frederick is to avoid any unnecessary stimulus, and that, to my way of thinking, includes sunlight!"

'"It most certainly includes your raised voice," muttered Nurse.

'"*What?*" cried Mrs Crabbit. "*What* did you say to me?"—not that she managed to cow her any. The woman walked right up to her with her eyes a-blazing, saying, "Your uncle is in great pain, Mrs Crabbit. What he needs is a good deal of quiet. So be so good as to keep his best interests at heart, and for pity's sake lower your voice!"

'"His *best interests*? *At heart*? How dare you imply I do anything *but*!"

'While the two of them were going at it hammer and tongs, the master beckoned me over to his bedside.

'"Pull back the curtains for me, Gladys," he whispered, and I was only too happy to oblige him.

'That niece of his froze like a statue when she saw what I was up to. Then she turned to the master and addressed him coldly: "If you wish to speed your own death along, far be it from me to prevent you. Since I'm clearly not needed or wanted here, I shall go up to London and order a bolt of black crepe. We will need it for the mirrors soon enough! You, girl! Inform Cook that I shall be back in time for supper." And,

184

without batting an eyelash, she stalked out of the room.

"'I fear I have made a dreadful mistake," sighed the master, "and it behoves me to put it right while I still may. Gladys, fetch me my writing case from the bureau in the drawing room. I must summon my lawyer at once."

'I glanced at Nurse and she gave a little nod. Well, I brought him his case and he wrote his letter, even though you could see how much the effort was costing him. He sealed it it in an envelope and handed it to me, with instructions to have Miss Moss's boy deliver it.

"'I'm sure Mr Thomas would be happy to take it for you," I ventured to tell him, but the master shook his head and wouldn't hear of it.

'So I came here to the Limes and knocked at the kitchen, only to be told that the boy was on an errand and not expected back until the afternoon. *What to do?* I wondered, as I returned to the house, and it's there, in the entrance hall, that Mr Thomas came upon me in a perfect dither.

"'He wants his lawyer, you say?" he asked, once I'd blurted out the story.

"'Oh, sir! It's my belief that he wishes to change his will!"

"'Why don't you let me take the letter?" he said. "I'll see it gets delivered."

'Well, I couldn't see how this would hurt any, so I gave it to him, but, as misfortune would have it, his lawyer couldn't be summoned, for he was away in the country on business.

'The master was most distressed by the news and called again for his writing case. "It seems I have no choice but to write the document myself." That's what he called it, *a document*, though we all knew what he meant was *a will*. He insisted that everyone leave the room, but Cook and I were to remain outside until he called us back in. He made us watch while he signed it, then she and I put our names to it, along with our respective positions. Cook put "cook" and I put "housemaid".'

George gave her an encouraging nod as I popped the last of my sandwiches into my mouth. *Keep quiet and let him get on with it*, I told myself. *Since she's clearly not interested in me, let's see what George can get out of her.*

'Did he let you see what he'd written?' he asked.

'Apart from where it said, "witnessed by my two faithful servants"?' Gladys shook her head and adjusted her cloak. 'No. There were two sheets, and he kept them both covered up.'

'And was there anyone else in the room with you at the time?'

'No, Nurse had gone to her quarters to get a little shut-eye, and I'm not sure where Mr Thomas was. It was just Cook and me.'

'And what did he do then?'

'Well, he folded the pages in two and sealed them up in an envelope. He gave this to Cook and told her to place it in the bureau downstairs, then bring him the old will, for he wished to destroy it. It took her quite some time to find it, too; she was gone a good twenty minutes.'

Twenty minutes? *That*, I thought to myself, *was a*

fact worthy of considerable attention. The sooner we located this Agnes Butterworth, the better it would be for everyone. If the theory I had constructed was correct, she may well hold the key to the will's authenticity... *or its lack thereof.*

Again Gladys took up the tale. "'Sorry," said Cook, when she finally reappeared, "It was right there in front of me the whole time, but do you think I could find it?"

"'Throw it on the fire, Miss Butterworth," the master commanded. "I need to see it consumed by the flames."

"'Are you quite sure, sir?" said Cook, and her tone was grave. "A thing that is burned cannot be unburned. Are you quite positive that this is what you wish?"

"'Burn it for me, Agnes. I shall have no peace of mind till you do."

'Stony-faced, Cook moved to the fireplace and cast the old will on the coals. The master stared as the edges began to char, catching here, catching there, until suddenly it burst into flame. He looked drawn and haggard from all the exertion, but he also looked content.

"'Not a word of this to my niece," he warned us both. "Let her discover the consequences of her cantankerous ways once I'm dead and buried. And you can tell her from me that I never wish to set eyes on her again.'"

'Gladys,' I said, for I just couldn't help myself, 'did Mr Eldritch ask her to burn any other papers for him? Or did he ask you? Think carefully now.'

'Did your little friend over there say something?'

she inquired of George. 'I was sure I heard a squeak.'

George glanced at me and I nodded. 'Did Mr Eldritch ask you or Cook to burn any other papers for him?' he asked, paraphrasing, but paraphrasing quite acceptably.

'No, just the will,' she said. 'So, can I get on with my story now? And don't look to him for an answer!'

Again I butted in. 'Was Mr Eldritch mobile, Gladys? Was he able to get about on his own?'

George sighed and repeated my question.

'Not without help,' she replied, directing her answer as always to George. 'Nurse would call me in if she needed to move him. Now can I get on with my story?'

George glanced at me and nodded uncomfortably.

'Well, there were ructions at Blackthorn that night, I can tell you! Mrs Crabbit fairly had a fit when she learned she was no longer permitted in her uncle's rooms.'

This seemed to accord with what Miss Moss had called "silly nonsense". Had the chief clerk's wife been embarrassed by this sudden loss of face in the household? Of course she had. But embarrassed enough to make her think twice about confronting her cousin when she found him going through the bureau? It was unlikely. No. She'd *wanted* him to find the will. She'd *wanted* him to see who the beneficiary was. Unbeknownst to her, of course, her uncle had just made a new one.

'Well, first she blamed Nurse,' Gladys went on, 'then she blamed Cook, and then she blamed Mr Thomas.'

'What about you?' said George.

Gladys favoured him with a sly smile. 'Oh, she didn't try to blame me. I expect she didn't think I was important enough. When Miss Moss looked in, she got a right earful about the lot of us. How Cook and I were always trying to undermine her in little ways, how Nurse had overstepped her authority, how Mr Thomas's presence in her uncle's house was an affront to All Things Decent. The strange thing is, not one of us—not even Mr Thomas, who *could* have spoken out—put up much of a fight. So the more the woman went on about it, the more ridiculous she managed to sound.

'Miss Moss had come to see how the master was doing, but, when she found Mrs Crabbit in such a state, she quietly took charge of the situation. Oh, don't look so surprised! Miss Moss isn't the blushing wallflower you might think; she's made of sterner stuff than she looks. She ordered Cook to make a camomile tea with a little valerian root thrown in, and, when it had brewed, she sat with the woman and made her drink it all down. Then, once the tea took effect, she had me take her up to her bedchamber and settle her in for the night.'

George, ask her to tell you Cook's current whereabouts.

'Did Miss Moss go and see Mr Eldritch?'

'She did, but she didn't stay long. As it was bucketing down outside and almost as dark as Hades, Mr Thomas offered to escort her home. Old Vinegar Lips can say what she likes about him, but Mr Thomas is the perfect gentleman. Servants know, you know.'

Cook's current whereabouts, George!

'Go on,' he said, giving her another nod of encouragement, and I found myself biting my lip.

'Anyway, I was lying in bed, unable to sleep, and listening to the sound of the rain on the roof, when all of a sudden there came a knock at my door. It was Nurse. The master had taken a turn for the worse and was burning up with fever.

'She and I tended him through the night. I'd go fetch pails of ice-cold water from the kitchen garden water-butt, then we'd both soak towels and apply them as compresses to try and bring his temperature down. All night and most of the morning we worked, until Cook and Miss Moss came to take over. Nurse popped off home to look in on her husband; I took to my bed to get some sleep. Come evening, I was back in the sickroom again.'

Ask her about Cook, George!

'So you were there when Mr Eldritch died?'

Gladys shivered and gave a subdued nod. 'Funny thing, death. One minute you're there, and the next you ain't.'

I could see she was preparing to wind up the conversation, and George showed no sign of asking her what I needed him to.

'Please, miss,' I blurted out. 'Do you by any chance know of Cook's new address?'

She gave me a scornful look. 'I'd better be getting back. Miss Moss will be wondering what's become of me. So…aren't you going to ask me, then?'

'Do you know Cook's address?' George repeated faithfully, if not exactly word for word.

She pulled a face. 'Not that, silly!'

'Then what?'

'What I'd like to do on my afternoon off, of course.'

She threw him a saucy wink, pulled her cloak tightly about her shoulders, and disappeared through the gates into the gathering gloom.

CHAPTER SIXTEEN

'YOU'RE VERY QUIET,' SAID George, as we made our way back towards the high street.

'I was just thinking,' I replied.

'Oh? About what?'

'About one of Mrs Crabbit's better suggestions, George.'

'Really? Which one?'

I was in half a mind not to share it with him, but in the end I relented.

'That, if the will is indeed a forgery, then Gladys and Miss Butterworth conspired with Mr Ryman in its creation.'

'Are you trying to tell me that Gladys was involved?'

'Do *you* think she was involved, George?'

George considered the question for little more than a second and promptly answered, 'No.'

'You sound very sure of yourself. Why?'

'Because she wanted to have a big family.'

I stared at George, perplexed to the core. 'What has wanting a big family got anything to do with it?' I asked, though I privately questioned the *precise* meaning behind Gladys's words.

'It means that family matters to her. You heard her talk about how all the staff pitched in with the nursing. I could tell she thought of them as family— with Mr Eldritch as its head. She wouldn't do nothing that went against his wishes. I doubt whether any of them would have.'

He was probably right. While I could just about imagine Gladys throwing her lot in to assist Mr Ryman—for a wink and a nod, as Mrs Crabbit had put it—I couldn't see the cook, who'd been in Mr Eldritch's service most of her life, going along with it. Besides, the theory I had constructed suggested a very different scenario. *Oh, if we could only find this cook!*

'All right, I'll give you that,' I conceded. 'So here's another question for you. If the will was forged—'

'By Mr Ryman, you mean?'

'Perhaps. *If* the will was forged, how can it have any bearing on the attempt on Mrs Harmon's life and the actual murder of Miss Brahms?'

'Maybe Mrs Harmon knew something? Something about the will.'

Again I nodded. 'But how?' I asked. 'How could she know anything?' I would need to ask her, and impress upon her the importance of telling me the truth.

We tramped along in silence for a bit. 'George, the night Miss Brahms was stabbed…when Mr Ryman let go of your hand—'

'*If* Mr Ryman let go of my hand,' George corrected me. '*If* he let go of my hand, Octavius, it was only for a second.'

'George, think: what was Mrs Harmon—or Miss Brahms, if the substitution had already occurred—doing exactly?'

'I don't know; it was dark.'

'George, close your eyes and think. Was she still taking deep breaths?'

Huffing, George came to a halt and closed his eyes. In no time at all, he suddenly exclaimed, 'Oh!'

'Oh?'

'He *did* let go of my hand. But it was just for a second, like I told you.'

'Long enough for him to go and stab the medium?'

'No, Mrs Harmon was breathing; I am sure of it. Then her husband started asking if she was still with us. It was right about the time that Mrs Crabbit got stung.' His eyes were still closed and he had a peculiar frown on his face. '*Oh!*' he exclaimed again.

'What, George, what?'

'He let go of my hand again! When that trumpet blew and startled us all—but honestly it was just for a second.'

Had Mr Ryman deliberately lied about not breaking the circle, or, like George, had it just slipped his memory?

'Octavius?'

'What, George?'

'Can I open my eyes now?'

'Yes, George, you may.'

He opened them and blinked. For my part, I tried to get to grips with this new information.

'What are you thinking, Octavius?' he asked.

'I'm thinking that that sting was awfully convenient.'

We were on Flask Walk, almost at the high street, when I decided to pay Nurse Tully another call. Luckily for me, I found her in.

'Miss, did Mr Eldritch ask you to burn any papers for him?'

The nurse frowned. 'Papers? No, he did not.'

'Are you quite sure about that, miss? It's very important.'

She stared down her nose at me and narrowed her eyes. 'I swear he did no such thing.'

'Then, thank you, miss; you've been most helpful. We'll bid you good day.'

With that nugget of information under my belt, I led the way to the stables where George and I hired ourselves a cab.

'Why all those questions about Mr Eldritch getting people to burn papers for him?' he asked, as the driver set off on the precarious journey down the hill.

'Remember when I talked about the right kinds of questions to ask? Well, that was one of the right kinds of questions.'

'What's so right about it?'

'It's the type that rules things out, George.'

I gazed out the window at the darkening sky and waited for his anticipated response. It was much longer in coming than I might have hoped.

'Rules out things like what?' he said at last.

'Like whether Mr Eldritch, in his great distress, changed his mind and made a *second* will.'

'Beyond the one he's already made?'

'That's right.'

'Isn't that a third will?'

'If you wish split hairs, my friend. But think: if he happened to have made a further will, he would have needed help to burn the existing one.'

'But nobody burned anything…apart from the old will, that is.'

'Ah! Exactly!'

'So? How does that help us any?'

'It tells us, George, that he never changed his mind.'

'He never changed his mind?' he repeated.

'That's perfectly correct. He never changed his mind.'

We returned to the offices in Gray's Inn Square expecting to submit our receipts, only to discover that there was nobody to give them to; Mr Crabbit was curiously absent.

One of the junior clerks who had the misfortune of having a desk near his door saw us knocking and furtively beckoned us over.

'Haven't you heard?' he whispered.

'Heard what?' we both asked.

'Mr Bruff, Mr Crabbit, and all the articled clerks are down at the Bow Street Station House. They found a knife hidden in the mews behind Mr Crabbit's building, identical to the one that was used to kill that woman. Mr Crabbit's wife's been arrested. She's going to be charged with murder!'

George and I spent most of that Friday evening in the company of our colleagues at the Metropolitan Police's Bow Street Station; he to show his support, me to see if I could get a glimpse of this second dagger. I did, but only at Mr Bruff's insistence; Sergeant Snipe seemed set against showing it to me.

'Sir, may I please see the two together, so I might compare them side by side?'

Again the determined sergeant proved unwilling; again Mr Bruff insisted. The murder weapon was produced and placed next to its twin. Both handles were made of ivory adorned the same crescent-moon design; both blades were six inches long and both had a double-sided cutting edge. There was no doubt about it: they were a pair.

'Where and when was this second dagger found, sir, and, if I may ask, by whom?'

Sergeant Snipe thrust his chinless face out at me as pugnaciously as he could, and said, 'Why, I found it myself this very afternoon. It was hidden in a clump of brambles at the side of a stable block.'

'In the courtyard at the back of Pratt Street?'

'That's right. Off Passmore Place'

'Were you making a routine inspection of the courtyard, sir, or was there a particular reason for your presence?'

'I just happened to be in the vicinity, when I noticed something glinting in the bushes. It was the sunlight reflecting off the mother-of-pearl.'

Answering a call of nature, I'll be bound, given his reluctance to explain why he was there. 'And you think Mrs Crabbit placed it in the bushes?'

'It was right behind her house. Of course she did!'

'You have to admit, she didn't hide it very well, did she, sir?'

'*Eh?*'

'If *you* could see the handle glinting, then she didn't really try to hide it.'

The sergeant levered himself up on to the balls of his feet, lowered his head, and tried glaring down at me with his large, dark eyes. The trouble was, not only was I *not* seated—so we were practically on the same level—my eyes are naturally larger than his and I'm more than capable of doing a little staring myself!

'Someone get this blasted boy out of my sight!' he railed at his underlings, which led to my untimely, ill-mannered removal.

Well, I'd done my best. There's only so much a fifteen-year-old can do when it comes to challenging an officer of the law—especially one like Sergeant Snipe who seems determined to be dimwitted!

The next day, a Saturday, was another bright day, and another day where George was too busy to assist me. *Hmmm.*

After a late and leisurely breakfast of toasted crusts and a rasher or two of nice, fatty bacon, I parcelled up some of my older clothes and made my way along the tow-path to examine the stable block for myself.

It was not a commercial stables, as you might expect to find in any number of London's back streets; it was simply a shed where local people kept their animals, taking on their feeding and grooming themselves. I introduced myself to the two current residents, both donkeys; they seemed faintly bemused by my presence and chose to ignore me.

Quitting the interior, I made a tour of the perimeter. I found only one clump of blackberries, which was all but buried under a mound of snow that had built up against the shed wall. Apart from some gouges that looked rather like fingermarks, the surface of the mound was pristine. If this was where the sergeant found the second dagger, then the person who put it here had made a spectacularly bad job of hiding it. Why leave the handle visible, when you could plunge it under the snow? The obvious answer was that who-ever had put it there wanted it found, and found in the vicinity of the Crabbits'.

It was roughly two in the afternoon when I rounded the corner into Pratt Street. Suddenly I was forced to make a quick retreat, for who should I see crossing the road from the church, but my apprentice and his mother! George, once again, was in his Sunday best— even though it was only a Saturday. His mother was equally well attired, in a bonnet that could not help but impress.

I peered round the corner and watched as they mounted the steps. They knocked; they waited; they disappeared inside. *Too busy, indeed? My foot!*

By four o'clock I was wending my way through the bustle of market porters and flower woman, fashionable young rakes and out-and-out misfits, who on market days thronged to the Bucket of Blood in search of a drink and good cheer. Dressed as stylishly as any of the rakes—though each of them several stone heavier— Alex and Charley stood guard at the foot of the stairs. I nodded and made my way up.

I had wondered how well Mrs Harmon would adjust to her new surroundings; to a considerable degree, by the looks of things. When I arrived, she and Bertha were sipping glasses of sherry while watching Cassius teach young Walter a card trick.

'It's called a break,' Cassius explained, as he positioned the boy's middle finger partway through the deck.

''Tis what they call "*a break*",' repeated Walter, in an effort to commit the term to memory. He frowned and added, 'But if the deck is broken, sir… *what use is it to anyone?*'

''Cause when it's broken, you can do this,' said Cassius, deftly manoeuvring the cards in Walter's hand so the lowest ones slid unhindered to the top. 'And that,' he said, 'is called a pass.'

''Tis what they call "*a pass*".' Walter's forehead wrinkled. '*Oh, my; oh, my! So many new words to remember.*'

''Ere, Octopus! Were you any good at card tricks?' asked Bertha. Walter attempted a pass on his own and sent the cards splaying into the air.

'I might have been,' I replied, treating my friend to a knowing smile. As a pickpocket, I was naturally quite gifted at prestidigitation. 'What about you, Bertha?'

'Not with these 'ands, I weren't! Best I could ever manage was *Find the Lady*.'

'The four-card variety, I take it?'

Bertha sniggered and told me to help myself to a drink. I handed Cassius the parcel I'd been carrying and explained that I thought he might fancy a change of clothing, for all he had with him was his livery. He grinned and thanked me, and hurried away to get changed. As I poured myself a small sherry, Mrs Harmon asked me how the case was going. She seemed nervous about mentioning it, and even more nervous about hearing what I might have to say. I told her of Mrs Crabbit's arrest.

'But that's ridiculous!' she cried.

'I agree. But Sergeant Snipe, who is in charge of the investigation, thinks he has proof. There were hairs on the dagger that came from Mrs Crabbit's head.'

'Wot's 'e like, this Snipe?' asked Bertha.

Having dampened everyone's spirits slightly, I managed to lighten the mood again by describing the sergeant's antics. By the time I was on to my third drink, I was miming his use of a magnifying glass, and standing on tiptoe to stare down at my friends like a none-too-intimidating stoat. The fire crackled merrily in the hearth, the curtains were drawn tight against the encroaching night, and the smell of pine cones and lavender permeated the room from the bowl Bertha kept on the table. For a short while the world seemed normal again. Despite her good friend's murder and her own uncertain future, even Mrs Harmon seemed susceptible to the mood She was perched on the arm of a chair, her hair glowing like burnished gold in the firelight, smiling as she gazed across at Cassius.

'Look at him,' she said. 'He's almost back to his old self. I am grateful to you all for that.'

'Miss, there are one or two questions I should very much like to put to you.'

She glanced at me. 'Will they help find Sarah's killer?'

'They might.'

'Then ask me whatever you wish.'

'Think back to the sitting on Friday the tenth, the first time Mr de Ath attended. How did you know his name wasn't Winter?'

'Ah.' Mrs Harmon smiled guiltily. 'Sarah Brahms was not merely my assistant, young man; she had a

201

second, more important role. Like you, she was an investigator.'

'An investigator? A *female* investigator?' *Would wonders never cease?*

'Do you find the idea objectionable?'

'I find it strangely exhilarating, miss.' I admit I may have had one sherry too many.

Mrs Harmon laughed. 'When Mr Winter wrote me requesting a place at the sitting, I sent Sarah to carry out her regular checks. And what did she find? As soon as she saw him, she recognized him from the Prerogative Will Office, where she'd had occasion to consult Frederick Eldritch's will. His name was in fact de Ath; he worked for a Mr Devlin, the proctor to the law firm that handled Mr Eldritch's affairs. It wasn't hard to put two and two together. He was either there to keep his eye on me or his eye on Mrs Crabbit.'

'How is it that Mr de Ath failed to recognize her when she greeted him in the lobby? Surely he must have seen her before, if only when she consulted the will?'

'Sarah had a penchant for disguises. She was extremely good at it, actually; but then she was extremely good at her job.'

I gave a little whistle, for I was greatly impressed; Mr Death was not someone who was easily fooled.

'Women can be just as resourceful as men,' she observed.

'When Miss Brahms investigated Mr Eldritch's will, what, may I ask, did she find?'

'Not a lot. There was no proof it was a forgery. Then again, there was no proof that it was not.'

'And yet you claimed at your last sitting that Mr Eldritch would speak. Who were you going to disappoint? Mrs Crabbit or her cousin?'

'Neither.' She gazed at me steadily, trying to judge how far she could trust me. 'The trick is simple,' she said at last. 'Keep the story going; keep giving people hope. Do that simple thing, and they will always come back for more.'

She held out her left hand and straightened her fingers, then, starting at the top of her forehead, she ran her palm steadily down her face. It was as if she were wiping away all trace of expression, for when her features were once again revealed, her eyes were closed and her mouth was perfectly at rest. Then slowly—almost imperceptibly—her lips began to part.

'*Niece…nephew…*' The voice was deep, not exactly like a man's, but very, very close. '*You and I need to…*'— her chest rose dramatically as she drew in a breath— '*…talk…*' She exhaled loudly and raggedly, and it was quite some few seconds before she spoke again. '*Why did you do it?*' she said at last. '*Why did you go against my wishes?*' A long, rattling breath in; a long, rattling breath out. '*Why do you not honour the true terms of my will? You must honour the true terms of my will…*' The voice faded as she uttered these final words, and with it there came a shudder, giving the impression of some entity quitting her body.

Suddenly her eyes opened and she smiled. 'See? It could have been meant for either of them.'

She must have seen the look of distaste on my face, for she immediately went on, 'You think I'm a fraud, don't you?'

I considered her question for all of two seconds. 'Mrs Harmon, you make money out of people's misery!'

'If you think Mrs Crabbit or Mr Ryman were saddened by their uncle's passing, then you are nothing but a fool! All they cared about was his money. Besides, I wasn't always this way, you know. When I was sixteen, I *had* the gift. The spirits used to use me to rap out their messages. Soon I even began to hear their voices. I still do, but these days it comes and goes. Maybe Uncle Frederick would have come through to me; maybe not. People don't pay good money to watch me fail, so I do what I have to do.' Mrs Harmon gave me a pitying look. 'I can see you are still sceptical, but you should know: there is someone who is desperate to contact *you*.'

Unimpressed with her nonsense, I cut her short. 'Mrs Harmon, as fascinating as this may be, I have one further question for you.'

'Yes?'

'Miss Brahms didn't happen to trace the whereabouts of Mr Eldritch's cook, did she?'

'His cook? I don't think so. And, as I said, Sarah Brahms was very good at her job.'

CHAPTER SEVENTEEN

'WHO IS IT, JULIUS?'

It was early Sunday morning, my head was throbbing, the room was freezing, and I was down on my hands and knees in front of the stove trying to get the fire lit.

'It's a boy,' my brother called back to me from the doorway. 'He's asking to speak to Mr Guy. I think he means you, Octavius.'

I glanced up from the floor to see a neatly dressed boy, a little younger than my brother's age, gazing at me earnestly and hopefully. His dimpled face looked impossibly clean, as if he'd spent the last half an hour scrubbing it.

'Mr Guy?' he hazarded, as he ventured a smile. 'Are you Mr Guy?'

'I am Octavius Guy,' I replied. 'And who the hell might you be?'

The cursing didn't faze him in the least. 'Perkins, sir,' he immediately came back. 'Mr Smalley's personal messenger boy. My master sends his compliments, and asks if you will be so good as to join him down-stairs. He awaits us in his landau.'

'His landau?' I hobbled to my feet and wiped my ash-smothered hands down the seat of my trousers. Despite my best ministrations, the stove remained unlit. The dog, who'd been watching my progress from her basket, lowered her head with a whimper.

'There have been developments in Hampstead, sir,' the boy explained. 'Your presence is therefore requested.'

'What developments?'

Perkins cast his professional if distinctly younger eye over my brother Julius and declined to say. 'Wrap up warm, sir,' he advised me. 'It's almost as cold in the landau as it is in here.'

Julius took over from me as I went to get my coat. I grabbed a slice of stale bread from the table, gave the dog's ears a parting rub, and followed Perkins down the stairs to the waiting carriage. I was relieved to see that it was fully glazed and its roof had been installed.

'Mind your head,' he warned me, as I clambered inside, then he jumped in behind me and fastened the door. Mr Smalley leaned forward and tapped the front glass, and the vehicle lurched forward with a jolt.

'I apologize for dragging you from your breakfast,' said the lawyer, noticing the crust of bread in my hand. I expect I must have looked exceedingly rough; I know I certainly felt it. I suddenly wished I hadn't brought the bread, and promptly slipped it into my pocket.

'Are you all right, sir?' asked Perkins, peering at me intently. 'If I may say so, you look a little green.'

I chose to ignore him, but the truth was I *was*

feeling bilious. *Oh, why did I drink so much sherry?*

'Perkins here tells me there have been developments,' I prompted, fighting back the urge to heave.

'There have,' Mr Smalley replied. 'Yesterday, just as night was falling, the body of a young woman was discovered on Hampstead Heath.'

'She'd been *strangled to death*,' the boy added, in what felt like a wholly gratuitous manner.

'Was it Miss Moss?'

'No,' said the lawyer, 'I believe it was one of Miss Moss's maids.'

'It was Gladys, wasn't it? Gladys Bland?'

Mr Smalley nodded. Despite Gladys's indifference towards me, I could not help but feel depressed.

'Who found the body, may I ask?'

'I understand it was one of the attendees at Mrs Harmon's sittings…a Miss McVeigh.'

Miss McVeigh? Yet another murder where the woman was present! 'What was Miss McVeigh doing on Hampstead Heath, sir? From what I hear, she lives nowhere near the place.'

'Though I have yet to interview her in person, I believe she *claims* that Mr Ryman asked her to meet him there.'

'Mr Ryman?' *Curiouser and curiouser.*

'Wrote her a letter, apparently, although she can't seem to produce it, and Mr Ryman denies categorically ever having penned such a thing. It was nearly dark when Miss McVeigh arrived, and she quite literally stumbled across the dead maid's body. Her subsequent screams attracted the attention of two passing constables.'

'Was she acquainted with Gladys Bland?'

'She says not.'

'So how is it that Gladys came to be identified?'

'A letter was found on the maid's body, tucked inside her cloak. The envelope bore Miss Moss's address. Miss Moss was prevailed upon to view the corpse. There is no doubt as to the girl's identity.'

'And this letter, what did it say?'

The lawyer brushed a non-existent speck of lint from the breast of his overcoat. 'It purports to be from Miss McVeigh, asking the girl to meet her there. She'd drawn a map with directions to the glade.'

'Has Miss McVeigh been arrested, sir?'

'No one has been arrested yet, but given the wealth of evidence against her, Miss McVeigh has been detained. The constables requisitioned a room at a nearby inn—The Spaniards—where she was obliged to spend the night. By all accounts, she was none too happy about it.'

'Sir,' I said, for the carriage had made good progress, and was even now wending its way through Camden Town, 'might I prevail upon you make a short detour? I wish to inform my colleague of these events, for I feel sure he will want to accompany us.'

I could not have been more wrong in my assumption. When we arrived at George's house (to find George outside on the front steps, sprinkling them with a mixture of cinders and salt), he outright refused to come.

'I can't,' he said awkwardly. 'It's a Sunday.'

'What's so special about it being a Sunday?'

'Well, I got church to go to, ain't I?'

'*Church*? Gladys Bland has been murdered, my friend! It is our sworn duty to investigate!'

That pulled him up short.

'Is she really dead?' he asked, looking sick to his teeth. 'We were just talking to her two days ago—and now she's dead. It don't seem fair.'

'You're right, George; it's not fair. So we need to look into it. How else are we to avenge her murder?'

'But I can't,' he repeated, as he stared down at the freshly-gritted steps. 'I got church.'

'Think of Gladys,' I tried to persuade him. 'Gladys who brought you the sandwiches—Gladys who winked at you so prettily that it brought a glow to your cheeks. She'd only take questions from you, George; only from you!'

'Not today. I can't do it today. Today's the first day they're reading the—' His cheeks flushed scarlet as he broke off his sentence; he buried his head in his hands to avoid meeting my eye.

'George, please—'

'I CAN'T!' he roared, turning his back on me. Ignoring the faces that sprung up at the window, he threw open the door and charged inside, then slammed it shut behind him.

His behaviour had not gone undetected by those waiting in the carriage.

'Your friend, he didn't want to come?' inquired Mr Smalley, as I climbed back in.

'It's a Sunday, sir,' I replied, 'and George is most devout. Some might say to a fault.'

'Ah,' said Perkins, with a patronizing air that bordered on the impertinent. The boy was barely eleven, yet clearly felt able to pass judgement on his elders and betters. *Hmmm, indeed!*

Once again the lawyer rapped on the front window; once again we got underway. Up Haverstock Hill and Rosslyn Hill we went, eventually passing the East Heath Road, where Miss Moss and Mr Ryman resided. Still we kept climbing, though now we had woods to either side of us. At various points the canopy was so dense that the morning sun barely bled through. Presently I heard a *"Whoa,"* and the horses slowed to a halt. Perkins opened the door and jumped down, then reached up to help me out.

'Well done, sir,' he said, as I landed on the ground beside him. I had neither needed nor wanted his help, and was dismayed to find that his attentions were not to stop there.

'What are you doing?' I gasped, as he started brushing imaginary dirt off the sleeve of my coat.

'Just brushing away the dust of a long, hard journey, sir.'

'It's winter! There's snow on the ground! There is no dust! Go and attend to your master, boy, and leave me be!'

As Perkins went to brush the dust of a long, hard journey off his employer's coat, I took a good long look around me. This was indeed a desolate spot, the only habitations being a rambling old inn on the brow of the hill, a hundred yards or so further above me. Three vehicles—some minus their horses—were parked in the grounds outside. Mentally I ticked their owners off on my fingers: the local police, the local coroner, and someone from the Yard, in all likelihood.

Although the crime scene wasn't visible from the road, it was easy to discern in which direction it lay. Uniformed constables in their tightly-buttoned tunics and black silk hats moved back and forth along a trail that might have been considered a bridle-path had it just been a wee bit wider. Rejoining Mr Smalley and his fawning messenger boy, I fell in behind them and let them lead the way.

In no time at all the track opened up into a small wooded glade. A yard or so inside the entrance, a makeshift tent had been erected over an armature of scavenged branches. Though it hid what it could of Gladys Bland's body, her head had been deliberately exposed. Crouching beside her, examining the ligature marks on her throat (with his trusty magnifying glass and pair of tweezers, it goes without saying), was none other than the indefatigable Sergeant Snipe. *Could it possibly be that there were* no *other Detective Sergeants on the force?* A few paces behind him stood another man. Since he exuded an air of authority, yet seemed most put out by Snipe's presence, I assumed he was the sergeant in charge of the local S-Division. Both of them scowled as they noticed our approach.

'What are you doing here?' snapped Snipe.

'My client's good name has been besmirched,' Mr Smalley replied, referring, I imagine, to the letter Mr Ryman was supposed to have sent Miss McVeigh. *Not* that Mr Ryman was in fact his client. As he'd pointed out to me in the past, his client was Mr Eldritch—even though Mr Eldritch was dead. 'I have every right to investigate,' he added coolly. 'I believe, sir, that you found a letter on the poor girl. May I be allowed to read it?'

Grudgingly Sergeant Snipe handed it to him. Mr Smalley angled the envelope in such a way that Perkins and I could peruse the address: *Miss Gladys Bland, Housemaid in the service of Miss Cicely Moss, The Limes, East Heath Road, Hampstead.*

With gloved fingers, he withdrew the single sheet of paper from inside:

Dear Miss Bland,

You don't know me. My name is Miss Evelyn McVeigh and I have information of great importance that concerns the safety of your mistress. If you love her, you will meet me at the place I have indicated on the map below, today at a quarter past four. Come alone. Tell no one. Please do not be late. I am a woman of considerable means and I will make it worth your while. Commit the map to memory and burn this letter, I beg you.

Your secret friend and your mistress's ally,
Evelyn McVeigh

Directly below was a roughly-sketched map of the heath, with a zigzagging line leading from the back of the Limes to the spot where we currently stood. Had the person who'd drawn this wanted Gladys to avoid coming by road? Were they scared that she might be seen? I stared at the trees to my right, in the general direction from whence she had come. I estimated it would have taken her half and hour to walk here, possibly longer. And what did she find when she got here? Miss McVeigh, waiting to throttle her? *Hmmm.*

I glanced down at the ground. Everywhere I looked, the snow had been rudely disturbed by an army of boots; any footprints that may have counted as evidence had been trampled into oblivion by the police.

'What do you think?' asked Mr Smalley, as he refolded the letter.

Perkins was only to happy to tell him. 'Miss McVeigh made a fatal mistake when she trusted her to burn it!'

I kept my thoughts on the letter to myself, though I too believed it to be significant. 'Sir, might we be allowed to talk to Miss McVeigh? I should like to hear her side of the story.'

'What say you, Perkins? Shall we go talk to this woman of mystery?'

'We should, sir, most definitely…if only to dot the i's and cross the t's!'

'Well said, boy!'

Dot the i's and cross the t's? Hmmm.

It was a ten-minute trudge up to the Spaniards, where Miss McVeigh was being held. The inn was clearly very old, with roaring fires in the most unexpected places and nooks aplenty where its patrons could merge wraith-like into the shadows. The various parts of the building were oddly mismatched, as if they had mushroomed out of the ground without thought or care. We received a warm and studious welcome; since the inquest would no doubt be held here, the landlord stood to profit rather nicely from Gladys's death. Leaving his wife to attend to the needs of his regular customers, he led us up a narrow staircase to the second-floor landing, where a constable, quite a young man, sat keeping watch. The lad looked as if he hadn't slept in days.

Taking the initiative, the landlord began the introductions. 'This is Constable Lamb of S-Division, sir. He is one of the men who was first on the scene.'

Mr Smalley beamed at the boy. 'My name is Smalley and I am a solicitor. I would be extremely grateful to hear your story.' To show just how grateful he could be, some coins were dispensed to the landlord, who departed with a grin on his face. 'Constable, perhaps you can describe to us what happened?'

'My partner and I were making our rounds when all of a sudden we heard screaming.'

Mr Smalley nodded. 'And when was this?'

'As close to a quarter past four as I can tell, sir.'

'Did you not think to consult your timepiece?'

The young constable blinked. 'I don't have no timepiece, sir.'

'Then how did you know what time it was?'

'Because we were just coming up to the Spaniards.'

Stumped by this logic, Mr Smalley frowned. I could have told him what the constable meant, but I let him explain it himself.

'We have a route, see?' he said, though I'm not sure the lawyer did see. 'It never varies. We always go at the same steady pace—the regulation two-and-a-half miles an hour, sir. Our sergeant is a stickler for it. Which means we get to the Spaniards at a quarter past four.'

'Every day?' Mr Smalley sounded surprised.

'Every day without fail, sir.'

Every London criminal worth his salt knows the local officers' routes by heart and will time his crimes accordingly. *God bless Mr Peel's Metropolitan Police and their patrols that run like clockwork!*

'So you heard screaming,' Mr Smalley prompted.

'A little way down the hill. My partner and I went to investigate and we found her'—Constable Lamb jerked his head in the direction of the door he was guarding—'in the clearing, screaming her head off. And then we saw what she was screaming about.' His face went white.

'I imagine it was quite a shock for you.'

'It was, sir.'

'Your companion, the one who was with you—?'

'Constable Scott?'

'Yes, Scott. What has become of him?'

'He had to go home, sir. He was no use to anyone. I don't think he'd seen a dead body before.'

'But you stayed.'

'I did, sir.'

Again the purse came out. 'Constable Lamb, the dinner hour approaches, and you look, if I may say so, as if you're in need of sustenance. Why don't you go and order yourself a meal and get something to wash it down with? My treat.'

'I cannot leave my post, sir.'

'I will have my boy Perkins stand guard for you. You have my word that Miss McVeigh will still be here when you get back.'

With a reluctance that I genuinely admired, the young constable took the proffered coins and retreated down the stairs, glancing back at us with a worried expression as he reached the turn.

Was there nothing in this world, I wondered, *not even an honest man's integrity, that money could not buy*?

CHAPTER EIGHTEEN

THE CHANGE IN MISS McVeigh's appearance was shocking to behold. Gone was the elegant smile, the easy demeanour, the scathing wit. In its place was the haunted, wary look of a baited animal, as she gazed at us, trying to assess if we were friend or foe. Like the young constable, I don't think she had slept, either. Her face was puffy, raw and red, and, divested of her bonnet, which lay beside her on the bed, her hair hung limply down in disarray. She kept her cloak wrapped around her for comfort, even though there was a fire that took the chill off the room.

Mr Smalley explained that we were there to help in any way we could, which brought a small speck of hope to her eyes. 'Why don't you tell us what happened,' he urged her.

'What good will it do?' she replied. 'The police don't believe me. Nobody does.'

'My good woman, WE will believe you.'

This seemed a very extravagant promise, given that we didn't yet know what she might have to say. Miss

McVeigh, however, took him at his word.

'Yesterday I received a letter,' she began, 'hand-delivered by some street urchin.'

'You took receipt of it yourself?'

'No, my maid did. She made a rather scathing remark about the lad who delivered it. She said his feet were so filthy, they practically looked like boots.'

'Go on.'

'Well, I opened it and read it. It was from Mr Ryman.'

The lawyer raised his hand to stop her. 'Excuse me; how do you know that?'

Miss McVeigh gave him a withering look. 'Because it was signed by Mr Ryman, of course.'

'I see. And do you still have this letter?'

'No, I burned it.'

'A great pity! But perhaps you can recall what it said? And word for word, if you please. Accuracy is our greatest ally, is it not?'

She seemed sceptical about the aphorism he chose; nevertheless she gave it her best shot. '"Dear Miss McVeigh," it began. "My name is Thomas Ryman. I imagine you remember me, since we shared the ordeal of attending Miss Brahms's inquest together. I—"'

Here she paused, blinking slightly as she considered her next few words. With her eyes slanted as far to the right as they could comfortably go, it appeared to me that she was not so much recalling them as fabricating them outright.

'"Certain facts have come into my possession,"' she said, '"and I would value your good opinion as to their merit."' She mulled over this statement for a second or two, then gave an imperceptible nod. Apparently content with it, she began again with a renewed confidence: "'Please, will you meet me at the place I have indicated on the map, today at a quarter past four.' He'd drawn a map at the bottom of the page, you see.'

Mr Smalley tilted his head in acknowledgement.

'Then it said, "Take a cab to the high street and from there make your way on foot. Come alone. Tell no one. Burn this letter, I beg of you."'

'So you burned it?'

'I already told you I did.'

'Did the letter say anything else?'

'It merely went on, "Please, *please*, do not be late. I shall be waiting. Your hopeful friend, Mr Thomas Ryman."'

'I have a question, if I may be so bold, miss?' I piped up. My hangover had cleared considerably by this point, and my brain felt like it had begun to function again.

Miss McVeigh blinked. 'You're one of the boys who attended Mrs Harmon's sittings.'

'I am, miss.'

'You work for Mr Sligo…or is it Mr de Ath?'

'Currently he works for me,' said Mr Smalley.

'Miss,' I persisted, 'if you burned the letter, how did you manage to find your way across the heath? Without a map, the route would be extremely hard to find.' *Nigh on impossible, actually.*

Miss McVeigh looked surprised. 'I didn't come across the heath,' she replied. 'The map indicated that I should take the road, the one leading up to the inn.

It's the most direct route. Why? Is it important?'

I had a gnawing feeling that it might be. It was a small detail, but one that lent credence to her story. According to the letter found on the maid's body, Gladys had been lured to the clearing across the heath, out of sight and sound of the patrolling constables. *If* Miss McVeigh was not her killer—and the letter she'd received *was* genuine—then the writer was only too happy for her to encounter the police. Given the precise nature of the hour mentioned in the letter, it was almost as if he had timed it that way.

Bristling impatiently at my continued silence, Mr Smalley swept on. 'So you came by the main road?'

'I did.'

'Can anyone verify that?'

'If you mean did I pass anyone, or meet anyone coming my way, no, I did not.'

'And what did you find when you got to the clearing?'

'It was getting dark, and I had trouble finding the entrance to the glade, for it was not as wide as I'd expected. As I made my way down the short, narrow path, I called out, "Mr Ryman! Mr Ryman! I'm sorry I'm late,"—even though I can't have been more than two or three minutes overdue at the most. When I got no reply, I thought it a little odd, considering how pernickety he'd been about my being punctual. My boot caught on something as I entered the clearing and I felt myself being propelled to the ground. And there she was. Some poor girl. Lying in the snow.

'At first I thought she must have perished from the cold, for her cheeks were like blocks of ice. Then I saw the bruises about her throat. I screamed and I screamed—I couldn't stop screaming—and then two constables appeared...though God knows from where. One of them was violently ill when he saw the girl's body. He brought me here while the other one stayed to guard her. I've been detained here ever since, for they don't seem to believe my story.'

'Had you ever seen this girl before?'

'No, never.'

'And yet you wrote her a letter asking her to meet you there.'

'How could I have written her anything if I didn't know who she was?'

'I have seen the letter with my own eyes, Miss McVeigh.'

'I thought you said you'd believe me!'

'My good woman, I do believe you. The question is, *will anybody else*?'

After explaining that there would be an inquest and offering her advice on how best to conduct herself, Mr Smalley terminated the interview and we took our leave. *So much for his promise to poor Constable Lamb!*

'So, Perkins, what do you think?'

'Was there even a letter, sir? It seemed to me she was making things up as she went along. The key question is why she would venture out on a cold winter's night to meet a man she hardly knows in a bleak, remote spot such as this? The plain answer is: *she didn't*. No, to my mind, sir, we just met with the housemaid's killer!'

To my mind—not that I was asked for my thoughts

on the matter—the key question was this: *why a quarter past four? Why not four o'clock?* And I already had an answer: it's when the local constabulary would be patrolling the area.

As to the problem of the letters, that was less clear. On the one hand we had a very real letter purporting to be from Miss McVeigh, the contents of which could not be disputed. On the other, we had a report of a letter to Miss McVeigh, the contents of which were dubious at best. Which was I inclined to believe? Actually, I was inclined to believe them *both*.

After a hearty lunch of roast leg of mutton, courtesy of Mr Smalley, the three of us repaired to Blackthorn House to question Mr Ryman. In light of what I knew— or, more accurately, what I suspected—of Mr Ryman's activities, I took a careful note of all that occurred.

Mr Ryman greeted us with far more deference than he'd shown to me on my previous visit. He ushered us in and directed us once again to the drawing room. Either the crates had been collected or he'd had the good sense to hide them, for the entrance hall and the oval drawing room were now bare—all that remained apart from the writing bureau were four singularly mismatched chairs. As our host went to stoke the fire to coax a little more heat out of it, I noticed he used his left hand. His right one, I saw, was bandaged. *Hurt in a struggle, perhaps? Clawed by a housemaid defending herself?*

'Having a little clear-out?' the lawyer inquired, as we each chose one of the available seats.

'I've been putting my uncle's things into storage to make room for my own,' Mr Ryman replied. 'But surely you haven't come to talk about that? You'll want to know about the letter. The local police questioned me about it all last night. I can only tell you what I told them: I know nothing of any letter.'

'And yet Miss McVeigh assures me that she received one.'

'She may well have done, sir, but *I* assure you, it did not come from me.'

'It was signed in your name.'

Ryman stroked the side of his moustache with the first two fingers of his left hand. His bandaged hand remained tense but immobile in his lap. 'I imagine anyone who can write could append my name to anything they so wished.'

'A fair point,' the lawyer conceded, then tried another tack. 'Tell me, where were you yesterday afternoon?'

'I was here.' His eyes began their staccato blinking.

'Here at Blackthorn? The whole afternoon?'

'Yes. I was moving my uncle's things into the attic. I never left the house.' Suddenly his brow furrowed. 'No, I tell a lie. At about three in the afternoon, I had occasion to go next door.'

'For what reason?'

'Something silly, really.'

Mr Smalley sat a little straighter in his seat. 'Why not let me be the judge of that?'

'With all the lifting, I'd managed to sprain my wrist. My uncle's neighbour, Miss Moss—' He paused, then frowned, and began his sentence again. 'No, *my* neighbour, Miss Moss, took one look at it and insisted on sending her boy to fetch the doctor. It seemed a lot of fuss over nothing. I came back here to await his arrival. As you can see, he did a grand job of patching me up.'

He raised his right arm and waved the bandaged hand.

'What time was this exactly, Mr Ryman?'

'Time?'

'Yes, time. Could it have been a quarter past four?'

'I really couldn't say; you'd have to ask Dr Kauffmann,' he replied. 'Ah, that's probably him now,' he added, rising as the shrill peal of a doorbell was heard out in the entrance hall.

The minute he'd left the room, Perkins evacuated his seat and took up position behind his employer. He jerked his head several times at me to indicate that I should do the same. I chose to ignore his suggestion; there were enough chairs available already.

'So; how is the patient today?' inquired the doctor, as he and Mr Ryman entered the room. 'You have been resting your wrist, yes?'

Ryman sat down and presented his hand for inspection. The doctor unwound the bandage and gently palpated the flesh.

'Doctor,' said Mr Ryman, 'do you happen to recall what time it was when you visited me yesterday?'

'Ach, it was just before four when I got here. I left over half an hour later. My pocket-watch showed the time as half past four exactly.'

So. At a quarter past four—when Gladys Bland was meant to meet her killer—Mr Ryman was having his wrist examined by the good Dr Kauffmann. *Hmmm.*

We detectives have a name for this particular

phenomenon; it's what we call *an alibi*—which has nothing to do with someone singing you to sleep, I might add. An alibi is to the guilty as green-tinged pork is to your average sausage: *it stinks to high heaven no matter how hard you try to disguise it, be it with sweet, honeyed phrases or the addition of sage and mace*. It should come as no surprise to learn that alibis occupy a special place in *Guy's Taxonomy of Opportunities for the Jobbing Detective*, to wit: *And what, pray tell, is an alibi? A chance that God sends the jobbing detective to prove that the suspect <u>lied</u>!* It is in fact the only entry to warrant the use of underlining in conjunction with an exclamation mark.

The trouble was—though I could not speak to Thomas Ryman's veracity—I believed Dr Kauffmann implicitly.

Mr Ryman forged the will. I was almost sure of the fact. But had he strangled Gladys? That was by far and away more problematic. It seemed likely to me that Miss Brahms's and Gladys's killer were one and the same. But if it was Ryman, why did he kill Gladys now? Why not several weeks ago? What had made her dangerous to him all of a sudden? A horrible thought occurred to me. Could she have been killed because George and I had been to question her?

With the interview concluded, the three of us trudged back to the coach.

'Any thoughts, Perkins?' Mr Smalley inquired, as he picked his way across the snow. It was not lost on me that he'd hardly consulted me the whole day. I wondered whether it was on account of my obvious signs of a hangover, the crust of bread that I'd stuffed into my pocket (which, by the way, was still there), or George's refusal to accompany us (all of which made us look unprofessional in the extreme).

'At least we know Mr Ryman is not involved, sir,' the boy replied.

'Ah. But is that necessarily a good thing?'

'Sir?'

'The longer we defer settlement, the more hours we can bill the Eldritch estate.'

Perkins positively beamed at him. 'I like how your mind works, sir!'

I had to wonder if my own employment had not been a way of racking up even more charges. *Hmmm.*

On the journey back I asked to be dropped off at Covent Garden. It was late afternoon and the frozen streets were all but empty. There were so few drinkers at the Bucket of Blood that only Charley stood guard on the stairs.

Up in his bedroom, Bertha was doing a spot of tidying. Well, when I say tidying, what I mean is, he would move a large stack of things from one place to another, take a sip of his drink, top it up, then move the stack back to where it had been.

'Sherry?' he said, as I popped my head round the door.

'No thank you, Bertha. I think I had more than enough last night, don't you?'

'Suit yehself.' He shrugged and went back to his tidying.

'Actually, I've come to see Mrs Harmon.'

Mrs Harmon, who was seated on Bertha's *chaise longue*, glanced up at me anxiously. She was no longer wearing the flamboyant green dress she had fled in;

today she wore a modest black outfit not dissimilar to the gown I had first seen her in—second-hand, judging by its appearance, but of reasonable quality. I sensed Bertha's generous hand at work.

'Do you bring news?' she asked.

'There've been developments, miss, but nothing you need to concern yourself with. No, what I want to know is this: did Miss Brahms discover anything of importance with regard to Miss McVeigh?'

A vivid pink suffused the medium's cheeks. 'Miss McVeigh? Why Miss McVeigh?'

'I need to get a sense of the woman, miss, and I've a feeling you never much liked her. What can you tell me about her?'

Mrs Harmon's colour heightened alarmingly. '*Miss* McVeigh,' she declared, 'is experienced in the ways of marital life.'

'She's what?'

'Experienced,' she repeated, gritting her teeth for emphasis. 'In the ways of *marital* life.'

'She's sayin' she's a slapper,' hooted Bertha.

Undeterred, Mrs Harmon went on. 'She is willing to share her experience with men of a certain class, who, in return, are prepared to lavish gifts of money or jewellery upon her.'

'See? Wot did I tell yeh? *Slapper*!'

At least I could now understand her reluctance to admit the exact nature of the letter she'd received. She would hardly want it broadcast that she'd come in response to an offer of a romantic assignation—whether genuinely made or not, as the case may be!

CHAPTER NINETEEN

MONDAY, DECEMBER 20TH ARRIVED like a cold, gloomy nightfall. Any sunrise there might have been was buried behind a dark grey blanket of cloud. It had snowed again during the night and, from the look of the sky as I trudged into work, I expected to see more snowfall before the evening.

The first shock of the day came as I was passing a newspaper vendor's billboard. There in big handwritten letters was the morning's headline:

*MESSRS HARMON, HARGREAVES, AND COX
TO STAND TRIAL FOR FRAUD.*

Mrs Harmon would not be happy when she learned of that!

The second shock came went I went to Mr Crabbit's office, for I still needed to present Friday's receipts. I didn't really expect him to be there, but he was.

'Enter!' he called, as I rapped on the door.

I found him standing by the little window with his

hands clasped behind his back, staring out at the bleak, grey scene outside.

'Well, what is it, boy?'

'If you please, sir, I have brought you my receipts from Friday.'

'And why are they late?'

I imagine the question was an automatic response. When a beat or two later he realized the answer, he silently moved to his desk.

'Give them here,' he said.

He studied each of them carefully, meticulously checking for any irregularities, then he placed them in the cardboard folder that would eventually be dispatched to Skipp and Smalley, Solicitors at Law.

I turned to leave, but Mr Crabbit wasn't through with me.

'The money you were advanced, it must be returned to me.'

'Sir?' I wasn't sure I'd heard him right.

'The money you were advanced by Skipp and Smalley, it must be returned to me this minute.'

'*What?*'

'This morning when I arrived to open up, I found a boy waiting for me in the street. He brought a message from Mr Smalley.'

Perkins!

'The gentleman declines to pay any further expenses on your behalf, and requires you to return his advance forthwith. As regards your employment, you and George will be paid for the remainder of the week, up until the close of business on Friday.'

It was a blow, believe me, and one I had not seen

coming. To give him his due, Mr Crabbit took no pleasure in delivering it. I handed over the not inconsiderable amount I had left, then grimly set off to tell George.

Our immediate problem was how we were going to get ourselves to the inquest, for as despondent as the removal of our funds had made us, neither of us felt like we could miss it. Walking was out of the question—we'd never get there in time—which left us only one other option.

'You're going to pay for a cab out of your own pocket?' George sounded incredulous.

'I can't see how else we can get there, can you?'

George scratched his head and frowned. 'What will it cost?'

'I've a feeling it might be a shilling,' I said, praying it wouldn't be more than that, for a shilling was all that I had.

'Where d'you get a shilling?' he asked.

'Christmas is coming, and I wanted to buy my brother a present. I've been saving my pennies for weeks.'

'What about Julius's present?'

'He'll just have to go without again, won't he?'

'It don't seem right,' muttered George, but right or not he soon acquiesced.

In the event, the cab cost us one and threepence and we were obliged to make up the difference out of George's dinner money.

The inquest was scheduled to begin at eleven; we were only a few minutes late. The jury had already been empanelled, though they numbered only twelve.

Presumably there had been some difficulty recruiting volunteers. The coroner was new to me, a gentleman in his mid-fifties, with a purple face, a belligerent countenance, and a bellicose voice to match. The room was overly hot, and the first thing we did when we entered was remove our coats. There were spare chairs by the doorway and, at my direction, we each took one and carried it across the room. I planted mine in the space next to Mr Smalley. George planted his uncomfortably close to young Perkins. I was gratified to see the boy gulp.

'I didn't expect to see you here,' the lawyer whispered.

'And yet here we are anyway,' I exclaimed brightly.

Constable Lamb had just finished giving his evidence. Gladys's employer, Miss Moss, was called next.

In truth, she looked rather haggard. Her skin, which was deathly pale to begin with, had an even greater pallor to it, and her eyelids were red and puffy from constant bouts of weeping. She described how a policeman had called at the Limes early on Saturday evening, requesting that she accompany him to identify a body. Though she thought there must be some mistake, she went with Constable Lamb, and was shown the wretched corpse of Gladys Bland.

The coroner thanked her for her evidence and called Miss McVeigh to the chair.

Would that she had taken Mr Smalley's advice, she might have made a better impression. Instead she insisted on wringing her hands, clasping and unclasping them as she blurted out her story, to the point that the coroner grew irate with her and issued a reprimand.

'Your hands, Miss McVeigh, your hands!' he cried. 'Can you not keep them still for even a moment?'

I saw George frown. I saw him frown, too, a moment later, when the coroner had cause to admonish her again.

'Miss McVeigh! Your hands!'

I watched the light dawn in his eyes.

He leaned round behind Perkins and whispered in my ear, 'The first séance. She was always letting go of the doctor's hand.'

'Very good, George. Which means?'

'She probably let go at the second one, too. That's why you think she lied under oath at the inquest.'

'That's why I *deduce* that she lied at the inquest.'

The problem for Miss McVeigh was that, if I was capable of deducing this, someone else might have deduced it as well.

At one o'clock, we adjourned for a spot of dinner. George and I shared a plate of bread and cheese between us, whereas the lawyer and his imp plumped for the roast.

When the inquest reconvened, Miss McVeigh was prevailed upon to produce a sample of her handwriting. It was compared with the letter discovered on Gladys Bland's body, and was found—unsurprisingly—not to be a match.

Mr Ryman's testimony was perfectly straightforward. He denied writing any letter. I had hoped they might take a sample of writing from him. They didn't. Nor did they investigate his alibi. Instead the coroner thanked him and began his summing up.

The verdict, as you might imagine, was entirely predictable. Murder by person or persons unknown. And once again the case was referred to Sergeant Snipe of the Yard.

When George and I emerged into the afternoon gloom, we found the weather much deteriorated. Snow flurries eddied all around us as we started the long, hard trek back into town. We'd barely started down the hill when Mr Smalley's landau came careering past us, forcing us to leap to the safety of the snow-covered verge. We watched it disappear into the haze before setting off after it, our steps delivered at the slow, plodding pace necessitated by the blizzard. By the time we reached the village proper, my feet were frozen. To take my mind off them, I began to discuss the case.

'So, what do you think, George?'

'I think it's cold,' he replied.

'I mean about the murders. Any insights or ideas?'

George tutted at me like I was being stupid. 'Why, have you got any insights or ideas?'

'Well, we know about the will,' I said. 'The question is now whether our two murders are linked to it in any way.'

George came to a halt. 'What do you mean, *we know about the will?*' he asked.

'Well, whether it was forged or not.'

'Hold on…are you telling me you *know?*'

'To my own satisfaction…why, yes, George. I thought that was obvious.'

'You *know?*' he repeated.

'That is what I said.'

George let out a howl of rage. 'So! Is it forged?'

'Well, yes and no. It is and it isn't.'

Another howl, louder, longer, and a sight more impatient in its nature. 'How can it be both?' he cried.

'Ah. That, my friend, is the question—though I will tell you this: the signatures are perfectly genuine.'

George peered at me warily. 'You're just making this up,' he said.

'Not at all, George.'

'How can it be both? Tell me this instant!'

I was shocked by the brusqueness of his tone, so shocked that I actually found myself answering for once.

'The second sheet is genuine. It's only the first sheet that's forged.'

George mulled this idea over, not that his face looked any less sullen. 'How do you know?' he asked.

'I took time to study Nurse Tully's blotter, the one she saved as a memento. Quite clearly in the top left-hand corner you can see the words, "to do with as they see fit"—not "to do with as *he sees* fit", as it appears in the will. Of course, there was always the possibility that Mr Eldritch changed his mind and drafted a second version. But, if so, he would have needed someone to burn the first one for him. Since I've asked everyone else, unless the cook, Agnes Butterworth, helped him do it—and I don't think she did—then there *was* no second will.

'As to what the real will said, well, remember what Gladys told us—how Mr Eldritch sent Cook to fetch the old one, and how long it took her to find it? And when she did find it, how reluctant she was to burn it, for all that it favoured Mrs Crabbit, whom she almost certainly despised. "A thing that is burned cannot be unburned", she said. Deduction: she'd somehow learned the terms of the new one, and, for whatever reason, they were not to her liking.'

George had gone as white as a sheet; his mittened hands, which were balled into fists, hung trembling at his sides.

'Our problem is we can't prove this,' I went on, 'not without her testimony. Our task, therefore, is to find this good woman, and find her as soon as we can.'

'You've known for all this time,' said George, 'and you didn't bother to tell me?'

'I hoped you might work it out for yourself.'

'You've known for *all this time*, and you *didn't* bother to tell me?'

'Well, I'm telling you now.'

'You didn't bother to tell me!'

'George—' I hazarded to no great effect, for I should have seen there could be no calming him.

'What am I to you?' he bellowed. 'What am I exactly? Am I just here to witness the great Octavius Guy make his brilliant deductions? Am I here so people can compare me to you and see how much more clever you are?'

'It's not like that, George, I promise you.'

George shook his massive head. 'No, not this time, Octavius, for that's *exactly* what it's like! I'm the dimwitted friend you lead about to bask in the light of your glory!'

'How can I lead you about, George, when you are

never there to be led!' It takes a lot for me to lose my good humour, but when it abandons me, there's no getting it back.

'What?' said George, as if he had misheard me. '*What did you say?*'

'You're never there for me, George! You're always too busy to be there! But if you had been, you might have worked out how Ryman forged the will for yourself!'

'*How?* How was I supposed to do that?'

'If you'd not been so intent on asking dumb, pointless questions, you might have thought to examine the blotter! Oh, do not blame me for your missed opportunities! Do not blame me for you lack of commitment! Do not blame me if you fail to see clues that are right in front of your nose!'

'We were meant to be a team!' he howled.

'Oh, George, for once, I quite agree!'

For one long, ghastly second George gaped at me. Then abruptly he turned and stormed away, ploughing through the snow like a man possessed.

I watched him go. A tiny spark rooted deep in my belly implored me to go after him. It flared brightly for an instant, and then died.

Arriving at work on Tuesday morning proved to be awkward, since he and I bowled up in the square at exactly the same moment. I stood back to let him enter the building first; glaring silently at me, he did the same. The impasse was only settled with the arrival of one of the clerks, who insisted that we either go in or get out of his way. Under the circumstances, I felt it best to capitulate.

Things might have continued in this vein but, as it happened, George took himself off out—heavens knows where—while I made an excursion of my own. Mr Smalley may have robbed me of the means by which to investigate, but he could not—nor would not—stifle my inquiring mind. As I saw it, my professional reputation was at stake, and so, in the spirit of leaving no stone unturned, I spent the day making a number of visits.

The first was to Mr Sligo at his shop in Great Russell Street. When challenged, he readily admitted that Miss McVeigh had let go of his hand on several occasions. When asked why he had lied about it at the inquest, he replied:

'I was simply being gallant. I *can* be gallant on occasion, you know.'

The second was to Dr Moran's Harley Street practice. The doctor was more than willing to see me. He solemnly swore that Mr Sligo had kept hold of his hand throughout and had never once broken contact.

My third visit was to Mrs Emmaline Vine, the woman from the first séance who had disapproved so vehemently of Harriet, whose address I had acquired from Mrs Harmon. I included her for the sake of completeness, for I really did not believe that on the night of Miss Brahms's murder she had somehow managed to infiltrate the inner room. She was only too happy to answer my questions. Though she took pains to deny it, it was evident that she'd been following the whole sordid affair in the newspapers; she was even to be called as a witness in Mr Harmon's upcoming trial.

I first inquired as to why had she not attended the Tuesday séance. Because the fourteenth had been her dear husband's sixtieth birthday, she replied. Where was she on Saturday last, the day that Gladys was murdered? At a sewing circle hosted by her church, repairing clothes for the poor and needy. The whole day? No, only the afternoon. She'd spent the morning wrapping Christmas presents for her servants. A discreet word with said servants on my way out confirmed her story on every count.

The trial of Mr Harmon, Mr Hargreaves, and Mr Condon—at which Mrs Vine was due to testify—began the following day, and lasted till the Friday. The three were charged with obtaining money by deception and young Mr Cox had been hired to defend them. As much as I wanted to stay and observe the proceedings, I had urgent business elsewhere.

Gladys had claimed that the cook retired to the seaside—to a cottage left to her by her deceased brother. Presumably there'd been a will; if so, I knew just where to find it: the Prerogative Will Office, where a copy of every will must be recorded. This presented me with two minor obstacles. Firstly, each will I consulted would cost me a shilling—a shilling that I didn't have. Secondly, the last time I visited the Prerogative Will Office, I'd caused a bit of a stir. If I were to show my face again, the clerks in all likelihood would probably summon the police.

Obstacles, albeit minor ones. But what, pray tell me, are obstacles? Why, chances that God sends the jobbing detective to allow him to prove his worth! In this case Octavius Guy would require a disguise!

CHAPTER NINETEEN

I briefly considered borrowing the livery Cassius had worn at Mrs Harmon's sittings—I even went to the Bucket of Blood to try it on—but when I saw its ostentatious detailing afresh, I realized it was bound to attract more attention than it would deflect.

The real problem was my trademark bowler hat and my somewhat protrusive eyes. The hat I could simply remove. It was my eyes I needed to deal with. But how? A porter's cap pulled down low to shield them from sight? No, it would make me look shiftless. A gauze bandage to cover them up, as if I'd been blinded in an industrial accident? As much as this idea appealed to me, it would have made it impossible to see.

It was Bertha who came up with the solution. He marched me along to a second-hand goods stall in St Giles, whipped my hat off me, chose some spectacles from the three pairs on offer, and, without further ado, poked the frames boisterously over my ears. He then took a small pot of rouge from his handbag and applied a dot of colour to each of my cheeks.

'There,' he said, picking up a poorly-silvered mirror from the display. 'Wot d'yeh think?'

I could barely recognize myself. I looked like someone who might grow up to be a mop-headed, eccentric inventor.

'How much to borrow these, sir?' I asked of the stall holder. 'I shall only require them for two or three days at the most.'

'*Borrow*?' The man seemed bemused. 'You don't borrow them, son, you *buy*.'

'Borrow,' insisted Bertha, in no uncertain terms.

Thus attired, I entered the premises of the Prerogative Will Office and, studiously avoiding the two clerks at the desk on the right, I made my way over to Mr Death's cubicle. As he was engaged in copying some text or other, I waited patiently in the doorway. He eventually came to the end of the document and finally looked up.

'How can I help you young man?'

'It's me, sir; Octavius. I have need of your assistance again.'

Mr Death stared. Then he stared some more. 'Upon my word!' he exclaimed.

I explained what I hoped to achieve and described how I'd been reduced to impecunious circumstances.

'Never fear,' said Mr Death. 'If there is such a will we shall find it.'

By the end of the day we'd managed to locate five wills by persons named Butterworth, though none of them mentioned a sister called Agnes. Thursday proved equally as unproductive and I began to lose heart. It was on the Friday morning—Christmas Eve—that we finally struck gold.

'Look here, Mr Death!'

'Need I remind you that it's *two* words, young man? You pronounce it "*dee Arth*".'

'Yes, yes; look! "To my sister, Agnes, a cook in the service of Mr Frederick Eldritch of Hampstead, I leave my fisherman's hut on the outskirts of Orford."' I jabbed my finger at the writing in the ledger. 'Where's Orford?' I asked.

'It's in Suffolk, I believe. A small town, but it boasts an historic castle.'

'*Suffolk?*' I let out a wail. Suffolk was miles out of London.

'You are quite sure this Agnes Butterworth can tell us for certain whether the will is a forgery?'

'As sure as I can be, sir. It's my belief she was privy to its contents.'

Mr Death grinned broadly. 'Then I think the time has come for us to inform Mr Devlin. I'm sure he can handle Mr Smalley.'

CHAPTER TWENTY

WITH TRAVEL PLANS SET for the Boxing Day, there was nothing to do but relax and spend Christmas as best as we could. Julius and I woke early. As he went to take Tricky for her morning walk, I got busy with the stove. By the time they got back, there was a nicely-laid fire, the bread was sliced, ready for toasting, and a small, flat package sat adorning the table.

My brother's sharp eyes missed nothing. 'What's this?' he asked, drawn towards the wrapped trinket as if it were a magnet.

'It's your present.'

'What is it?'

'Open it and see.'

The layer of paper was quickly discarded. 'A handkerchief!' he cried. 'I love it! And look! It matches the one I got last year!'

It did indeed. Both bore the embroidered monogram "*O. G.*". Mr Bruff's choice of Christmas present is nothing if not predictable.

'Did you get Tricky a present?' he asked.

'Why? Did she get me one?'

Julius frowned. 'She wanted to.'

'Well, I wanted to get her one, too.'

My brother considered this carefully. 'I suppose that's all right, then,' he decided.

When the fire had burned down to a gentle glow, we toasted the bread on our toasting-forks, with the dog eagerly watching my brother as he made her the first piece. Afterwards we pottered about till it was nearly noon, then the three of us set off for the Bucket of Blood.

The day was bright, the sky was clear, and, for once, people seemed to be enjoying the snow. We came upon several groups of children building snow-men and throwing snowballs; Julius took one in the side of his head, and merrily joined in. Tricky lived up to her name by turning in circles as we walked, leaving the strangest patterns trailing behind us in our wake.

When we arrived at the pub, there was nobody guarding the stairs. Alex and Charley had been enlisted to help move furniture. The big room at the front on the second floor—the one with the newly repaired window—was in the process of being transformed. While the two lads struggled to get the massive wooden table they were carrying through the door, Florrie, the girl who ran Bertha's flower stall, placed sprigs of holly along the mantelpiece, deftly skirting around Cassius and Walter, who were trying to light the fire. Once the table was installed, Mrs Harmon went to work, spreading it with a white damask tablecloth, and laying it with plates, bowls, and spoons. Having finished the mantel to her satisfaction, Florrie started on the table, strewing sprays of foliage in artistic little groups. The smell of clean, green leaves permeated everything.

The only person who didn't seem to have a job to do was Mr Moss, the tailor who had a barrow on the market. It was he who kept Bertha and the boys kitted out so stylishly. He stood on one side, watching this flurry of activity with a faintly bemused expression. I found myself wondering if he was somehow related to Miss Cicely; I rather doubted it, for they came from such different walks of life.

'Chairs, Charley!' Mrs Harmon called out. 'Bertha says we'll need eleven of them.' Once again she was in her serpent-green dress and Cassius was wearing his livery. In the ten-or-so days since they'd first arrived, they'd gone from being a pair of helpless wretches to being part of Bertha's great big family.

At last sufficient chairs were found, the candles were lit (despite how bright the day was outside), and we all took our seats. It was then that Cassius noticed Julius staring at him.

'Is there a problem?' he inquired.

Julius shook his head and continued staring.

'Are you sure there's not a problem?'

'You and the lady talk funny, don't you?' Julius replied.

'We *talk* funny?'

Julius nodded.

'*We* talk funny?' the young man repeated.

Undaunted, Julius nodded again.

'But *you* don't talk funny?'

Dismissing the idea as ludicrous, my brother shook his head.

'Drum roll, please!' boomed Bertha's voice, roaring up the stairs, presently to be followed by Bertha himself, bearing a huge tureen.

'Go on, then, 'and us yeh plates,' he said, as he laid it on the table, and for several minutes he ladled out soup until each of us had a bowlful. One place-setting remained untouched in front of the one and only vacant seat. I wondered if someone was late, though I couldn't imagine who that someone might be.

'Anyone for more?' asked Bertha, when he'd drained his bowl.

There were numerous takers. It might not have been a goose, but it was delicious nonetheless, and it appeared that Bertha had made it by the cauldronful.

'What sort of soup is this, Bertha?' inquired Mrs Harmon. 'Whatever it is, it's delicious.'

'It's Pea an' 'Am.'

Mr Moss's spoon dropped noisily into his soup plate. 'It's what?' he gasped.

'Pea an' 'Am,' repeated Bertha, unaware of the man's religious bent and the subsequent dietary restrictions this entailed. 'Only without the 'am,' he added. 'I couldn't stretch to meat, see?'

Cautiously the tailor tasted his soup and, satisfied as to the lack of cured pork, resumed eating it with much relish.

When the meal was over, Bertha brought out the sherry. It seemed churlish not to accept, so I had just the one. Walter was dispatched to fetch the presents, and returned with a mountain of brown paper packages stacked in his arms. Surprisingly they all had name tags; Cassius's or Mrs Harmon's handiwork, no doubt.

Alex, Charley, and Walter got new shirts. Florrie opened hers next, revealing a very nice blouse. There were *oohs* and *ahhs* as Mrs Harmon displayed a veiled hat, rather along the lines of Bertha's own model. Cassius grinned as he held up a bowler hat, the quality of which rivalled mine, no less. It seemed to me an extraordinarily generous present.

It occurred to me that most of these gifts had come off Mr Moss's barrow, and I thought I understood the reason why the tailor had been invited to join us: since Bertha was temporarily strapped for cash, he'd made him the presents for free. But, in this, I was wrong.

'No, no, no, it was just the lady's hat,' he confided in me later, when I tackled him on the subject. 'I have profited greatly from your friend's patronage. Once she had explained her straightened circumstances to me, I felt it was the least I could do.'

He himself received an extremely handsome banner for his stall. Alex and Charley held it up between them so we could all appreciate its merits:

Mr Moses Moss
Dealer in Apparel of the Finest Designs
By appointment to a Lady who in turn is by appointment to
the Queen

As clumsy as the last line was, I felt sure I could detect the improvements that Bertha's sign-writing friend must have made to it.

Mr Moss was quite taken aback. 'You're by appointment to the Queen?' he asked.

Bertha's brow furrowed. 'Yeah…yeah…well, we don't talk regular, like…but yeah.'

'And I can use it? I can display it on my barrow without fear of falling foul of the authorities?'

'You use it all you like, my son; it ain't no skin off my nose!'

At first glance Julius's present was a bit of a mystery: a single, extremely thick leather glove, which was made to be worn on the left hand.

'What's it for?' he asked, after telling Bertha just how much he loved it.

'It's for you, when yeh're openin' h'oysters, Sprat. Yeh don't want to go cuttin' yer fingers off, do yeh?'

Even Tricky had not been forgotten. She'd been sniffing her gift in my brother's lap, and, when he finally handed it to her, she set about ripping at the wrapper to reveal a bone that was almost as big as she was.

As I tore away the string on mine, I felt a lump rise in my throat. I was the proud recipient of a magnifying glass and a pair of tweezers.

'Now you go catch your murderer!' bellowed Bertha.

There was one present left, the only one that didn't have a name tag. If I had to guess, I would have said it was another magnifying glass and tweezers set.

'Who's it for?' I asked, imagining it to be for the missing guest.

'For yer mate,' he replied, 'the one wot you do all your sleuthin' with. I 'oped you might bring 'im along. 'Ere, Octopus! Wot's the matter?' he added, as tears threatened to well up inside me.

'It's nothing…nothing,' I stammered. 'I just got

something in my eye.' I can't imagine anyone was fooled.

'Nah, nah, nah! You can't be sad!' he insisted. 'Not on a day like today! C'mon we'll 'ave a toast. Walter, fill the glasses. A toast! A toast to our friends wot ain't 'ere!'

'To absent friends,' I echoed glumly, feeling no less miserable than before.

I wasn't allowed to remain so for long, however, for as soon as the entertainment got underway, things instantly went wrong, and I was called upon to help. Mrs Harmon and Cassius had planned on performing their rapping routine. Walter was sent to fetch paper, pen, and ink. He returned with the end of a pencil stub and a few yellowed old sheets, which I suspected had come from the landlord's supply. It's then that they realized their plan's fatal flaw: nobody apart from myself and Mr Moss could write.

'You can write out the questions for us,' Bertha urged me.

'How will I know what you want to ask?'

'We can whisper it to yeh, can't we?'

'Why don't I just go out of the room?' Mrs Harmon suggested. 'You can call me when you're ready.'

As people came and huddled round me—whispering their questions, changing their minds, then promptly changing them back again—Cassius began to look increasingly alarmed. I understood the problem; he needed to know from whom each question had come.

'Enough!' I said. 'I cannot think straight. Everyone go sit at the table and I will deal with you one at a time.' The relief on Cassius's face was unmistakable, but soon another difficulty arose. There were questions to which he wouldn't necessarily know the answer.

'Don't worry,' I whispered to him. 'Just tell Mrs Harmon to make sure she looks at me.'

The sky was growing dark outside when she finally re-entered the room. At Bertha's request, Walter drew the curtains. Using a wooden tray in place of his usual silver platter, Cassius circled the table retrieving the folded sheets of paper. He moved with all the grace of a footman, and no one was left unimpressed.

Mrs Harmon smiled and picked up the first sheet as she glanced around at the company. If she caught me looking to my left and pulling on my earlobe, she gave no sign of it, for her gaze swept across me and was immediately gone again. Two explosive raps rang out in quick succession.

'The answer is most definitely no!' She opened it up and read out the question: '*Am I always doomed to mess things up?* Yours, I believe, Charley. You have had a run of bad luck, but I can assure you it is over. This coming year portends great things for you.'

Everyone applauded, especially Charley, who was beaming from ear to ear.

She selected the next question and held it aloft. I looked to my right and tugged at my ear. One rap resounded like thunder.

'Yes, yes; I tell you, thrice yes!' she cried. She opened this one and read it out: '*Will there ever be another Christmas as good as this one?* Of course there will be, Walter. With you there, how could there not?'

More applause, more squeals of delight. It seemed to me that with each passing question the room became a little brighter. Were only George here to share in our joy! We continued in this vein until it was Mr Moss's turn. Having written his question out himself, I had not been privy to its contents, so— when Mrs Harmon held it up—I had no other recourse than to stare at the ceiling. Cassius, however, was glancing to his right, and fiddling with his earlobe as he did so. Yet another loud rap ensued.

'Of course the answer is yes,' Mrs Harmon insisted. '*Will she marry me*? She certainly will, Mr Moss! And if she doesn't, she's a fool to herself!'

As the entertainment came to an end, the only person who seemed less than cheered by it was Cassius. 'You did all the work,' he whispered glumly, when I asked him why.

'Fine! Then you do something,' I challenged him. 'You're good at card tricks. Impress me.'

'Very well. I will.'

Cassius drew my brother aside and murmured something in his ear. Julius nodded several times, then, taking Tricky with him, he left the room. Presently he returned with a deck of playing cards.

'The landlord's not very friendly, is he?' he observed, as he handed them to Cassius. Cassius bade me to sit at the table and then sat down in the chair opposite. He removed the cards from their box and passed them to me.

'Shuffle,' he said, and I did as he commanded. I was about to give them back, when he stopped me. 'Just spread them out with a sweep of your hand, face-down on the table.'

Sensing that something exciting was about to happen, people began to flock to my side. I had Julius and Walter on my left, and Alex and Charley on my right. I fanned out the cards with the palm of my hand into a perfectly-shaped horseshoe.

Never once taking his eyes off me, Cassius rested his fingertips lightly on the table top. 'Choose a card, Octavius. Pick it up, look at it, but don't let me see it, not even the back…I wouldn't want you to think they were marked, now.'

I chose a card—the Knave of Hearts—which reminded me oddly of Thomas Ryman; it was the tightly-clenched jaw as much as the neat moustache and boyish good looks that did it.

'Memorize it,' he said, 'and place it back anywhere in the deck.'

At this point I expected him to gather up the cards, making what is called "a break", then performing a quick pass to produce the one I'd picked. He didn't. His hands remained poised and unmoving on the table.

'Is it red? Is it black?' he asked aloud, as if posing himself a question. His sculpted lips pursed arrogantly as he closed his eyes. 'It is red!' he proclaimed with a shout, as inspiration seemed to come to him. He gave Julius a big wink before continuing. 'So the question is, is it a diamond or a heart?'

Again he looked at me, his eyes boring into my head.

'Hearts? *Really?*' Now came a smirk. 'A picture card, perhaps? Why, of course it is! A king? No. A queen? No. Which only leaves the Jack. The card you chose is the Jack of Hearts. Oh, my, you look surprised, Octavius.'

Cassius rose amidst a tumultuous round of applause. He moved over to the fireplace and began to stoke the fire. As the people around me dispersed, I flipped over a few cards at random, to assure myself that it was not a deck composed entirely of Knaves of Hearts.

How had he done it? *How?* Had he somehow managed to commit their order to heart? No, the idea was unthinkable. I'd shuffled the cards myself—which meant there could be no predetermined order. And yet he had guessed the one I had chosen without even touching them! *How?*

I rose and, noticing Bertha asleep in his chair, I went to give him a shake. Walter intercepted me before I could.

'No, leave him, sir,' he implored me. 'All is well. Mr Bertha will wake in a few hours and I'll see him to his bed.'

'Walter, does this happen often?'

'Oh, no, sir, no,' the boy answered, nodding sadly as he did so.

'Look after him, Walter, won't you?'

'I will, sir. I will.'

'You're very lucky,' said Mrs Harmon, as she came to join me. 'You have such lovely friends. Bertha is truly charming.'

'She is, miss; I agree.'

'You and your brother look so alike. He tells me he works on a fish stall.'

'He does, miss.'

For quite some few seconds we stood in companionable silence, watching the antics of Alex and Charley as they tried to tempt Florrie with a sprig of mistletoe.

Florrie was having none of it. Cassius was back at the table, teaching Julius and Walter a card game. Mr Moss had taken his leave of us some time before.

As conversationally as I could put it, I said, 'You haven't asked me yet how your husband's trial went.'

'I didn't want to spoil the day,' she replied.

'The day is almost over, miss.'

'So it is,' she said wistfully. 'Very well. Tell me.'

'Your husband, Mr Hargreaves, and Mr Condon were all acquitted of obtaining money by fraudulent means, miss. Their lawyer successfully argued that any fraud perpetrated had been orchestrated by you and Miss Brahms between you. He questioned the witnesses most carefully. Each swore that it was always she who took their payments. The police are still trying to trace you, but you'll be safe enough here. You cannot however be reunited with your husband, for they will no doubt be watching him in the event that you try to make contact.'

'I can't stay here for ever, though, can I?'

'I suppose not, miss.' She and Cassius seemed to fit in so well, I hadn't given the matter any thought. 'So what do you intend to do?'

'Try to find safe passage back to America. Build a new life for Cassius and myself. Pray that my husband finds me some day.'

'Safe passage won't come cheap.'

Mrs Harmon smiled a joyless smile. 'Lucky, then, that I have sufficient funds at my disposal. When we fled, I made sure I took all the money we'd made.'

Suddenly I saw red. 'You have money, yet you did not think to buy Bertha a present? And after all she's done for *you*!'

The joyless smile transformed itself into a real one. 'You are wrong,' she said. 'I bought Bertha exactly what she asked for.'

Slowly the penny dropped. 'It was you who bought all the presents.' *No wonder Cassius's bowler had been so nice!*

'It was I who paid for *some* of them,' she corrected me. 'And, believe me, it was worth every cent.'

When the time came to bid our friends farewell, I took Cassius aside for a parting word.

'Tell me how you did it,' I begged him. 'How did you know which card I picked?'

The young man broke into a smile, revealing two rows of perfect, white teeth. 'Is it so hard to believe that I was able to read your mind?' he asked.

Given his predilection for trickery, I quietly thought that it was.

CHAPTER TWENTY-ONE

'WHO IS IT, JULIUS?' It was early Boxing Day morning, the room was freezing, and I was down on my hands and knees trying to get the stove lit. My head, I am pleased to report, was perfectly pain-free and clear.

'It's that boy back again,' my brother called out to me from the doorway. 'He says his master sends you his complaints—'

'His compliments, Julius.'

'—and he's got some bloke called Alan Dow waiting downstairs to see you.'

I didn't bother to correct him on that one. 'Just tell him I'll be down in a minute.'

Having lit the fire, stroked the dog, and checked that Julius knew what to do in the event of trouble, I swaddled myself in scarves and headed on down.

It was Mr Death who opened the door for me and hauled me up inside; Perkins remained steadfastly rooted in his corner, looking smug and aloof. Mr Smalley barely acknowledged me as he leaned forward and tapped the front glass, signalling the driver to get underway. A landau, which is designed for rich folk to be seen in as they are ferried about town, isn't really the kind of coach you want for long-distance travel, nor is it especially good on rural terrain. That said, at least it was fast, for this time it was being drawn by a team of four horses.

'Remind me,' said Mr Smalley, as we sped ever eastwards, 'exactly why I'm obliged to leave the comfort of my home—on Boxing Day, no less—to travel miles to see some woman whom I've already spoken to before?'

'Sir, I am fairly confident that Agnes Butterworth knew the terms of Mr Eldritch's will.'

'And why is that?' he asked.

'Because of her reluctance to burn the old one.'

'Her *reluctance*?' The lawyer looked horrified. 'You have committed us to this trip because of a cook's reluctance?' He turned to Mr Death. 'And remind me again why Mr Devlin is not here to accompany us?'

The old man shrugged. 'He felt that I should be his humble representative on this occasion.'

Mr Smalley scowled and fell into an irritable silence, for which I was surprisingly grateful. Not that it was to last, for Perkins produced a map from his pocket and began charting our progress with a running commentary.

'Bow! Famed for its bells, sir!'

I sat back and stared out the window, pondering Cassius's card trick as the buildings flashed by. It occurred to me that the way he'd presented the trick was somewhat unusual. All those questions! *Is it red?*

256

Is it black? Is it a diamond or a heart? A picture card, perhaps? A king? No. A queen? No. Which only leaves the Jack.

Questions! Of course! Silly me! He'd used a variation on Mrs Harmon's "Questions". That big wink at Julius should have alerted me to the fact! *He'd had the temerity to enlist my brother as his accomplice, someone who had seen my card and could signal with his eyes! Same trick, different setting.*

'Ilford!' cried Perkins, making me jump.

As evening approached, we broke our journey at a place called Colchester, a town that, according to Mr Death, lost more of its inhabitants to the Great Plague than did the entire City of London—5,259, to be exact. *Hmmm.* A terribly precise figure, to my way of thinking—but then I expect he of all people should know! We arrived quite late at the coaching inn, only to find that the food had run out.

'What is that, then?' Mr Smalley demanded of the landlord, as we watched great steaming bowls being set before a party of fellow travellers.

'The last of the stewed chicken, sir,' the man replied. 'It's Boxing Day; we weren't expecting so many customers. I could do you some bread and cheese, if you like?'

The bread turned out to be stale and the cheese was served in astonishingly meagre portions. We were forced to watch the other table mopping up their plates while we chewed through our tough, parsimonious fare. Nor were the accommodations up to much, either; the mattresses were lumpy, the pillows sparsely filled, and the blankets could have done with a damned good airing. It was almost a blessing to get underway again the next day.

Only Perkins seemed unaffected by our stopover. He cheerily recited the names of the places we passed through: Manningtree; Ipswich; Woodbridge. As the morning wore on, however, even he fell silent. Lulled by the rhythmic rocking of the coach, I began to nod off.

I was awakened by a sudden cry of, '*There!*'

Mr Death was pointing out the carriage's right-hand window. I craned my head round to look. Away in the distance, towering above the treeline, the tall battlements of a castle could be seen etched against the sky. Soon the snow-covered fields gave way to human habitations, and presently we found ourselves driving down the narrow lanes of a sleepy, old-fashioned village. It was a far cry from the hustle and bustle of London. The few people I spied moved slowly as they went about their labours, as if they had nothing of any great importance to do and all the time in the world in which to do it.

We stopped in the market square, where Perkins hopped down to inquire of passers-by the way to the fishermen's huts. 'Follow the road past the church and go straight on until you reach the estuary,' seemed to be the general consensus. 'Peter Butterworth's hut is the seventh on the left.'

When the road petered out at the water's edge, we were obliged to dismount and walk. Perkins led the way along the icy shingle track with the wind whipping about us, carrying the sharp smell of brine to our nostrils. Hauled-up fishing boats lined the shore to our right, interspersed with nets hung up to dry from the occasional tall pole. To our left, some rotten timbers had been fashioned into a fence, marking out what appeared to be a boat-repairs yard. Presently we came to the first of the fishermen's huts, a tiny wooden building with a sharply pointed roof, no bigger in size than our room at my lodgings. It was, I thought, not unlike something my brother might draw, were he to sketch a house and forget to put in windows.

Agnes Butterworth's hut had little to distinguish it from the others we'd passed. A stout pair of boots hung by the door from the planks that clad the exterior; an abandoned work bench sat half-buried in the snow in the small patch of ground at the front. Mr Smalley strode up to the door, raised his cane, and tapped smartly three times. Within seconds the top half of the door swung open.

The face that peered out at us was feathered with lines, but very few of them could accurately be termed wrinkles. Miss Butterworth's eyes were of the palest blue, her cheeks were full and round, and her hair—or what could be seen of it, for she wore a bonnet of intricately-ruched cloth held in place with a fine woollen scarf—was pure white, as white as the snow surrounding the cottage. Judging by her ample figure, I thought she might be an excellent cook.

Mr Smalley, as always, took charge of the situation. 'Miss Butterworth,' he said, 'perhaps you remember me? My name is Smalley. I was your late master's solicitor.'

'Why, yes, of course, sir; I know who you are,' the woman replied.

'These are my associates: Mr de Ath, my proctor's clerk; my boy, Perkins; and this young man, who calls himself Gooseberry. May we be allowed to come in?'

Agnes Butterworth unlatched the lower portion of the door and stepped aside so we might enter.

The hut was, as I'd imagined, just a single room, the focus of which was the fireplace at the far end. A modest fire burned in the grate, sufficient to heat the tiny space several times over. A kettle and teapot sat to one side of the hob, gently simmering away. Much use had been made of the interior walls; in addition to the odd framed picture, several coils of rope, two storm lanterns, and even an old fiddle hung from hooks attached liberally to each of the papered surfaces. As for furnishings, there was a small folding table and two wooden chairs. A serviceable mat covered most of the floor and a bed-roll stood propped up in a corner.

Having secured both parts of the door, Miss Butterworth reclaimed her seat by the fire and quietly resumed her knitting. Neither Mr Smalley nor Mr Death took the remaining seat; instead the four of us stood awkwardly in a circle around the table.

'Miss Butterworth,' I began, 'I know Mr Eldritch asked you to burn one will for him. May I inquire if he asked you to burn another?'

Before I had even finished my sentence, I felt Mr Smalley's cane pressing against my chest and pushing me aside. Miss Butterworth saw this; her face hardened, she brought the two needles together and slowly set down her knitting. Mr Death had seen it too. He'd raised not just one but both of his eyebrows, and was stroking the right one with the tip of his ring finger.

'Miss Butterworth,' Mr Smalley took over, 'it has been brought to my attention that when your master requested you burn a will for him, you were reluctant to do so. Can you tell me why?'

'A thing that is burned cannot be unburned, sir,' she answered cautiously.

'Is that all you have to say for yourself?'

'Why, sir! What more would you have me say?'

'I cannot believe that I allowed myself to be dragged all the way to this hell-hole to have some woman spout platitudes at me.'

'Come, let us go, sir,' said Perkins, casting a filthy look at both Miss Butterworth and myself. 'She clearly has nothing to tell us...at least nothing of any import.'

'No, wait!' I cried. 'Please! We can't go yet!'

Once again it was Mr Death who came to my assistance.

'I apologize for our wretched behaviour, miss,' he said, smiling graciously at the cook. 'My esteemed colleagues and I are in a snappish mood for want of sustenance, comfort, and rest. Can you suggest a suitable hostelry nearby where we might obtain a much-needed meal?'

'This were never a fashionable resort,' she replied, 'not even in the old days. Still, there's one or two good inns what cater to the carriage trade. You might try the Crown and Castle, sir; they should see you right. You'll find it on the other side of the marketplace, near the castle what it's named for.'

Mr Death bowed. 'Much obliged to you, Miss Butterworth. Octavius, are you coming?'

'I shall catch you up presently, if I may, sir.'

When my colleagues had departed, the cook latched the door, then went and busied herself at the hob.

'Your employer doesn't think much of you, does he?' she observed, as she topped up the teapot from the kettle.

'He is not my employer, miss; he merely pays for my services.'

'I hope he pays you enough, then…though I can't imagine he does.'

She poured out some tea and started buttering a few scones that she'd first warmed briefly on the griddle.

'Well, sit yourself down,' she said, 'but not in my seat, mind. Pay no attention to those dirty dishes on the table. I haven't got round to clearing them yet. As to your question, the answer is no. The master only asked me to burn the one will for him. One will; nothing more. Here, get this down you,' she added, placing the cup in front of me and handing me a plateful of scones. 'I'm sure you're just as peckish as that lot was.'

'Thank you, miss.' I took a bite as she refilled the kettle with water and set it to boil. 'They're delicious, miss,' I told her, and quickly began snaffling down the rest.

'A light hand is what's needed with scones,' she remarked, gratified by my obvious enjoyment.

I took a slurp of the tea. It was heavily stewed, but it was milky enough and not too overly sweet.

'Miss,' I said, once I'd drunk my fill, 'I know you read the will your master wrote.'

'Really? Now how could I have possibly done that,' she asked, 'when the master had gone and sealed it up in an envelope?'

'How is not really important,' I told her, as I watched the urgent jet of steam issuing from the spout of the kettle. *A light hand is what's needed with scones*, I reflected.

Miss Butterworth had the temerity to blush. She rose and moved the kettle back to the side of the hob where the temperature was less fierce.

'Whatever it said must have upset you,' I continued, 'for you were reluctant to burn the old will, even though it favoured his niece, Mrs Crabbit.'

The cook's eyes narrowed at the mention of the woman's name.

'You had no love for Mrs Crabbit, miss, and yet you begged your master to reconsider. In your eyes, whoever he was planning to leave his money to was someone even less suitable than his niece.'

'Let's say I did happen to see it,' she posited. 'How could I explain such a thing to that awful employer of yours, the one what pays for your services?'

I gave the matter some thought. 'You used to sit with Mr Eldritch, did you not, to give the nurse a break? You can claim that he was troubled about the wording of one of its provisions, and asked you to fetch it for him. He opened it in your presence and had you read it out to him. Once he was satisfied and his mind was at rest, he sealed it up in another envelope and had you return it.'

Miss Butterwork smiled. 'You've a bit of the devil about you, haven't you, boy?'

'So what did it say, miss?'

'It said,' she said, clearing her throat and adopting what she undoubtedly saw as a posh accent, '"In light of recent experiences, I bequeath the h'entirety of my h'estate to the Hampstead Society for the Welfare and Protection of Stray Cats and Dogs, to do with as they see fit." The cheek of it!' All the pretence at poshness had vanished. 'Money should stay in the family. It oughtn't never go to no strangers!'

This explained a lot. I'd never been happy with the language found on the genuine sheet, especially the phrase: *"Though it pains me to adopt this extraordinary course of action"*. How might leaving his estate to his nephew be considered in any way extraordinary? How could it hope to cure Mrs Crabbit of her *"mean, uncharitable ways"*?

'Miss,' I said, 'did you not think to remark upon how the will had changed? Surely it would have been the first thing you noticed?'

'When Gladys told me what the will said, lad, of course I remarked upon it!'

Oh, my God! She had, too! I recalled Gladys quoting her on that very subject, that Friday afternoon in Miss Moss's studio: '"I was scared he might go and leave it all to some Home for blinkin' wayward cats and dogs!"'

Since that wasn't quite what I'd meant, though, I tried again. 'Miss, did you not think it *odd* that the provisions of the will had changed overnight?'

She rose and began to clear the table. 'I have no idea how the master managed it,' she replied, 'but it struck me as being fortuitous for all concerned. Here, this ain't going to affect Mr Thomas's inheritance none, is it?'

I didn't—nor couldn't—reply. My eyes had come to rest on the spot where the plates had been, or, more specifically, on the green leather notebook that had been lying beneath them.

'That notebook—is it yours, miss?'

'Bless me, no. The other lad left it here.'

'What other lad, miss?'

'The one who was here earlier. Funny, ain't it? He was asking questions about the master's will as well.'

'A big lad? Older than me? Goes by the name of George?'

'Aye, that be right.'

How on earth did George find this address? And how did he manage to get himself here?

I must have spoken these questions aloud, for the woman promptly answered, 'Mr Thomas hired a rig and drove him down himself. Proper gentleman is Mr Thomas!'

A chill went through me that no fire could hope to shift. Thomas Ryman, forger of wills and probable murderer, had somehow got George in his clutches!

'Miss, this is extremely important. What did you tell him?'

'Well, not what I told you.'

That was good.

'And when did they leave?'

'About half an hour before you turned up. Mr Thomas offered to buy the boy lunch and then show him the view from the castle.'

'The castle, miss?' That sounded ominous.

'They say you can see halfway to France on a clear day. You'd never get me traipsing up all those stairs to find out, mind!'

I had a bad, bad feeling about this. Warning her to bolt her door or, better still, seek out safety in the company of friends, I made my excuses and left, then raced along the icy path back into town. Seagulls wheeled in the sky overhead, forming and reforming patterns—not unlike those, I might say, that were reshaping themselves in my mind. Thomas Ryman's substitution of the first page of the will had been a trick—a simple, opportunistic trick, but a trick none-theless. Could the same trick have been employed to bring about Gladys's murder? I suddenly saw that it could.

The man writes three letters. The first he sends to Gladys, asking her to meet him on the heath in the early afternoon—*early* afternoon, note—which she's only too willing to do, bringing the letter with her. He strangles her and replaces it with a second letter, this one purporting to be from Miss McVeigh and specifying an appointment for much later in the day. He then calmly sets about creating his alibi. As with the will, it was a simple matter of substituting one page for another.

The third letter he writes is to Miss McVeigh—for he has decided that she will take the fall for Gladys's murder—inviting her to an assignation at a quarter past four, a time when he knows that there'll be constables patrolling the immediate area. Of course, by this point, Gladys is long since dead.

Was there any proof that Gladys had died earlier than was

initially believed? I thought there might be. There was Miss McVeigh's statement, "At first I thought she must have perished from the cold, for her cheeks were like blocks of ice." Hardly damning, but certainly indicative.

If I were Ryman, and I wanted to rid myself of anyone who was aware of the will's true provisions, I would be desperate to do away with Cook. But first I'd have to deal with George—George, who had accompanied me here; George, who could speak to my presence. *George, how did you even find her address in the first place?*

I went tearing through the marketplace like I had the Devil on my back, much to the consternation of the mild-mannered locals. The Crown and Castle was coming up on my left, a low, extremely long, two-storey building that sat hard against the shoulder of the lane. Dashing from window to window, I peered in at the various diners, but there was no sign of George or Mr Ryman. *Could they have gone somewhere else to eat?*

Mr Smalley's party was installed in the second-to-last of the rooms. I rapped on the pane to get their attention, then signalled with urgency for them to join me outside. Without waiting for them to appear, I sped on.

Ahead of me loomed the castle itself, on the crest of a gentle hillock. My stomach lurched as I caught sight of two figures on the roof of the tallest tower.

Up the snow-covered knoll I ran, throwing the occasional glance behind me. Perkins was following at a fair-paced trot, but he was still many yards away; Mr Smalley and Mr Death had only just emerged from the building. They seemed disinclined to stir themselves so quickly.

The door to the castle was up a steep flight of steps. Once inside, it appeared that the only way up was by a spiral stone staircase in a room to my right. I flew up the broad steps, passing several floors, and then, having reached the top, I found a window to climb out of on to a circular patch of roof.

I found myself surrounded by the castle's three towers: the one I'd just crawled out of, another to my left, and a third to my right, which was the tallest. Against its stones stood a battered, old ladder. I grabbed hold of the rungs and started to climb. As my eyes drew level with the parapet, they were greeted by a heart-stopping sight.

George was perched perilously close to the edge, peering over the side; Ryman was standing just a foot or two behind him, with his body taut, his jaw clenched, and his palms poised, ready to push. Slowly he leaned back to give himself purchase.

'George!' I called out in warning.

George turned just as Mr Ryman struck, and over the side he went. A shriek filled my ears, filled my brain, filled my head, that felt divorced from my throat, which was its source.

Mr Ryman turned and stared. Seeing me clambering on to the roof, he heaved a sigh of annoyance and started towards me.

Then we heard the cry: 'Help me! Please help!'

It was George. All I could see of him were his two sets of fingertips clinging to the edge of the parapet.

Mr Ryman saw them too.

CHAPTER TWENTY-ONE

'Please!' cried George. 'For the love of God, please help me!'

But Ryman wasn't helping; he was bent over, trying to dislodge the lad's fingers. Even as I charged towards him, I could hear Perkins scrabbling up the ladder and gasping as he realized what I was about to do.

Caught off balance—and hit by the full force of my thrust—Ryman went floundering over the edge. A howl of fury rent the air, but only for a second. When I peered over the side to see what had become of him, I saw his body lying in a queerly-contorted heap only yards from a gibbering Mr Smalley.

CHAPTER TWENTY-TWO

'YOU KILLED HIM!' SCREAMED Perkins. 'You just killed a man!'

'Only because he was trying to kill George! Now get over here and help me pull him up!'

'What?'

'Here, God damn you! Grab George's hand and help me get him up!'

George, once he was back on the roof, fell to his knees and was violently ill. Neither of us could stop shaking. Somehow we managed to get down to the ground, where we were shepherded back to the inn. Blankets were produced and brandies fetched for the shock; I took one sip of mine and abandoned it. George, I noticed, did the same. Through chattering teeth I asked him how he came to be in Orford, and in the company of Mr Ryman, no less. It turned out that, George being George, he'd been doing some sleuthing of his own. He'd taken himself off to Hampstead, where he applied to Miss Moss, who had allowed him to go through Gladys's room. After a fruitless search, it occurred to him that there was a surprising lack of personal items.

'And that's when I knew,' he said.

'Knew what?'

'That she kept her whatnots in an envelope *t-t*-taped to the underside of her bedside table.'

I blinked. 'May I ask what *d-d*-drew you to this extraordinarily specific conclusion?'

'I *deduced* it,' he replied, as proudly as he could, given that he too was shaking uncontrollably.

'*B-b*-based on what, George, *m-m*-may I ask?'

'*B-b*-based on the fact that that's where my sister Annie likes to keep her things.'

Ah. *Of course.* That *kind of deduction.*

He had found, amongst other things, a birthday card from Agnes Butterworth with a return address on the back of the envelope.

'But why involve Mr Ryman?' I asked. 'You knew he'd forged his uncle's will, right?'

'Miss Moss said she didn't believe that to be the case. She said I owed it to the man to let him prove me wrong. Besides, he offered to drive me down here. It was my one chance to question the cook, so I couldn't pass it up, now, could I?' George rubbed his eyelids with his fingertips. 'I figured if he tried anything on, I could take care of myself. I was bigger and stronger than he was.'

I rather suspected that Ryman had taken this into account when plotting poor George's demise.

The inquest was held on Wednesday, 29th at the Crown and Castle, where we had taken lodgings in order to attend. Mr Smalley insisted that I limit my testimony to only the things I could prove.

'Don't go trying to tie Ryman to the murder of that little housemaid,' he warned. 'Stick entirely to how the man forged his uncle's will.'

'Don't worry, sir,' I promised—and I meant it— for, although I was certain I was right, the theory I'd evolved was simply that—*a theory*—and one that contained any number of holes. If I was correct in my assumptions, Gladys's murder had been triggered by her mention of the true recipients of Mr Eldritch's estate. But how had it come to Ryman's attention? Had she realized the significance of the words, perhaps, and approached the man for money?

The inquest—and the story that came out of it— caused quite a sensation. I imagine the locals will talk of little else for months and months to come. I testified to seeing Ryman push George off the edge. Mr Smalley and Mr Death corroborated my story, while George talked about how the man had tried to prise his hands free. But the real star of the inquiry was the cook, and the testimony she gave about the will. When she was made to understand that she would have been Mr Ryman's next victim, she was only too willing to testify.

'Steaming open a will—well, that's hardly a crime, now, is it?' as she put it.

Despite the very welcome verdict of *chance medley*— manslaughter mitigated by extreme provocation (a charge which the Superintendent of the Ipswich Police Force was not keen to pursue, for what reasonable man would not have acted in the same way that I did?)—I still felt dissatisfied. Ryman's death left us with an awful number of unanswered questions. George, too, seemed rather distant and preoccupied. He barely picked at his supper that night, and then went off for a walk on his own. When he returned, I sensed that something had changed, for he had a feverish look in his eye.

'I know how he did it,' he said, slumping down on to the bed next to mine.

'How he did what, George?'

'How he killed Sarah Brahms.' His forehead glistened in the light from the oil lamp.

Please, oh, please, don't let this be another of your deductions, George! 'Would you care to share your theory?' I hazarded.

'It was dark, right? The whole room was dark?'

'Agreed…'

'Well, when Ryman let go of my hand the first time, that's when he made his move.'

'But you said it was only for a second.'

'What if it wasn't *his* hand I ended up holding?'

Oh.

'Go on…'

George crossed his legs and leaned forward. 'What if it was Miss Moss's? She was sitting next to him, right? Her hands are just as big as his.'

'But why, pray tell, would she do such a thing?'

'I reckon she was in on it.'

'Even if that were true, George, she was seated at the end of the table; that's quite a distance for her arm to stretch.'

'Then she moved seats.'

'What about Mrs Crabbit?'

'She didn't need to hold Mrs Crabbit's hand—Mrs Crabbit had broken the circle.'

My eyes narrowed. 'That's right, because she'd been stung…I've always had my suspicions about those stings. The first of them, I am fairly sure, was when somebody yanked out her hair.'

George leaned even closer. 'What if the second was a jab from the dagger?'

'Yes…to get her to her release her hands…' George was right. Ryman had had a partner.

Suddenly his whole body seemed to crumple before me.

'What's the matter, George?'

'We're forgetting something, aren't we? It was dark. How could anyone stab Mrs Crabbit's hand if they couldn't see where it was?'

'They'd know where it was if they were holding it…which brings us right back to Cicely Moss.'

'What if Miss Moss killed Miss Brahms on her own?'

'She couldn't have, George. To stab Mrs Crabbit on the wrist, her left hand needed to be free—and that's only possible if Thomas Ryman willingly and knowingly relinquished it. Here's my theory—'

George stopped me with a peremptory cough. '*Whose* theory?' he asked.

'Our theory, then. Miss Moss somehow delayed Mrs Crabbit from entering the room, so that, when she did, the only available seats were at the end of the table.'

'Why's that important?'

'Because, for their plan to work, she needs to be

sitting between Mrs Crabbit and Ryman. In fact, she chooses to sit next to Miss McVeigh, knowing that when Ryman turns up, she can offer to change seats with Mrs Crabbit.'

'I *think* I see,' said George, screwing his face up with the effort. 'Actually, I'm not sure I do.'

'Don't worry; it's really not that important. Listen: the lights go out. Miss Moss lets go of Ryman's hand, nabs a strand or two of Mrs Crabbit's hair—the *first* sting—which she wraps round the dagger's hilt before giving her a poke on the wrist.'

'The *second* sting?'

'Irrefutably. As Mrs Crabbit lets go of her hand, she passes the weapon to Ryman, who, using the walls to guide him, goes and stabs Sarah Brahms in the back. The deed done, he returns to his seat—'

'Where Miss Moss is sitting—'

'—and she vacates it, just as Mrs Crabbit is ready to link hands again. Before he has a chance to sit down, however, Ryman receives a nasty shock.'

'A shock?'

'Cassius blows a trumpet in his ear.'

'How d'you know that?'

'At the time, I thought Ryman had jumped out of his seat. I now believe he was standing.' I sighed. 'That dagger, as we know, was part of a pair, and when the police are slow to arrest his cousin, he plants the second one behind the Crabbits' lodgings. Do you recall the first time we interviewed him at Blackthorn—when his boots were making puddles on the floor? Considering when that dagger was found, I think that he'd just come back from planting it.' I sighed again. 'You realize Miss Moss had a hand in Gladys's murder, too?'

George nodded. 'Yes, she gave Ryman his alibi.'

'She may have *helped* him with his alibi; but, no, that's not what I meant. I think it was she who alerted Ryman to what Gladys had said.'

'About leaving his money to a home for stray cats and dogs?'

'Yes. And, from this, we can deduce precisely what, my friend?'

George furrowed his brow and thought. 'That Miss Moss has a good memory where words are concerned?'

I threw him a disparaging look and urged him to try harder.

'That either she visited him or he visited her *after* we interviewed Gladys?'

Another look; sharper, more withering.

'*Oh*!' George's eyes widened as it finally came to him. 'She knew the provisions of Mr Eldritch's will!'

'Very good! Unless she knew what the will said, that remark would have meant nothing to her.' Now it was my turn for my shoulders to droop. 'The trouble is, it's all conjecture. We've not a single shred of evidence between us. We don't even know *why* they wanted Mrs Harmon dead, for it was she who was clearly their target.'

My despondency was infectious; George's shoulders buckled too. 'And it's not like we can just ask her,' he reflected.

I blinked. I blinked again. *Ah. And the sooner we asked her, the better*, I thought.

Early the next day we set out on the first leg of our journey home. We were bound for Chelmsford, a town we had passed through on our way to Orford, which happened to have a direct train service to London—a fact that the annoying Perkins had pointed out so chirpily. Since we seemed to be back in Mr Smalley's good books, it wasn't hard to talk him into buying George and me a pair of tickets for the overnight train—third class, naturally; though even these set him back a cool eight shillings and sixpence—chargeable to the Eldritch estate, of course. I did not explain the purpose of the trip to George; I felt it best to keep him in the dark for as long as possible. As someone who had yet to experience train travel, he simply imagined I was arranging a bit of a treat.

'You'd think the First Class passengers would want to ride up front,' he observed, as we took our places in the carriage next to the engine. 'Isn't it strange that they ride at the back of the train?'

Not if they thought the engine was going to explode, I mused, though I was careful to keep this idea to myself.

The whistle blew and the wheels screeched in protest as the train juddered into motion.

'Will you still...you know...?' asked George.

'Will I still what?'

'You know...teach me...to be a detective.' The words came out haltingly as our carriage clacked and clattered its way over the first of the viaducts.

'I will if you want me to, George.'

He nodded, withdrew a monogrammed square of linen from his pocket, and blew his nose. 'I don't want no more taxonomy, though,' he added, referring to my list of opportunities for the jobbing detective. Sniffing to underscore the point, he stuffed his handkerchief back inside his jacket. 'No,' he said, 'I want real skills this time.'

Real skills. 'How might you feel about learning to pick pockets?' I asked.

'You can pick pockets?'

I held out my balled-up fist and slowly unfurled my fingers. I allowed him to behold the crumpled square of linen that had been residing in his jacket only seconds before.

'Oh!' he cried, noticing the letters "*G. C.*". 'It's *mine*!' He blinked. 'But how did you do it? I didn't see nothing! I didn't feel nothing!'

'I'm so pleased you asked, my friend! We have a long journey ahead of us, and these hard wooden benches threaten to render my backside permanently numb. Why don't we distract ourselves from our impending ordeal and begin your lessons immediately?'

II

The train pulled into Bishopsgate at a little after six in the morning. The streets were still dark as I bundled George into a cab. When it dropped us off in Long Acre and I steered him down the side street towards the Bucket of Blood, George's sense of adventure began to desert him.

'Why have you brought me here?' he gasped, as he stared with misgiving at the pub's facade. 'It looks like a nest of thieves and cut-throats!'

'Prepare yourself, George. All is about to be revealed.'

Slowly revealed, as things turned out, for everyone was still in bed asleep. After much hammering on the door, I managed to wake Charley, whom I set to work rousing the others. I showed George up to the big front room where my friends and I had spent our Christmas, sat him in a chair, and then proceeded to sweep out the fireplace and build a fire. A succession of sleepy faces appeared in the doorway, only to scamper away again—presumably to get washed and changed—once they'd ascertained what was going on.

'You've been harbouring a wanted criminal,' observed George, after Mrs Harmon and Bertha put in one such appearance.

'*I* haven't been harbouring anyone, George. My friend Bertha has.'

'Yeah…about your friend, Bertha. Isn't she a—'

'Whatever else she may be, my friend Bertha is *my friend*,' I insisted, before he could get the words out. *A thing that is burned cannot be unburned*, as a wise old cook once said.

Eventually a fully-dressed Walter arrived bearing a tray full of cups. Hard on his heels came Cassius with a teapot the size of a pumpkin. One by one the others turned up and helped themselves to tea. Now modestly attired in black and with her hair pinned up, Mrs Harmon entered the room, shortly followed by Bertha, in his beloved widow's weeds.

He advanced on George, who shrank back in his chair as Bertha pressed a parcel into his hand.

'What's this?' he asked.

'It's your Christmas box, ain't it? Go on…might as well open it, then.'

Egged on by Walter and Cassius, George fumbled with the string and tore away the paper, revealing a magnifying glass and pair of tweezers that were a match for my own.

'This is for me?'

'Yeah. Well, now you and Octopus 'ere can go and be real detectives, can't yeh?'

'Thank you kindly…'

I sensed he was about to leave it there, so I gave him a nudge with my elbow.

'…miss. That is really most generous of you, I'm sure.'

Bertha beamed.

Together George and I related the events in Orford and expounded our theory of Miss Moss's involvement. Was there anything Mrs Harmon could tell us that linked her with the murderous Ryman?

'Do you remember the first time he attended a sitting?' she asked. 'When he forced his way into the room? That was before Sarah had had a chance to investigate him, of course. And yet she came up to me and whispered something rather odd in my ear.'

'What, miss?'

'How, when she'd been looking into Miss Moss, she had observed her and the intruder walking arm in arm on Hampstead Heath. It seemed too good to ignore, so I included it into the act.'

'The act?'

'When I was prancing about in the dark, pretending to be Henrietta. *Cicely's got a* boy*friend, Cicely's got a* boy*friend*!' she chanted. 'Surely my dear Sarah wasn't murdered because of *that*?'

'I have a terrible feeling that she might have been, miss,' I replied. 'It rather looks as if they were trying to keep their relationship secret, though I can't think why.'

'It's no use,' said George. 'We still can't prove any of it, can we?'

I shook my head. 'True, but I may have an idea.'

George looked at me strangely. 'Please don't tell me you're planning to kill her,' he begged.

'*What*? No, of course I'm not!' I tried to laugh it off, but his remark left a lasting impression on more than one of those present. 'What I meant was we still have two advantages in our favour.'

'What advantages?'

'One: she loves him. And two: *she doesn't yet know that he's dead*.' I turned to Mrs Harmon, who was still studying me with a frown. 'How would you feel about giving one last performance, miss?'

Once I'd explained what I wanted everyone to do, Bertha and Mrs Harmon got to work transforming George's appearance, applying the ashes I'd swept from the fireplace. Mrs Harmon stepped back to survey the effect, shook her head, and promptly sent me out to buy raspberry jam. Quite where I was meant to find raspberry jam in Covent Garden on New Year's Eve somewhat eluded me, until Bertha suggested I try knocking door to door. I eventually found a woman who agreed to sell me a few spoonfuls for the princely sum of tuppence—such an outrageous price that I demanded she write me a receipt. As the door closed in my face, leaving me to ponder whether I should have asked her to use the general term "supplies" (rather than the more specific phrase "raspberry jam"), a gently drifting snowflake flew across my line of vision and landed with a puff on the ink's still tacky surface. I tried to blow it away, which only served to disturb the ink more.

By half past two that afternoon, everyone was in position. Bertha and Walter were stationed by the gates to Miss Moss's house, ready to hail the patrolling constables, who were due to pass by in about thirty minutes time. George, looking ghastlier than ever, was hiding in the trees on the heath at the rear. Dressed in her serpent-green brocade, and accompanied by Cassius in his livery (and me in—*well*—my bowler), Mrs Harmon strode up to the door and knocked. When the footman answered, she pushed her way past him into the hall and, resisting all attempts to be silenced, called out loudly and repeatedly for Miss Moss to appear.

'Forgive the intrusion,' she began, when the lady of the house finally arrived, 'but earlier today, while I was communing with the spirits, one of my spirit guides came to me and told me of a newly-arrived soul who was desperate to get a message to you. Miss Moss, I felt it my bounden duty to come!'

Miss Moss dipped her head with that curious pecking motion of hers. 'Quite,' she said, looking very ill at ease.

Mrs Harmon closed her eyes and raised her hands, moving them slowly through the air as if trying to feel for some invisible presence.

'*Tsk!*' she declared, and opened them again. 'This

house positively blocks the vibrations! Never mind. I felt a spark of something coming from that direction.' She hooked her arm through Miss Moss's to spur her into action. 'This way, my dear.'

She led Miss Moss by the route I'd described through to the studio at the back. Cassius and I followed behind. Both women may have been of a similar age, and one of them may have even been mistress here, but it was the shorter, red-headed Maria who was in control.

'Oh, yes!' she said. 'This room is *much* better.' She moved about the brightly lit studio, admiring the tapestry and running her fingers over various pieces of furniture. 'Cassius! Octavius!' she cried. 'Bring the chairs!'

'Come, miss. Sit here,' I said, positioning one of the bow-legged chairs so that it faced the mirror. Though clearly not wanting to, Miss Moss complied. Cassius placed another directly opposite her for Mrs Harmon to sit in. I adjusted my hat in full view of the windows to give George the pre-arranged signal, then Cassius and I brought chairs of our own, and the circle was complete.

'Everybody link hands!'

Watched by a very apprehensive Miss Moss, Maria Harmon began taking a series of long, deep breaths. The medium's eyelids began to flicker as she rocked her body back and forth, moving ever more wildly and recklessly with every lurch. Suddenly she sat bolt upright. Her face was expressionless and her eyes were closed, but her lower lip had begun to tremble.

'*Faughhhh…faughhhh…*'

The deep, guttural sounds that issued from her throat hardly seemed human. I felt Miss Moss's hand tighten in mine.

'*Faughhhhl…am…faughhhhl…I am fal…ling…falling…*'

With a gasp and a whimper, Miss Moss cowered back in her chair.

'*He…poooooh…poooooh…pushed me…*'

'No…don't tell me these things!' she squeaked. 'I don't want to know!'

But the spirit seemed in no mood to be silenced. '*He threw…yes*, threw *me…to my death…*'

Without warning, I felt a grip so tight that it threatened to break my fingers. I glanced at Miss Moss, who was staring at the mirror, gazing in horror at the reflection of George lumbering across her back lawn. His skin was as grey as any corpse's, and the right side of his forehead appeared to be a mass of congealed blood. A shard from a broken bowl that stretched from his matted hair down to his brow line might have been a piece of his fractured skull, so convincing did it look. There was something about the woman's expression that recalled to mind a poem, a half-remembered ballad from my youth:

> *Out flew the web and floated wide;*
> *The mirror crack'd from side to side;*
> *"The curse is come upon me," cried*
> *The Lady of Shalott.*

'Do not break the circle!' cried Cassius, as Miss Moss leapt to her feet.

'Look! Can none of you see it? The boy has returned

to haunt me!' Her fingernails dug into the flesh of my palm, threatening to penetrate the skin.

'What's that you say, miss? Someone has come back to haunt you?'

'There! There! Can't you see? He has come to wreak his vengeance!' Tears of anguish were streaming down her face.

'*Over…the edge…I am cast…as if I'm…expected to fly…*'

'Why would anyone wish to wreak their vengeance on you, miss? I don't understand…'

'Because Thomas killed that poor boy, and now he's come back to haunt me! Oh, do something to stop him, I beg you, I beg you!' She let out a shriek as George's grey knuckles appeared at the window and rapped with great solemnity on the pane.

'*The frozen ground…rushes up to greet me…ripping apart my flesh…shattering my skull, my bones…*'

'I didn't want him to kill him,' she wailed. 'I didn't! I didn't! I argued with Thomas, but he said he had to— the boy knew Cook's address!'

'Calm yourself, miss; that's just my friend, George. I think he wants to come in.'

She turned to stare at me. 'Do you not understand? Your friend George is dead! Mr Ryman killed him.'

'George is probably a bit cold, and could do with a wash, but he's perfectly fine, miss; I promise you. It wasn't he who went off the tower.'

'*What?*'

'It was Mr Ryman.'

'*No!*' The roar lasted several seconds and, as it died away, the voice that issued from Mrs Harmon's mouth delivered its final words:

'*He's telling you the truth, Cicely…it's me that they killed…me, your beloved Thomas…*'

Abruptly the tears ceased to fall. Miss Moss's eyes, normally so pale, had gone utterly dark. Her lips now cut across her face like a gaping, raw wound. She tossed our hands aside and took three faltering steps across the carpet, where she crumpled to a heap on the floor, murmuring over and over, 'He cannot be dead.'

She did not notice when Cassius and Mrs Harmon slipped quietly from the room, leaving her and I alone together. I sat down beside her and put my arm around her shoulder.

'Miss…miss,' I coaxed her, 'this all started with the will. Won't you please help me understand what happened?'

'What?'

'The will, miss. What happened?'

'What happened?' She gazed at me blankly. 'That afternoon—Mr Eldritch's last afternoon—I came downstairs and found Thomas in the study. When he looked up with a terrible, guilty expression, I realized what he was doing. He was forging his uncle's will. But when he showed me who the new beneficiary was to have been, I couldn't help but agree with him; Mr Eldritch was not in his right mind when he drafted it. It was the only thing to do; it was the *right* thing to do; and when it was done, he walked me home—and, on the way, he professed his love to me.'

'But why did you feel the need to keep your love a secret?'

'He wanted to protect me. He feared that if what he'd done ever came to light, people might think I had a hand in it.'

It seemed like twisted logic to me, yet I let it pass unquestioned. 'Why did he try to kill Mrs Harmon, miss? What threat did she pose to him?'

'That horrid little Harriet seemed to know all about us. He was scared of what else she or others of her kind might decide to reveal.'

'And you allowed it?' *She'd more than allowed it; she'd helped.*

She turned her cavernous eyes on me and glowered. 'Have I no right to happiness?' she asked. 'Why should I not feel as cherished and loved as the next woman?'

I found myself nodding. 'Tell me about Gladys, miss.'

'Gladys practically quoted the will at me…here, in this very room.'

'Actually, she quoted the cook, miss.'

'Cook; yes, Cook.' Miss Moss frowned. 'How could she have known what provisions Mr Eldritch had made? Of course, Thomas realized he had to get rid of her.'

'And George, too.'

'Well, he found her address.'

Murder only seemed to beget murder, I reflected. Given the secretive nature of their relationship, I wondered if Miss Moss might have been the next in line.

'Do you think Mrs Harmon is right?' she asked.

'About what, miss?'

'That when people die, they see the Gates of Heaven opening before them, and their loved ones are waiting there to welcome them into their arms?'

Hmmm. 'Undoubtedly, miss.'

The smile she gave me chilled me to the bone. I stayed with her until, summoned by my friends at the gate, Constables Lamb and Scott arrived to find a pliable if somewhat withdrawn woman, ready to accept her fate. She was taken into custody, questioned further and then charged, and some four hours later Mrs Crabbit was released.

III

Monday, January 3rd, 1853. A brand new year; a cold, bright morning. I was in the chief clerk's office presenting him with the last of my receipts.

'And what is this?' he asked, quietly removing his spectacles—never a good sign.

'A receipt for four spoonfuls of raspberry jam, sir.' A *water-stained* receipt for four spoonfuls of raspberry jam, if I were to be exact.

'Raspberry jam?' He replaced his glasses and peered more closely at the blotchy blue-black lettering. 'Is that what it says?'

'It is, sir.'

Mr Crabbit threw me a look, then reached for the file labelled *Skipp and Smalley*.

'I don't quite know how to thank you,' he said, as he placed it inside with the others.

Luckily for me, I happened to have one or two ideas of my own on that account.

THE EPILOGUE

'I DON'T SEE WHY I should be the one to wash the window,' grumbled George, as he wrung out his soft leather cloth and applied it to the pane.

I did not point out to him all the things that I myself had done. I'd scrubbed down the chairs and desk with wire wool and white vinegar, then dried them off, applied beeswax, and buffed them till they shone. I'd whitewashed the walls and stripped the polish from the floorboards, replacing it with a layer of my own. I'd splashed out on a bamboo coat-rack and a nice umbrella stand; with a little bit of cleaning they looked as good as new. I'd hired Bertha's sign-writing friend to make a plaque for the door. In tasteful black lettering on a muted gold background it proclaimed:

Octavius Guy
Investigator-in-Chief
Discretion is our byword

Below this it read (in equally large letters):

George Crump
Investigative Assistant
No case is too big or too small!

The crowning glory for me, though, was the potted fern that I'd picked up at the flower market. Its dark green fronds provided a welcoming splash of colour even on the dullest of winter days. Oh, yes! 1853 looked set to be a truly promising year.

'Even detectives-in-training need to know how to clean windows, George,' I replied.

'What about proper detectives?' he moaned. 'Or don't they like getting their hands wet?'

'Just be grateful that Mr Bruff has seen fit to make you a full-time investigator.' *And me a chief investigator, no longer simply in name.*

Though Mr Crabbit had given me his word that the office was to be mine, it was not until he removed his list from the wall (*No illegible receipts—No indecipherable receipts—No torn receipts—etc., etc.,*) that I knew it was truly the case. To show my appreciation, I made a trip to the Bucket of Blood, and the next day I was able to return to him all the money his wife had squandered on the sittings she'd attended. One might think that should take care of any illegible, indecipherable, or torn receipts I might present in the future—though, knowing Mr Crabbit, I don't suppose it will.

'Done,' said George, stepping back to admire his handiwork. Wiping his hands down the sides of his breeches, he came round the back of my chair and peered over my shoulder. 'What are you working on?' he asked.

I rapidly folded the sheet of paper on which I'd been writing and stuffed it inside my jacket. 'Nothing,' I lied, conscious of just how popular *Guy's Essential Stratagems and Ruses for Working Undercover* might prove. I perceived a lightening-fast movement from the corner of my eye, and instinctively my hand shot up, grabbing hold of the wrist that was attempting to infiltrate my jacket's interior.

'George, George, George! You will have to do better than that if you ever hope to pick *my* pocket!'

In the days and weeks that followed, much came to pass. Under Mr Devlin's and Mr Death's supervision, Frederick Eldritch's estate duly passed to the Hampstead Society for the Welfare and Protection of Stray Cats and Dogs. Mr Smalley was so impressed with how I'd concluded the case that he begged me to come and work for him, and at nearly double the rate I received from Mr Bruff. *Just me*, however. *Not* George. Naturally I declined. He might think money can buy everything, but it cannot buy loyalty. Besides, I doubt that the post came with an office. I do hear tell that Perkins was offered the job. *Good luck with that, Mr Smalley*!

On Tuesday, January 11th, George and I attended Miss Moss's arraignment at the Old Bailey. Miss McVeigh and Mr Sligo attended too. I became aware of a certain frostiness developing between them, which I put down to Miss McVeigh's new-found distaste for smart words and gossip. Such was the interest in the case that the public gallery was full to overflowing, and we were lucky to get a seat. It amused me to see the judge bring in flowers (freesias, obtained, no doubt, from Covent Garden that very morning). For a brief second, I wondered if he was about to present them to Miss Moss.

I glanced at George; he glanced at me. 'Weird,' he muttered. I couldn't have agreed more. In the event, he simply set them down on his bench.

Miss Moss was asked to stand as the clerk of the court read out the charges against her.

'Cicely Moss, you are hereby charged with four counts of conspiracy to murder. To the charge of conspiring to murder Miss Sarah Brahms at Condon's Hotel on Jermyn Street on the evening of the fifteenth of December last, how plead you?'

'Guilty.'

'Miss Moss, you will need to speak louder than that.'

'Guilty,' she repeated, in the same quiet, breathless voice.

'To the charge of conspiring to murder Miss Gladys Bland at Hampstead Heath on the eighteenth of December last, how plead you?'

'Guilty.'

'To the charge of conspiring to murder Mr George Crump at the Suffolk town of Orford on the twenty-seventh of December last, how plead you?'

'Guilty.'

'To the charge of conspiring to murder Miss Agnes Butterworth at the Suffolk town of Orford on the twenty-seventh of December last, how plead you?'

'Guilty.'

I went to see the hanging; George declined, preferring to concentrate on our very first client's case: the disappearance, yet again, of Mr Tibbles, feline serial absconder *extraordinaire*. St Sepulchre's tenor bell tolled solemnly as Cicely Moss was led from her holding cell for the very last time. Watching her make her way up to the gallows, I was once again reminded of the poem that the teacher at my Ragged School used to recite to us:

> *Under tower and balcony,*
> *By garden wall and gallery,*
> *A pale, pale corpse she floated by,*
> *Deadcold, between the houses high,*
> *Dead into tower'd Camelot.*

Say what you like about poets, when it comes to conjuring up a divine sense of creepiness, they know what they're doing—provided they can stay off the drink, that is!

Sergeant Snipe had proved so ineffectual at his post that his superiors demoted him. He is no longer a *Detective* Sergeant; he is merely a Sergeant. He runs V-Division, out Battersea way, I believe. He'll be fine there; there's not a lot of crime amongst the potteries and the cabbages.

I never learned what became of Miss Brahms's intended, Mr Hargreaves, but Mr Condon lost his hotel to his lawyer, when he couldn't meet the bill for his defence. It's now Cox's Hotel, and I'm pleased to say that George's brother is still gainfully employed there.

As for Mr Harmon, with Bertha's help a regular passage was booked for him, departing from Liverpool, bound for New York. The following week, two highly irregular passages were found aboard a cargo vessel—also bound for New York—departing the Port of London on the fifteenth day of January.

The long-awaited thaw had come by then, and at last the streets were clear of snow. It was a dull, grey winter's day, with clouds that constantly threatened to rain but never quite managed to do it. Our little party—consisting of myself, Bertha, Walter, Alex and Charley, and our two American friends—might have been a cortège, such were our moods and our manners of dress. Warehouse workers and wharf hands all removed their caps as we passed by (presumably out of respect for Bertha), adding an even more funereal touch to the proceedings.

The *Hornet* was a clipper moored up in St Katharine's Dock. There's something quaintly old-fashioned about clipper ships, yet I am assured they are remarkably swift.

'Is that her?' inquired Mrs Harmon, staring up uneasily at the flurry of activity on board the ship's deck.

Bertha nodded. 'Don't you worry, Maria. It'll get you there before yeh know it!'

'Looking forward to seeing your homeland again?' I asked Cassius.

He pondered the question for a moment, and then, without speaking, raised his emerald eyes skywards, idly gazing at the clouds just as he might gaze at a ceiling. *I don't know.*

'I guess this is goodbye,' he said, shaking me by the hand. 'Thank you for all you have done for us, Octavius.'

'You are most welcome.' A thought suddenly occurred to me. 'Cassius, before you go, tell me something… Henrietta's ghostly touch. How did you manage that?'

The lad began to laugh. 'I filled a silk glove up with cold jellied aspic and tied it off at the wrist. Then, just before the sitting, I put it out on the window ledge in the snow for twenty minutes.'

Ah.

'And the raps? How were they produced?'

'Are you sure you want to know? You'll be very disappointed.'

When I nodded he drew close to my ear and whispered.

'The heel of her boot? Is that all?' He was right. I *was* disappointed.

'We really cannot begin to thank you and Bertha enough,' said Mrs Harmon.

'I wish you a safe and tranquil voyage, miss, and a joyous reunion with your husband.'

The medium smiled, then opened her mouth to speak, but for a moment the words seemed to stick in her throat. 'I really do have the gift,' she said, 'and I cannot leave without telling you this. There is someone who is desperate to talk to you. She speaks English, I think, but with a very strange accent; I've never heard the like of it before.'

She took hold of my hand and wetted her lips with her tongue, then, frowning, she began to manoeuvre her jaw into one shape after another, finally settling on one where her mouth formed a great big O.

'"*Oak*"—no, that's not quite right—"*Owk*"—"*Awk*"—that's more like it—"*Awk*"—'

I'd seen too many of the woman's performances to be impressed.

'"*Awk-tay-vi-us*"—"*Awk-tay-vi-us, I'm so proud of you, Awk-tay-vi-us…solving murders*"—no, not quite—"*solving mirrr-ders, the way you do.*" Yes, that's better.'

It was just a voice, I told myself. It wasn't my mother's voice. It was just the voice of someone who might possibly have a Birmingham accent.

'"*I watch you every day, son. You will do great things, I know it. Don't judge your father too harshly; it's just his way. He has his own family to think of, see?*"'

Pulling my fingers free of her grasp, I found myself muttering quite incoherently. As I backed away, Maria Harmon mouthed the words, *She loves you*, and then turned and ascended the gangplank to the ship.

The reason for George's many absences finally became apparent to me when, quite out of the blue, I was invited to his wedding. *His wedding*! Well, not exactly his wedding as such, but to the reception in the churchyard afterwards. He was to marry Mary Moody, eldest daughter of Mrs Moody, who you may recall was the Crabbits' landlady. It transpired that on Saturdays he and his bride-to-be were encouraged to court—under the watchful eyes of their mothers, of course. That Sunday when he'd been unwilling to accompany me to Hampstead Heath, the banns were to have been read in church for the first time.

'Mary wanted me to be there,' he explained, 'and not just for that one but for all of them. As things turned out, I could have come with you to Hampstead after all.' He was referring to the fact that his Boxing Day flight to Orford had caused him to miss the second reading. 'She made the vicar start again. He read the third of them yesterday.'

'Congratulations, George! That's wonderful news!' *Well, it was extraordinary news, at least.* I wasn't quite sure how I felt about it. I'm not sure he knew how he felt about it either.

'You can bring your brother, if you want,' he said, then paused and added, 'and your friend.'

'You mean Bertha?'

'Yeah. Bertha. You can bring—'

'I'm sure she will be delighted to come,' I butted in, before he could add, *him too.*

The union of George Crump and Mary Moody took place on Saturday, January 22nd, at the church on Pratt Street in Camden Town. Did I mind that I wasn't invited to the actual service? No. Church affairs don't interest me; marriage is but a civil contract, when all is said and done. The real celebration occurs when people come together to toast the happy couple afterwards.

I would like to be able to report that the day was balmy. It wasn't; but at least the sun was out and the sky was blue, and there was little chance of rain. A long trestle table had been set up outside against the brickwork of the church, and on it sat plates of biscuits and various sweetmeats. A large, dense fruitcake, as dark as a tinker's pot, took pride of place in the centre. George's brother, William, who had stood as his best man, had been charged with cutting it up. His sister, who, only weeks before, I had spied on her way to the shops, moved through the guests, handing out wedges. She glanced over at the wall, where the three of us (and the dog) were huddled under the tree, and proceeded to make her way over.

'Don't tell me,' she said, 'you're Octavius; the one George used to call Gooseberry.'

Up close—and without the muffler I'd seen her wearing—I judged her to be no older than sixteen. Her hair was blonde, her eyes were blue, and the look on her face was mischievous in the extreme. The smile that was for ever in flux only heightened the effect.

'It was a nickname, miss, that's all,' I replied.

'Well, how do you do, Mr Guy? My name is Annie. I'm George's younger sister.'

'It's very nice to meet you, Miss Crump.'

'George tells me that you saved his life. Is that true?'

'I'm sure he exaggerates, miss.' I was aware that George had deliberately played down his brush with death in order to spare his family any anxiety.

'Would you care for some cake, Mr Guy?'

'Thank you, miss,' I said, helping myself to the smallest piece.

'You're modest, I see,' she observed. 'I like that in a man. So. Aren't you going to introduce me to your friends?'

I wasn't sure this was such a good idea; William had seen us talking to his sister, and was even now heading across the lawn to intervene.

'Well?' she said. 'I'm waiting.'

'This is my brother, Julius, miss.'

'How do you do, Julius? Would you care for some cake?'

'You're pretty,' he said, taking a slice. Tricky barked in agreement and circled her feet in a figure-of-eight.

'And who is this?' she asked, turning to Bertha— but, before I could answer, William stole up behind her and laid his hand on her shoulder.

'Mother wants a word with you, Annie.'

'Oh, hush, William! Mother wants no such thing! You were saying, Mr Guy—?'

'This is my best friend, Bertha, miss. She's a little shy,' I added hopefully.

'Not so shy I can't speak for meself!' grunted Bertha.

Annie laughed while her brother looked on indignantly.

'You are most welcome here, miss,' said Annie, treating Bertha to a radiant smile. 'Would you care for some cake?'

'Thought you'd never bleedin' ask,' replied Bertha, with a deep, earthy chuckle.

'I said Mother wants *a word*,' William tried again, but Annie displayed not the slightest intention of leaving.

'There's to be music,' she announced, addressing us while at the same time handing her brother the plate of cake she was holding. As if taking his cue from her, a man stepped forward from the assembled revellers and began beating rhythmically on a kind of hand drum.

'What's that he's playing, miss?' I asked.

'It's called a bodhrán,' she replied.

'A *what*, miss?' It was a term I was not familiar with.

'A bodhrán.' She pronounced it something like *bar-ron* or *bor-ron*.

As I watched, George—who, it has to be said, was looking extremely out of his depth—took his new bride by the hand to begin the dancing. Seeing this, a second drummer joined the fray and the first burst gruffly into song:

'*The first time I saw her, she moved through the fair…and I smiled as she passed with her goods and her gear…*'

'So, Mr Guy,' said Annie, 'are you going to ask me to dance?'

I felt my throat constrict to the point I could hardly speak. I glanced up at the Crabbits' window; I stared wordlessly at my boots.

'*I was naught but a wee lad when I heard her to say*: "*It will not be long, love, till our wedding day.*"'

'I can't, miss,' I said at last.

'Why not?'

'Because nobody ever taught me to, miss.'

A woman fiddle player now pitted herself against the singer, stealing snatches of the man's melody and making it her own. Whether plucked or bowed, her notes sounded oppressively sweet and mournful in equal measure.

'Then I shall just have to teach you myself, Mr Guy!'

'Will you teach me?' begged Julius.

'I will,' replied Annie. 'But first I'm going to teach your brother.'

'*When I met her next, I was a man in my prime…she*

looked not one day older for all of that time…'

'Place your palm here, Mr Guy,' she said, and, taking my wrist, she placed it firmly in the small of her back. 'Now give me your other hand.'

'Not a single day older when I heard her to say: "It will not be long, love, till our wedding day."'

'And…one—two—three…one—two—three…one—two—three…one—two—three…'

I did my best to follow the pattern of her moving feet, terrified that at any minute I would trample on her toes.

'One—two—three…one—two—three…that's it! Keep going! Don't look down. You're dancing, Mr Guy! You are dancing!'

And now I am old; I am long in the tooth
Though I'm crippled and weak, she still clings to her youth
When she passed by my window I heard her to say:
"It will not be long, love, till our wedding day."

I saw her today as I moved through the fair
And she smiled as she passed with her goods and her gear
Then she turned and she kissed me, and this she did say:
"We have tarried too long, love; this is our wedding day."

♆

AUTHOR'S NOTE

On the Origins of Octavius Guy

In 2014, my Crime & Thrillers reading group tackled *The Moonstone*, which Wilkie Collins originally wrote as a serial for Charles Dickens's weekly magazine *All the Year Round*. I was particularly struck by one of the minor characters who pops up towards the end of the book, the lawyer Mr Bruff's office boy, Octavius Guy, better known by his nickname, Gooseberry. Collins gave Gooseberry the small but extremely important role of being the only person capable of identifying and following the villain when he redeems the diamond from the bank.

As I read I began to realize that Gooseberry would make a perfect protagonist for a novel, and over the summer I applied myself to doing just that. Reprising many of the original characters, I wrote and published the novel *Gooseberry* on Goodreads, one chapter each week, just as Collins had done with *The Moonstone* almost a hundred and fifty years before.

The Real Maria Harmon

Early spiritualists were often extremely forward-thinkers, espousing such causes as the abolition of slavery, women's suffrage, vegetarianism, and equality for all. The rapping-style séances that originated in and around America's Eastern Seaboard in the late 1840s were introduced into Britain at the tail end of 1852 by a certain Mrs Maria B. Hayden (1826-1883) and her husband, a doctor from Hartford, Connecticut.

In addition to causing random raps to be heard (merely signalling the presence of spirits), Maria was also a "test" medium, in that she fielded yes-or-no-type questions where the answers were known only to the person who asked them. I'm not sure if Charles Dickens himself attended her séances, but her husband reports that two of his friends did, and with the intention of having various things go wrong—early ghost-grabbers-in-the-making!

The séances in *Big Bona Ogles, Boy!* are divided into two parts. The first half, where the medium answers written questions, would be perfectly recognizable to Maria Hayden. The second, where spirits are manifested when the lights go out, would not. These kinds of séances developed slowly over the next twenty-or-so years. You can read more about Maria B. Hayden and Florence Cook, who provided the inspiration for Mrs Harmon's materializations, on my website.

The Lady of Shalott

Alfred, Lord Tennyson's poem, *The Lady of Shalott* (written in 1832; published in 1833; revised in 1842), draws on Arthurian legend for its subject matter. The lady in question is fated to live in isolation on an island in the middle of a river that flows into Camelot, and to spend her time weaving tapestries at her loom—based on what she can see of the world outside reflected in her mirror. She is aware of a curse hanging over her; she may not stop her weaving, nor look directly out of her window, lest it trigger this curse—though quite what its effects will be we are never told. One day she glimpses the reflection of Sir Lancelot in her mirror, and runs to her window for a better look. Falling in love with what she sees, she takes a boat and quits the island, but by the time she reaches Camelot she is dead.

Hampstead Heath

Hampstead Heath, at roughly 350 acres, is the largest single area of common land in Greater London, the bulk of it acquired for the general populace by London's Metropolitan Board of Works. Parts of it are perfect for picnics and sports, but much of it is moderately dense woodland. It provides the setting early on in Wilkie Collins's *The Woman in White* where the hero Walter Hartright first encounters the ghostly woman of the title. The Spaniards Inn on the north-west edge of the Heath is an historic London pub dating from the late 1500s. It was mentioned in both Charles Dickens's *The Pickwick Papers* and Bram Stoker's *Dracula*. Amazingly it still operates as a pub, with inglenooks aplenty and roaring fires in the winter.

Though it was over thirty years ago, I myself dropped in for the odd pint.

To Orford and Back

The town of Orford in the county of Suffolk was once a prosperous medieval port, but by the early 1700s it had fallen into decline. Orford Castle was built by Henry II in the twelfth century, but by 1852, when the book is set, all that actually remained of it was the keep, which today is one of the best preserved examples of its kind.

Orford Castle, photo by Gernot Keller, www.gernot-keller.com

The train that Gooseberry and George take was run by the Eastern Counties Railway Company from the end of the line in Chelmsford to its London terminus, Bishopsgate Station, which was eventually destroyed by fire in 1964. It was a journey of 51 miles, and, as Third Class fares were a penny per mile, each of their tickets would cost four shillings and threepence—

about £43 in today's money. Still, that's cheaper than the £85 it would cost to go First Class.

She Moved Through the Fair

She Moved Through the Fair is what is termed a "traditional" Irish air, which might lead you to think that it's as old as the hills. Well, it is and it isn't. In the standard version that everyone sings, the music was "collected" by Herbert Hughes—but the lyrics were specifically written for it by the poet Padraic Colum. It was first published by Boosey & Hawkes in Hughes's *Irish Country Songs* of 1909. In this version, the singer's true love ends up dying before the pair can be wed. There are, however, a number of other folk songs that share some of Colum's lyrics: notably *I Once Had a True Love* and *My Young Love Said to Me*, where the singer's true love proves herself to be less-than-true, and slips out of the window to abscond with another man. It occurred to me to write my own variation for the wedding guests to dance to, using many of the phrases these three songs share in common, but this time as a *memento mori*—a reminder that, even in life, there is death.

On the Cover

Once again the cover is taken from John Thomson's collection of photographs *Street Life in London* (published by Sampson, Low, Marston, Searle, and Rivington

[1876/77], with text by Adolphe Smith). You can download your own free PDF copy of it from the London School of Economics' Digital Library at: http://digital.library.lse.ac.uk/collections/streetlifeinlondon —Do! It is truly fascinating.

And, once again, I am also indebted to *The Great British Bobby—A History of British Policing from the 18th Century to the Present* by Clive Elmsley; published by Quercus (2009, updated for the paperback edition 2010) for its insights into early policing.

Michael Gallagher, 2016.

BIG BONA OGLES, BOY!

And there's more…

Receipts Both Ancient and Modern

(Arranged in ascending order of complexity)

Property of
Octavius Guy

and his brother
Julius

Funeral Biscuits

[*Editor's note: these genuine Victorian recipes from "Everybody's Confectionary Book" (sic) are intended for your entertainment and edification only, not for actual cooking.*]

Take twenty-four eggs, three pounds of flour, and three pounds of lump sugar grated, which will make forty-eight finger biscuits for a funeral.

French Rolls

[*Editor's note: these genuine Victorian recipes from "Everybody's Confectionary Book" (sic) are intended for your entertainment and edification only, not for actual cooking.*]

Rub an ounce of butter into a pound of flour, mix one egg, well beaten, a little yeast, not bitter, as much milk as will make a dough of a middling stiffness; beat it well, but do not knead, let it rise; bake on tins quickly.

Spanish Fritters

[Editor's note: these genuine Victorian recipes from "Everybody's Confectionary Book" (sic) are intended for your entertainment and edification only, not for actual cooking—though you are probably safe with this one!]

Cut the crumb of a French roll into lengths, as thick as your finger, in what shape you will. Soak in some cream, nutmeg, sugar, pounded cinnamon, and an egg. When well soaked, fry off a nice brown; and serve with butter, wine, and sugar-sauce.

Mince Pie

[Editor's note: these genuine Victorian recipes from "Everybody's Confectionary Book" (sic) are intended for your entertainment and edification only, not for actual cooking.]

Of scraped beef free from skin and strings, weigh 2lb.; 4lb. of suet picked and chopped, then add 6lb. of currants nicely cleaned and perfectly dry, 3lb. of chopped apples, the peel and juice of two lemons, a pint of sweet wine, a nutmeg, a quarter of an ounce of cloves, ditto mace, ditto pimento, in finest powder; press the whole into a deep pan when well mixed, and keep it covered in a dry cool place.

Half the quantity is enough, unless for a very large family.

Have citron, orange, and lemon-peel ready, and put some of each in the pies when made.

Gooseberry Fool

[*Editor's note: these genuine Victorian recipes from "Everybody's Confectionary Book" (sic) are intended for your entertainment and edification only, not for actual cooking.*]

Put the fruit into a stone jar, and some good Lisbon sugar; set the jar on a stove, or in a sauce-pan of water over the fire; if the former, a large spoonful of water should be added to the fruit. When it is done enough to pulp, press it through a colander; have ready a sufficient quantity of new milk, and a tea-cupful of raw cream, boiled together, or an egg instead of the later, and left to be cold; then sweeten it pretty well with fine Lisbon sugar, and mix the pulp by degrees with it.

Bride Cake

[*Editor's note: these genuine Victorian recipes from "Everybody's Confectionary Book" (sic) are intended for your entertainment and edification only, not for actual cooking.*]

Take four pounds of fine flour well dried, four pounds of fresh butter, and two pounds of loaf sugar. Pound and sift fine a quarter of an ounce of mace, and the same of nutmeg; and to every pound of flour, put eight eggs well beat. Wash four pounds of currants, pick them well, and dry them before the fire. Blanch a pound of sweet almonds, and cut them lengthwise very thin, take a pound of citron, a pound of candied orange, the same of candied lemon, and half a pint of brandy. First work the butter to a cream with your hand, then beat in your sugar a quarter of an hour, and work up the whites of your eggs to a very strong froth. Mix them with your sugar and butter, beat your yolks half and hour at least, and mix them with your other ingredients.—Then put in your flour, mace, and nutmeg, and keep beating it well until the oven is ready; put in your brandy, and beat in lightly your currants and almonds. Tie three sheets of paper round the bottom of your hoop, to keep it from running out, and rub it well with butter. Then put in your cake, and place your sweet-meats in three layers, with some cake between every layer. As soon as it is risen and coloured, cover it with paper and bake it in a moderate oven. Three hours will bake it.

OH, NO, OCTAVIUS!
Octavius Guy & The Case of the Quibbling Cleric (#4)

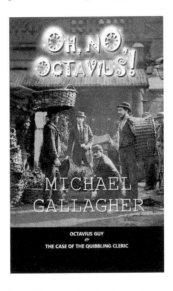

The well-heeled residents of Highbury have a problem: the Reverend Allaston Burr, the rector who's been foisted upon their congregation by an ancient yet legally-binding right known as an advowson. When a final appeal to Queen Victoria—as the head of the Church of England—fails to remove him from his post, they turn to Gooseberry for help.

Join Octavius Guy and his ragtag bunch of friends on their fourth adventure as they investigate the detested cleric, only to discover that someone has a far more permanent form of removal in mind.

From Seventh Rainbow Publishing, London
Coming in 2018.

Fancy a sneak peek? Read on...

THE PROLOGUE

Highbury, on the outskirts of London.
Monday, September 5th, 1853.

"'I CAN'T *THINK* WITHOUT thinking about you; I can't BREATHE without thinking about you; I can't LIVE without thinking about you,'" George quoted at me from memory. He narrowed his eyes and came straight to the point. 'It looked like *your* handwriting, Octavius.'

It was; not that I was about to admit it.

'Was it signed?' I asked, knowing full well it was not.

'No, but the writing was cursive like yours is, all spiky L's and T's. This is my little sister we're talking about.' He stressed the words *little sister* again and glowered at me some more.

Oh, why had Annie kept my note? Why had she hidden it where George was bound to find it? Surely she knew that her brother pried—if only where she was concerned? He was angry, very angry—anyone could see that—so angry that it was distracting him from the task in hand.

'Concentrate, George. This is a crime scene, and we have precious few minutes before Mr Badger returns with all the constables of N-Division in tow. Come, observe whatever may be observed and tell me what you think.'

The big lad peered down at the body, which was sprawled across the aisle in the broad octagonal space where the transepts met the nave. Cool, early morning light filtered in through the church's east windows, amply illuminating the corpse.

'I think he's dead,' said George.

'It would certainly seem it. See how the whole of his face has been battered in? All that is left is a wet, pulpy mess.' The sight prompted in me a sudden memory.

When thou saidst, 'Seek ye my face,' my heart said unto thee, 'Thy face, Lord, will we seek.'

Prophetic words indeed.

'Hammer?' George suggested, as his professional curiosity finally began to exert itself.

'Perhaps…or some kind of mallet.' I cocked my head to the side. 'Such a frenzied attack! Someone was particularly determined that he should not survive it.' One of our own clients, presumably, who—frustrated with our efforts to date—had resorted to a much quicker solution to their problem.

George sniffed. 'Maybe they just didn't want us to identify him,' he posited.

I stared. It was a truly ingenious idea, though not one that was borne out by the evidence. I scrutinized the man's manner of dress: the fusty old frock-coat, the battered felt hat, and the telltale white gloves he habitually wore. If anyone was trying to hide his identity, they'd made a deplorable job of it.

'I was just saying,' George grumbled, when I pointed this out to him, 'if the murderer didn't want us to identify him, what better way than by bashing in his face?'

He crouched down to take a closer look. 'Poor bloke was trying to defend himself. See how he's cowering? Arms and knees drawn up in front of him to ward off the blows, and look at how his fingers are clenched. Here, what's this?'

George leaned forward and grasped the Reverend Burr's right hand. With a forceful tug he prised away whatever it was he had spotted.

'Looks like a torn scrap of parchment,' he opined, 'maybe from a letter…something the murderer must have snatched off him when he knew the old man was done for. There's writing on it, see?'

'What's it say?'

He held it up to the light, peered at it, and then shrugged. 'Your guess is as good as mine. Looks really old. Here, see for yourself.'

There *was* writing on it…of a sort. A single line that appeared to be in code:

++ *etomnialignaregionisplaudentmanu* ++

I scanned my eye back and forth along the text, noting the crosses and the faint but definite underlining. George was right; the script indeed looked ancient, with any rounded parts rendered not in a circular fashion, but formed instead with a flat-cut nib employing short, oblique strokes. No matter how I tried to group the letters, the only words I could make were "to" or "Tom", "I align", "a region is", and either "laud", "den", or "dent". And "man", of course, though, with the ensuing "u", I presumed we were missing the *-facture* or *-facturer* that would likely come next. A thousand pities that we had only this small portion to work with, I reflected. Had we more, what grand truths might we have discerned?

George watched as I stowed the scrap inside my pocket. 'Guy's Seventh Rule of Detection?' he queried, and I shot him a grin: *Never allow good evidence to fall into the hands of the police*. Well, it's not as if they would be needing it; if *I* couldn't work out what the message meant, then they, poor souls, hadn't a chance. Mr Peel's finest are not exactly noted for their brains.

'Has the clergyman anything more to tell us?' I asked.

George scratched his head. 'Well, his muscles are stiff.'

'Fully stiff?'

'They don't come no stiffer.'

I tried to recall what I had read about this—which proved a lot easier than having to apply it.

'Rigidity starts to take hold approximately two hours after death and reaches its peak some eight to twelve hours later. The muscles can remain fully stiff for a further eighteen. But…'

'But?'

'Well, it was a rather warm night last night, which may have sped up the process. The hour is now almost seven by my reckoning. Which means…'

'What?'

'The Reverend Burr met his end at some point in the past thirty-odd hours.'

George raised an unimpressed eyebrow. 'We both saw him alive at yesterday's service,' he said. 'It had to have happened since then.'

Ho hum. I should like to state in my defence that estimating time of death by observing the body's natural rigours is an imprecise science at best.

'We should check the church for more clues while we still have the chance,' I said, keen to put my little oversight behind me. 'You take that side; I'll take this.'

For the next few minutes we inched our way through the interior, starting at the altar then working down the nave, thence back along the side aisles on either wall. Though Gothic in style, it was a new church, and everything in it—save for a discarded lantern and the fresh pool of vomit made by young Mr Badger—was spotless. From the bible on the lectern—open, I observed, at the Book of Isaiah—to the rows of hardwood pews, there was not a scratch nor a scuff mark to be seen.

'Anything, George?' I asked, as we met up again by the body.

'Nah. You?'

'Only an impression, but rather an interesting one. The blood…or the lack of it, to be precise. His face was beaten to a pulp, and yet there isn't nearly as much blood as I would expect there to be.'

George glanced down at the floor and frowned. 'You're right. There should be more. A lot more. What can it mean, Octavius?'

'That one of the people who hired us cleaned up after themselves when they murdered him.' Though I was speaking in jest, my face was grim, for it seemed to me the most probable explanation.

The sound of rapidly approaching footsteps from outside the church put paid to any further speculation, however; it appeared that Mr Badger was back, now accompanied by the stalwart men of N-Division.

'Don't think I've forgotten that note to Annie,' George warned me as they came blundering in through the doors. 'She's my little sister, see?' He fixed me with a stare that was positively bovine.

Unfortunately for me, I saw only too well.

Five-star praise for the series
SEND FOR OCTAVIUS GUY

"Sometimes you see a book and just know you're going to love it…An absolute treat for fans of Collins' novel [The Moonstone] and a successful novel in its own right."
—Emma Hamilton, buriedunderbooks.co.uk, LibraryThing Early Reviewer
★ ★ ★ ★ ★

"Here is a sensational historical fiction who-dunnit that gives nothing away until the very end. To me, it reads like an old time radio show. It leaves you breathless."
—Connie A., LibraryThing Early Reviewer
★ ★ ★ ★ ★

"This is an absolute gem of a series and quite the most enjoyable set of books I have read in a very long time."
—Anita Dow, Goodreads Reviewer
★ ★ ★ ★ ★

"Thank you so much for writing these books, and for bringing these characters to life. I have a feeling they'll always be lurking around in my head. Excellent, excellent, excellent!"
—Laura Brook, LibraryThing Early Reviewer
★ ★ ★ ★ ★

"I was hooked from the start and spent as much time trying to guess the outcome as I did laughing out loud. I thoroughly enjoyed this novel and can't wait to read another of Mr. Gallagher's mysteries. Forget Sherlock Holmes, send for Octavius Guy!"
—Brittney L. Divine, author, Smashwords Reviewer
★ ★ ★ ★ ★

"My favorite Victorian boy investigator sets off to solve a new mystery…Words cannot describe just how much I enjoy Octavius."
—Bethany Swafford (TheQuietReader), Goodreads Reviewer
★ ★ ★ ★ ★

"Michael Gallagher is a marvellous writer and storyteller. Witty, warm, full of wonderful descriptions, dialogue and characters. Doesn't sound like a murder mystery? It certainly is."
—Alasdair Muckersie, Goodreads Reviewer
★ ★ ★ ★ ★

"A scholarly murder mystery without being staid…a masterpiece of misdirection and layers of creative storytelling. Trust me. Buy the books!"
—Laura Dogsmom (Laura in Wisconsin), Goodreads Reviewer
★ ★ ★ ★ ★

"Did I solve the puzzle - no, but I enjoyed every minute of Octopus's investigations."
—LizzieKillin (Liz Stevens), LibraryThing Early Reviewer
★ ★ ★ ★ ★

"When you read a book by Michael Gallagher be prepared for a total immersion—every bit of scene setting, speech, character and historical detail is perfect."
—Chris Keen LibraryThing Early Reviewer
★ ★ ★ ★ ★

"Pour some tea or a wee dram, put your feet up, and enjoy cover to cover."
—Gladread, LibraryThing Early Reviewer
★ ★ ★ ★ ★

ABOUT THE AUTHOR

Author Photo by Elaine Jeffs

Michael Gallagher is the author of two series of novels set in Victorian times. *Send for Octavius Guy* chronicles the attempts of fourteen-year-old Gooseberry—reformed master pickpocket—to become a detective, aided and abetted by his ragtag bunch of friends. *The Involuntary Medium* follows the fortunes of young Lizzie Blaylock, a girl who can materialize the spirits of the dead, as she strives to come to terms with her unique gift.

For twenty-five years Michael taught adults with learning disabilities at Bede, a London-based charity that works with the local community. He now writes full time.

Find him online:
on Twitter @seventh7rainbow
at his website michaelgallagherwrites.com
and on Facebook and Goodreads.

Follow Octavius Guy @sendforOctavius.